THE ISLAND'S VENGEFUL DEAD

EAST TIMOR CRIME SERIES № 4

Chris McGillion

coffeetownpress

Kenmore, WA

Coffeetown Press books published by Epicenter Press

Epicenter Press
6524 NE 181st St. Suite 2
Kenmore, WA 98028.
www.Epicenterpress.com
www.Coffeetownpress.com
www.Camelpress.com

For more information go to: www.Epicenterpress.com

All rights reserved. No part of this book may be reproduced or transmitted in any form or by any means, electronic or mechanical, including photocopying, recording, or any information storage and retrieval system, without permission in writing from the publisher.

This is a work of fiction. All characters are creations of the author's imagination.

The Island's Vengeful Dead
Copyright © 2025 by Chris McGillion

ISBN: 9781684922420 (trade paper)
ISBN: 9781684922437 (ebook)

LOC: 2024940286

Printed in the United States of America

Dedication

For Bill Blaikie

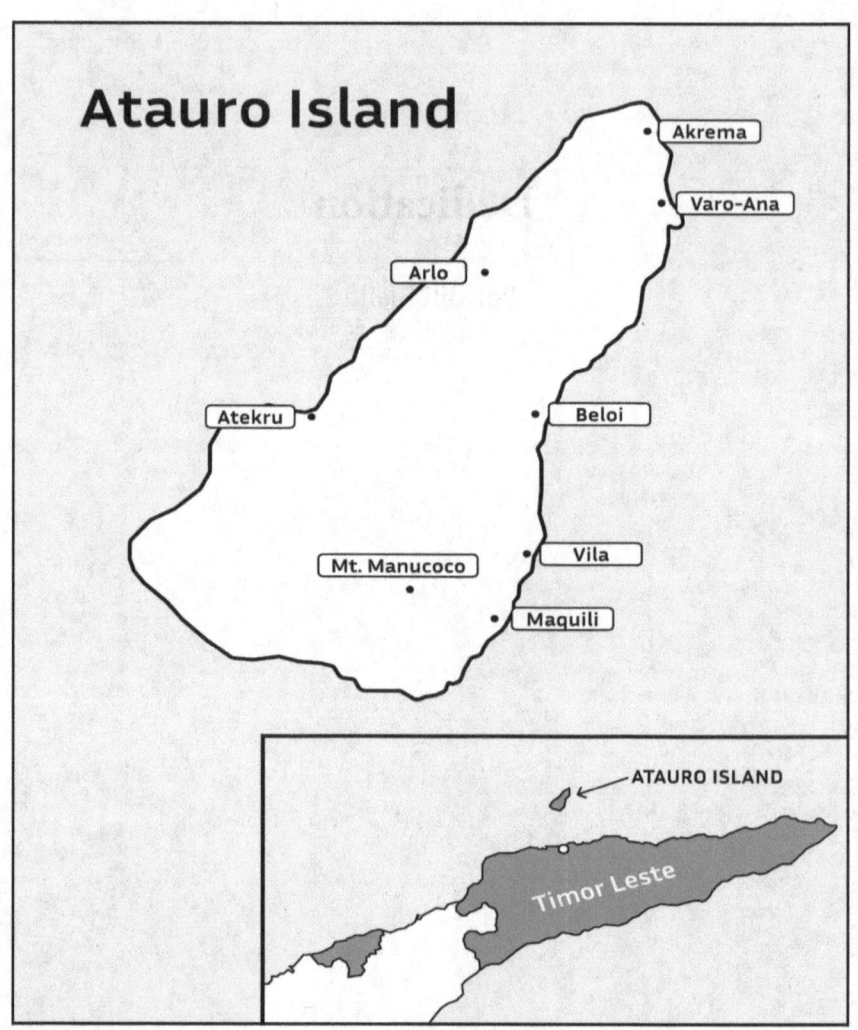

Map by Dominic Andrews

Author's note

While *The Island's Vengeful Dead* is a work of fiction, Atauro Island was used as a colonial prison by the Portuguese for centuries and as a place of exile by the Indonesians after they invaded East Timor in 1975. Over the next ten years or so, thousands of Timorese were uprooted from the mainland and sent to the island where many died of hunger, mistreatment, and neglect. The dead were buried on Atauro in improvised mass graves. The remains of some were being repatriated to their mainland origin villages by 2015—one year after this story is set.

Tales of a sixteenth century shipwreck off the coast near East Timor's capital, Dili, from which a priest and a few sailors were said to be the only survivors, and of a Portuguese-speaking patriarch of a group on Atauro who reached the island after several days adrift at sea, appear in the anthropological literature.

My thanks are due to Dr Sarah Frias-Torres, an oceanographer and marine biologist from Florida, for important insights into coral reef research.

1

Justino had drifted off to sleep just before dawn, but his head protruded from the ground and the glare of the sun woke him now. He raised an arm out of the soil and covered his eyes. When his vision had adjusted to the sharp light streaming onto the island of Atauro, 16 miles north of Dili, the capital of East Timor, he turned on his side, crawled out of the shallow hole that resembled a grave, stretched, and brushed the dirt off his body. It had been a full moon the night before and on full moon nights especially Justino liked to bury himself to draw energy from the earth and to make him strong. One day, he believed, people would see how strong he'd become, and they would have to respect him, perhaps even make him a leader.

The boy wore a filthy T-shirt, frayed shorts, and sneakers with the toes exposed. His hair was a tangle of dust and grass seeds, his arms and legs smeared with grime, and his dark eyes drooped as though he struggled to stay awake.

It was how he always appeared.

Justino was barely seventeen years old. He'd never gone to school and could neither read nor write. Usually, his mother was anxious about letting him leave their hut alone except to push a cart of coconuts through the village each morning to sell to make a little extra income. But occasionally, at night, he slipped away to climb the ridge behind his hut and bury himself until early morning like he had just done.

He worked the circulation into his skinny legs and reached for a necklace made from a length of rope he'd hung on a nearby sapling. He draped it around his neck. The dead bat and skin of a wolf snake hanging from the rope would ward off evil spirits lurking in the forest that separated his hole from the narrow coastal plain on which he lived.

Only this morning, as Justino walked down toward the village and the beach, he was to find that his talisman had lost all power to protect him.

• • •

It had just gone 8.40am and FBI Agent Sara Carter was finishing a breakfast of muesli, yogurt and fresh mango in her duplex apartment near the seafront in Dili's old Portuguese district of Motael. It was Tuesday and she was dressed for work in dark blue slacks and a light blouse. At thirty years of age she was lean and well-toned but she kept the blouse loose rather than draw attention to her figure in a country and among a people she was still getting to know, barely three months since leaving her office in Flagstaff, Arizona, to take up a temporary posting with INTERPOL.

She was enjoying a rich, dark Timorese coffee when her cell rang.

"Agent Carter. It's Hudson Taylor," the voice said.

Carter stifled a groan. Taylor was the US Ambassador to East Timor—a generally stupid as well as pompous individual which made him doubly irritating. Recently he had pressured Carter to sign up for a second three-month stint with INTERPOL because her work with the international policing organization gave him something to boast about in reports sent home. Eventually she'd agreed in order to maintain policing credentials so she could help her friend and interpreter, the young Timorese police officer Estefana dos Carvalho, rescue her fiancé from kidnappers involved in a drugs trafficking ring. Her reasons for re-signing were personal, but she resented Taylor's constant haranguing to stay on. Consequently she tried to keep her distance from him.

"Yes sir," she said for want of a more cordial greeting.

"Professor Frankston is dead," Taylor said.

"Frankston?" replied Carter.

"Yes Frankston. Professor Hank Frankston. The marine biologist from Hawaii," Taylor said in a tone of impatience. "If you'd come to the Embassy reception I invited you to, you'd know who I was talking about."

The scent of frangipani wafted in through her open window and carried the laughter of children walking past her building on their way to school.

"And you say he's dead?" asked Carter, ignoring Taylor's criticism.

"Yes. That's exactly what I'm saying. Dead. On the island. Atauro. His body was found about two hours ago. It's terrible, just terrible. I took a call this morning from police headquarters here in Dili."

She could hear Taylor shuffling papers and imagined him sitting at his heavy wooden desk while out the window behind him sprinklers kept a totally inappropriate lush green Embassy lawn from wilting in the tropical heat.

"Here it is," he continued. "They say he was killed, murdered. Found by the side of the road. It's the last thing we need."

Carter blew out a long breath, more to suggest concern rather than express it. After all, she didn't know Frankston, and INTERPOL was not in the business of investigating run-of-the-mill murders.

"I don't see—"

"I want you to get over there and take a look into it." She was about to say something but Taylor went on as though his instructions were infallible. "I've cleared it this morning with Jacobsen." Danique Jacobsen was the director of INTERPOL operations in East Timor and she felt she owed Taylor a favour for his role in Carter's decision to re-sign with her small force. "I'm sending my aide Gerard Miller as well."

"Sir, INTERPOL doesn't—"

"Do you know who Professor Fankston is—I mean was—married to, Agent Carter?" Taylor asked, obviously irritated. "Susanna Sheridan. Do you know who Susanna Sheridan's father is? A senator from North Carolina. He's an important man. Very important. Sits on the Committee on Foreign Relations. Are you getting my drift?"

Carter placed her coffee cup on the table and ran a hand through shoulder-length hair that had faded from brown to a shade of chestnut in the sun.

"Miller's there to comfort Mrs. Frankston and give her what assistance he can to get her home," Taylor added. "You're there to see that an acceptable solution to this…this tragedy is found so she can return to the States as soon as possible."

"Acceptable?" queried Carter but Taylor took no notice.

"I've arranged a flight across to the island with"—more paper shuffling—"MAF. Mission Aviation Fellowship. Some sort of church-based thing. The flight's at eleven."

"This morning?" she interrupted him.

"Obviously," Taylor said. "Gerard has made bookings on the island. Meet him at the airport at 10:30 a.m. sharp. And I suggest you pack for a couple of days."

Carter took another breath intending this time to complain but thought better of it. She picked up her coffee cup and drained the last of its contents instead.

"We need to get a handle on this quickly, Sara," Taylor continued, employing her first name by way of appeal. "I'm counting on you. The Timorese are sending over a special investigator—Cadato or Catano or someone. You may know him—"

"Cordero? Vincintino Cordero?" asked Carter.

"Whatever," said Taylor. "We need to make sure this thing's done properly. That's why I want you there. Mrs. Frankston has enough to contend with without the Timorese police causing her more grief."

Carter replaced her coffee cup on the table and walked to the window with her cell pressed to her ear. The day was heating up, the sun already blistering the sky.

"What more do you know?" she asked.

"Not much," answered Taylor. "This is coming from the island to Dili police and through their various channels to me. Apparently he was found in a place called Vila. Stabbed to death. That's all I know."

Each morning Carter could see the hazy outline of Atauro sitting across the Wetar Straight when she left for work or when she jogged or took a stroll along the waterfront. She was recalling it now. The island's shape reminded her of a lounging lion—a hump at one end like the animal's hips; a high mountain cresting at the other like a lion's mane. She had yet to set foot on Atauro and knew nothing about it other than it was remote, poorly developed, and for both reasons popular among foreigners who liked to dive and snorkel on its largely pristine coral reefs.

"It's terrible, just terrible," Taylor was saying to no one in particular. Carter turned from the window.

"I'll need my interpreter—the policewoman, Estefana dos Carvalho—to come with me," she said, ignoring the Ambassador's whining.

"What? No. Gerard speaks perfect Tetun," Taylor said. "He can interpret for you."

"And have the Embassy be seen to involve itself in a murder investigation?" Carter said. "I don't think you want that."

Taylor sighed.

"Of course, of course. You're right. No, we don't want that. Take your interpreter but make sure you keep me in the loop."

With that Taylor ended the call. Carter checked her watch, put one hand on her hip and bit a fingernail on the other. A murder investigation sounded much more interesting than the cold case war crimes she was documenting for INTERPOL. In fact it was exactly the kind of thing she preferred to be involved in. With her friend Vincintino Cordero on the case she knew she could be involved--centrally involved.

She slipped into the bedroom and pulled a travel bag from the closet.

• • •

"Sorry I couldn't give you more notice, Estefana," Carter said as she squeezed in alongside her friend in the tiny five-seater MAF plane most often used for medical evacuations from remote areas. "I wasn't given much notice myself."

Gerard Miller, the Embassy aide, sat next to the pilot. Carter had met him once or twice: he was not the sort of person who made a big impression. He was in his early twenties, she knew that, and on his first diplomatic posting. But with his crew cut, rosy cheeks, and poor excuse for facial hair he resembled an eager young intern in a realty office or a bank more than he did an officer in the Foreign Service.

Estefana was a pretty girl with flawless coffee-coloured skin, bright brown eyes and long dark frizzy hair. Typically she was excitable and talkative but now, strapped to her seat, she was withdrawn and, chewing her bottom lip as the single engine spluttered to life, appeared to shrink inside the folds of her light-blue police uniform.

She had been quiet since she'd arrived at the airport. She'd sat, head bent over her traveling bag, and, unusually for her, had asked no questions about what they were doing or why. Carter glanced at her, wondering if something was wrong.

"Is this your first time in a small plane?" she asked.

Estefana offered no reply.

Carter swiveled side on to face her as best she could in the confines of the plane.

"It's my first time in *any* plane, *mana*," Estefana said, referring to Carter by the typical informal Timorese designation for women of 'sister'. She stole a peek out the window but straightened quickly to focus on the back of the seat in front of her.

"I remember my first time in a plane," Carter said to reassure her, easing back in her own seat. "Scared the hell out of me. It's normal. Don't worry. Besides, they said it's only a twelve-minute flight. It'll be over before you know it."

"It's not that, *mana*," murmured Estefana.

Carter faced her a second time.

"Okay. What is bothering you then?" she asked.

"Atauro, *mana*," Estefana said and closed her eyes tight.

"Atauro?" Carter repeated but the plane had begun to jolt down the runway and the clamour of the engine rendered further conversation pointless. They lifted abruptly and swerved sharply over the lacquered blue sea toward the island.

Estefana's fingers clasped a silver crucifix that hung around her neck. Carter thought she might be mumbling a prayer although whether in fear of the flight or of the island to which they were heading she had no way of telling.

2

Vincintino Cordero of Timor-Leste's elite Scientific Police for Criminal Investigation unit had taken a maritime police boat from Dili to the only pier on Atauro at the village of Beloi, half way along the island's east coast. The water had been calm and the trip had taken only forty minutes. He'd arrived a little after 10.30am, found the maritime police building unattended, and so had to improvise on land transport. He'd noticed a man with a sunken chest and the remains of a T-shirt tied loosely around his head sitting on a *tuk-tuk*—a motorcycle with a metal tray attached to improvise a rickshaw. Cordero hired the man to take him to Vila, where Professor Hank Frankston had been staying and where his body had earlier been found.

Vila was also the administrative center of Atauro and the base of the local police headquarters. It had a population of less than 2,000 people spread out along the coast on a thin stretch of lush flat land between sandy beaches and foothills rising to the mountainous interior. It was a slow, jolting, dusty journey down an unsealed road fringed with coconut palms and acacia trees on the inland side and banana trees and fan-leaved palms on the other. Occasionally a break in the thick vegetation revealed aqua patches of coral reefs bordering the stark blue waters of the Wetar Straight separating Atauro from the mainland. Reefs encircled the island and were reputed to be one of the most biologically diverse habitats in the world—a magnet for marine biologists like Professor Frankston as well as adventurous tourists, but there were few people on the road or in their gardens now, the drowsy do-nothingness of a sultry tropical midday having set in. Cordero reached the outskirts of Vila feeling parched, bedraggled, more worn out than his forty years, and less steady on his feet than when he climbed into the rusting tray of the *tuk-tuk*.

He shouted over the noise of the motorcycle engine for the driver to pull up outside the *eskuadra-polisia* or police station on the northern approach to Vila. Cordero paid the driver the two-dollar fee—Timor having adopted the US dollar as its own currency— lifted his valise onto the ground, and dusted himself off as best he could. The *tuk-tuk* rattled and coughed and headed back to from where it had come.

The police station consisted of a three-room, tin-roofed, white cement block building set in a compound of withered dry grass behind a high wire fence. A Timorese flag drooped limp in the heavy heat from a pole outside the front door. A dual cab utility, its police decals smeared with dirt, was parked at the side of the building but there was no sign of life other than a mangy dog lying asleep as if dead under the utility's chassis.

Cordero picked up his valise and made for the front door.

He knocked and entered, noticing that inside was hardly cooler than the day outside. The front room was sparsely furnished. It contained a large desk with papers and manuals strewn across it, and a smaller desk supporting what looked like a radio transmitter. A wooden straight-back chair was set up at each desk and an old metal filing cabinet occupied the corner. A map of Vila and another of the entire island hung alongside each other with a calendar on the wall. A police officer lolled on a third chair beside a window. A fan had been placed on the sill and the blades were whirling to no obvious effect. The man wore socks—his boots parked beside the chair—and one leg was propped up on a trash bin, the ankle tied in thick bandages. The man was flicking through a magazine and he didn't look up.

Cordero placed his bag on the floor, took a kerchief from his pocket, and wiped his neck. Once more he knocked, louder this time, on the door frame.

"What?" the officer grumbled from behind the magazine.

"Sergeant Emilio Amparo?" Cordero asked.

The man lowered his magazine and straightened slightly in his chair. His leg remained poised on the bin. He was older than Cordero and much heavier. His police shirt was unbuttoned and hung, along with his stomach, over his trousers. His hair was thinning and a thick grey moustache covered his upper lip. His chin had gone unshaven for several days.

"You must be Cordero," he said. "The inspector they sent."

"I'm a police *investigator*," Cordero corrected him. "And yes, I've been sent to look into the death of the American." He surveyed the room. "I take it you're in charge while the police commander is in hospital in Dili?"

"That's right," the sergeant said. "Hernia or something I'm told. He'll be gone for a couple more weeks." He rubbed a hand coarsely across his stubbled chin. "The air conditioner doesn't work again this week," he added and pointed at a rusting model on the far wall. "Damn thing." He eyed Cordero more closely. "How did you get here?"

"Police launch and *tuk-tuk*. Couldn't find anyone in Beloi to give me a vehicle or drive me."

The sergeant chuckled.

"You won't find anyone here either," he said. "Everyone's gone to Dili. Training exercise."

"But not you?" Cordero said.

"No. Not me," the sergeant replied. He swung suddenly to swat a fly on the window sill with his magazine. He missed. "You didn't need to come, you know," he said lounging again in his chair.

"Tell that to my superior," Cordero said.

"I've got the one who did it," the sergeant said, his tone flat.

Cordero lowered his kerchief and questioned Amparo with his eyes. The sergeant flicked a thumb over his shoulder.

"He's out back," he said. "They call it a cell but it's really just a secure room where we hold people temporarily." Cordero waited. "Boy named Justino Ferrao. Picked him up this morning."

"You say he killed the American?"

Amparo nodded that he did.

"What makes you think so?" asked Cordero.

The sergeant took a deep breath. "Well for a start he's *bulak*," he said meaning crazy. "Always has been. I know this boy. What Timorese is going to kill a foreigner unless he's not right in the head?"

Amparo raised an arm and scratched the pit, in no hurry to lay out his case.

"Second," he continued but paused to shift his weight in the chair, "he's been in a fight and he's covered in blood. Third, he was found wandering around near where the body was found this morning like he was in a trance or something."

He raised an open hand.

"He's the one. No doubt about it."

"The American was stabbed to death, right?" Cordero said and the sergeant showed no sign he disagreed. "Did you find a knife or a blade of some kind?"

Amparo sniffed and pinched his nose. "It could be anywhere. Who knows? He might have wandered onto the beach and tossed it into the sea. The tide'd take it out on that coral and we'd never find it." Again he raised an open hand. "Or he could have tossed it into the undergrowth anywhere between where he killed the American and where he'd spent time wandering around."

"Has anyone taken a look?"

"Of course. I sent my cadet officer. That's as much as I could do. As I've said, most of the officers here were recalled to the mainland and the local villagers aren't reliable when it comes to searching for evidence. Apart from anything else it's too damn hot for them."

Cordero made no comment.

"You want to question him?" Amparo asked.

"Not until I know more about the case," Cordero said. He edged over to the maps on the wall. He focused on the map of Vila. "Where was the American's body found?"

Before the sergeant could answer his cell buzzed. He lifted a hip, fumbled for the cell in his pants pocket, and took the call.

"Sergeant Amparo," he groaned into the cell.

He was silent a long moment, listening to whoever was calling.

"When?" he asked finally.

The person on the other end answered.

"Let me guess," said Amparo. "Nothing taken."

He fell silent as the caller continued.

"Uh-huh," Amparo said. "Okay. Ask around and let me know if you learn anything. I'll come soon as I can."

With that he put the cell in his pocket and wiped a hand across his face as though removing an irritation. "Another *uma lulik* broken into," he said, meaning a sacred house, the traditional center of each village. "Like I said, we're understaffed right now. It took a while to get an officer down there from Biqueli."

"Another?" Cordero repeated.

"Fourth in just over two weeks," Amparo said and scratched his head. "First was up in Akrema. That's on the northern tip of the island. Second in Uaro-Ana and third in Biqueli. Now it's Beloi. Whoever's doing it seems to be making his way down the coast. Nothing ever taken. Just things disturbed, tossed around, and a mess left."

"Sounds like tourists up to no good," suggested Cordero.

"Doubt it. You know what *malae* tourists are like," said Amparo, using the Tetun expression for foreigners. "Things are very basic on this island. Before long, even the tourists who call themselves nature lovers are looking for a flushing toilet and a hot shower. So they leave."

He lent forward, lifted the leg on the trash bin with both hands, and put it down in a different position.

"No, tourists don't stay long enough to be involved in this business. Probably some local teenagers with nothing better to do. But it pisses the elders off, you know? So they piss us off by wanting us to put a stop to it." He sniffed his contempt for the interruption. "I'll have to put in a damn appearance, I guess. But that can wait. What were you asking? Oh yeah. Where was the body?"

The sergeant twisted uneasily and held out a hand toward the maps on the wall. "See the cemetery?" he said. "His body was found just up the road from there. In a ditch, covered with palm fronds." His eyes followed Cordero as the latter located the cemetery on the Vila map and ran a finger to the right.

"No, not that way," the sergeant said. "The other way. About fifty yards."

"And this boy you're holding—Justino was it?" said Cordero. "You say he was found near where the body was located? Where exactly?"

"Down the road," said Amparo. "About a hundred yards further on."

"North or south?" Cordero asked.

"Does it matter?" the sergeant protested.

"Maybe not but I like to know my way around," said Cordero.

"South," grunted Amparo.

Cordero traced his finger from the cemetery south down the road that ran alongside.

"Around here?"

"More or less."

"What time was the body found?" asked Cordero.

"Early morning," Amparo said. "Little after six. But we weren't told until near seven. I went straight out and checked. When I saw it was the American, I contacted Dili straight away."

"Why did it take an hour for the body to be reported?"

"The ones who found it had other things to do first," said Amparo as though it was obvious.

"Who found it?"

"Couple of women on their way to today's market. One had a small boy with her and he was playing with an empty noodle container. Kicked it into the ditch and saw the body when he went to retrieve it."

"And this Justino? What time—"

"About two hours ago. By the time we settled him in it was too late to get a message to Dili to say you weren't needed. My cadet found him—Sisko Ketakura. Lives out that way and was heading into work here."

"A cadet, huh?"

"Yeah. Hasn't completed the new community policing program yet. Got another few months of on-the-job training here in Vila before graduating."

"Where's he now?" Cordero asked.

"I sent him to check on a guy who's under house detention for almost killing his wife. Been twelve months now awaiting trial in Dili. I'm sure you know about the backlog."

Cordero did. "You have photos of the crime scene?" he asked.

Sergeant Amparo took a deep breath before answering. "I've been a police officer since independence in 2002. Nine years on the mainland and I've been a sergeant for three years here now," he said. "I know my job."

He paused and eyed Cordero.

"I also know this place and these people," he added. "You don't."

"You haven't answered my question," said Cordero.

"Sure I have photos. What do you think? They're on my cell. There's no way to print them here. The machine doesn't work these past few months and Dili's in no hurry to give us a new one." He lifted his chin toward the broken air conditioner. "That was a parting gift from the Indonesians," he added sarcastically. "This is a forgotten place."

Cordero nodded. "What's your guess as to the motive for the killing?" he asked.

"Like I said, the boy's crazy," Amparo answered.

"That's a little vague," Cordero commented.

"You telling me crazy behavior is exact?" asked Amparo.

Cordero wiped his neck a second time and replaced his kerchief in his pocket. "I'd like to see the body," he said.

"Of course," the sergeant said. "It's at the health clinic. The power comes and goes in Vila most days. So does fuel for our generator here at the station." He rocked himself to a more upright position. "The clinic has its own generator and a lot more fuel, for obvious reasons. We put the body there to ensure it was kept cool.

"Where's the wife?"

"You mean the widow," Amparo said. "She and her husband rented a place along the beach. She confirmed the body was that of her husband this morning and as far as I know she's at the house now. When we're ready to ship the body off to Beloi, I'll have Sisko inform her. She may want to go with it."

"Not all the way," said Cordero. Before Amparo could protest he added: "Until I'm satisfied you do have the right suspect."

"You're not suggesting—" Amparo began.

"Where do I find the clinic?" asked Cordero, cutting him off.

The sergeant stared at Cordero. "It's at the other end of the village," he said. "I'll drive you. I need to get the body to Beloi and off to Dili and if I've got to go and check on that sacred house break-in I might as well be the one to do it. The sooner we get the American's body off the island the better."

"Bring your cell with those photos," Cordero said. "I might want to look at them at the health clinic—if not, when we come back here."

"Have to put my boots on first," Amparo said. He slid into one gingerly, the leg that had been propped on the bin giving him obvious difficulty.

"What happened to your leg?" Cordero asked.

"Ankle," he corrected and squeezed his eyes in pain. "You know what they call this island, don't you?" he asked, but continued without waiting for a reply. "Goat island. The Portuguese brought them here. Now they're everywhere. Including in the church because the priest insists on leaving the doors open."

He picked up the other boot and slipped it on his good foot.

"I was trying to chase a goat around the altar and stumbled. The ankle's twisted but I can drive." He made a face as he stood. "The priest said he'd say a prayer for me. Lot of good that'll do. Bloody priest. Confessing girls in that church all alone. All of them sworn to secrecy."

"I take it you're not Catholic," Cordero said.

"Me? No."

"Protestant?" Cordero tried.

"Here they're mostly Assembly of God types," Amparo said. "The pastor's wife reeks of perfume."

"Why's that a problem?" Cordero asked.

"You don't need perfume in heaven," the sergeant said.

"She's not in heaven yet," Cordero countered.

"A pastor's wife in Vila?" said Amparo. "That's as close as she's going to get."

"So you're not religious?" asked Cordero.

"I don't go in for any of that stuff," said Amparo. He exhaled satisfaction as his foot settled in its boot. He left the laces untied. "You?"

Cordero ignored the question. "You want to get a new calendar," he said instead, looking along the wall from the maps. "This is last year's."

"Nothing much happens here from one year to the next," Sergeant Amparo explained. "Nothing that needs checking on a calendar, anyway."

Boots attached, if loosely, the sergeant reached across his desk. He sniffed, picked up his cell and the keys to his utility.

"I could have handled this myself, you know," he repeated. And with that he opened the door and hobbled out into the intense sunshine.

• • •

A local man working casually for the Mission Aviation Fellowship or MAF had chased three stray goats off the dirt airstrip before the small plane banked over the coral reef and shuddered to a stop alongside the road from Beloi to Vila. When Carter unbuckled her seatbelt and opened the cabin door the midday heat hit her like a blast furnace. She retrieved her overnight bag, threw it across one shoulder, raised a hand to shelter her eyes from the glare and squinted in the vain hope of a building that could afford some relief from the sun. No such luck. The best she could see was a flame tree toward the end of the runway. She stepped out and sought what shade it offered, her blouse quickly sticking to her body with sweat. Next came Gerard Miller, the Embassy staffer, a large overnight bag in one hand, a brief case in the other. His shirt was soggy by the time he made it to the shade of the tree. Only Estefana, last in line, seemed unaffected by the heat.

The MAF pilot gestured from the cockpit to the one-man ground crew, spun the plane sharply around, revved the motor, and hurtled down the airstrip before rising sharply into the glare of the sun. The man left on the ground doffed his tattered cap, slicked back his hair, and removed his hi-vis vest. He folded the vest under his arm and hurried off home. The goats returned to resume their grazing and the bougainvillea on either side of the airstrip, stirred by the plane's arrival and departure, resumed sagging lazily in the still rising temperature of the day.

Miller had arranged a *tuk-tuk* to pick them up at the airstrip and take them to what was impressively called a tourist eco-lodge in Vila where he had booked rooms. Before long the *tuk-tuk* arrived and they chugged down the road trying not to inhale dust kicked up from the tyres. As they passed the police station Carter noticed Cordero, valise in hand, following a heavy-set policeman who was hobbling toward a vehicle.

"Stop here a minute," Carter shouted to Miller above the rattle of the motorcycle. "Wait here," she added when it had finally come to a halt. "Tino!" she called—Cordero's nickname—as she jumped out of the *tuk-tuk*.

Cordero wheeled, recognized Carter, and broke into a smile. "Hi," he said. "They told me you were coming."

'They,' being his unit commander, had also told him to keep his distance from the FBI agent. *This is a Timorese police investigation*, the commander had said, *and we need to demonstrate that we're capable of conducting it professionally, effectively, and most importantly on our own.* That had annoyed Cordero because he didn't like being told what to do but also because he was fond of Carter and respected her abilities as a policewoman. He also figured that she would have access, through the Embassy, to information about the late professor which might prove useful if he could convince her to share it.

"You look hot and bothered," she said as she strode up, shading her eyes from the glare of the sun.

"You're looking good too," he said. "Haven't seen you for a few weeks. What have you been up to?"

"This and that," Carter said. "INTERPOL's kept me busy since I commenced the new contract but there's not a lot to show for it. You?"

"Same."

He took his gaze past her to the *tuk-tuk* spluttering on the side of the road.

"Is that Estefana with you?" he asked.

Carter looked over her shoulder. "Yeah. I wanted her along," she said. Cordero waved: Estefana acknowledged the greeting by raising a hand of her own. "And that's Gerard Miller in front," Carter added. "He works for the Embassy. He's green. First overseas posting. Very eager to please, especially when it comes to Ambassador Taylor."

Cordero nodded but paid the comment no mind.

"What are you meant to do here?" he asked.

She laughed. "Protect Ambassador Hudson Taylor's ass." She left it at that, and he didn't press the issue. "When did you get here?" she asked.

"About an hour ago," he said. "Maritime police."

"We flew. Just landed. We're staying at some kind of lodge in Vila. You?"

"Same place. Vila eco-lodge. It's the only lodge in Vila." He grinned slightly. "I'm told the district inspector stayed there last month."

"Inspector of what?" asked Carter.

"No one I talked to knew," said Cordero.

Sergeant Amparo had shooed the dog away from under the utility and managed to scramble into the driver's seat. He wound down the driver's window and Cordero noticed him eyeing Carter with interest.

"This is *Mana* Carter. She's from the US Embassy," he said to Amparo to keep it simple. "They sent her and another Embassy staffer here to help the widow. She doesn't speak Tetun." The sergeant acknowledged her by dipping his head. He turned the key on his ignition. "That's Sergeant Amparo," Cordero said to Carter. "He's the senior police officer in Vila. He doesn't speak English."

"Well that's a good start," said Carter. "Where are you off to?"

"I'm going to take a look at the body," Cordero said.

Carter glanced at the *tuk-tuk*. "I'll come with you," she said. "Give me a second to tell Estefana and Miller."

"I don't think that's necessary," said Cordero, a doubtful tone to his voice.

Carter faced him.

"What do you know about Professor Frankston?" she asked.

Cordero shifted uneasily.

"You'll want me along," Carter said. "On the way you can tell me what you know about the case so far and I'll tell you what I've learned about Frankston."

She hurried to the *tuk-tuk* and Cordero climbed into the utility next to Amparo.

"Pretty girl," the sergeant said.

Cordero peered at Carter.

"Headstrong too," was all he said.

3

Gerard Miller and Estefana dos Carvalho had continued on in the *tuk-tuk* to the eco-lodge—a small collection of stand-alone bamboo and galvanised tin huts arranged around a courtyard of crushed coral and stone with oleander bushes strategically planted to provide some privacy for the guests. An office and kitchen fronted the road and across from the kitchen on a short path through to the courtyard and huts was a slightly raised dining area under a thatched roof and enclosed by a waist high timber railing.

Miller and Estefana were directed to two huts: one containing twin beds for Estefana and Carter and the other a single for Miller. The remaining four huts in the lodge were empty, although one had been reserved for Cordero. Each hut was small but self-contained with an attached bathroom and toilet but there was no running water. All washing and flushing was done using a pail floating in a plastic water container. The huts were finished with a rickety table and plastic chairs, and each was decorated with Chinese and Indonesian kitsch of seashells, fish, and starfish on the walls.

The heat of the day was reaching its peak and the sky was leached of colour. Even the pink oleander shrubs dotted here and there between the huts seemed to be struggling in the dry, hard-baked soil. A small boy—no more than nine or ten years old—sat in the shade of a thin eave protruding from the side of the lodge's kitchen. He wore oversized shorts and a soiled 'Batman' T-shirt and seemed to have no qualms going barefoot in the stony surrounds of the kitchen and undercover dining area. He belonged to one of the woman working in the kitchen and, as was not uncommon, had skipped school.

The boy watched the newcomers as they went to their huts. For reasons only known to him, he took a particular interest in Miller. He sauntered over to Miller's hut and peeped through the partially open door. Miller caught sight of him and stopped unpacking.

"*Bondia*," he said, and asked the boy his name in Tetun.

The boy said nothing, his face blank.

Miller told the boy his name and asked him what he was doing. The boy remained silent before returning to his shady spot under the kitchen eave.

Estefana hesitated a moment considering which bed she should take. She decided on the nearest to the bathroom where the floor had sunk slightly. She placed her bag and Carter's down on each of the beds to signal the selection. She was staring at a battery-operated lamp hanging from the ceiling when there was a knock on the door, and she opened it to find Miller looking overdressed in a tie—rarely if ever worn by people in Timor—and a fresh business shirt. Under his arm he carried a parcel.

She regarded him uncertainly.

"I'm going to find Mrs Frankston," he said. "Someone here must know where she and her husband lived. I'll ask in the kitchen," he added.

"But *Mana* Carter said to wait until she returns," Estefana reminded him.

"I don't work for *Mana* Carter," Miller said. "I work for Ambassador Taylor. And I have my own instructions. You wait here for Carter. I shouldn't be too long."

With that he went to the office/kitchen area and Estefana heard him calling for someone who could assist him with directions. She slipped inside her hut and closed the door. She opened the mosquito net on her bed, sat and closed her eyes. She folded her hands across her chest and began to rock back and forth in an effort to block the thoughts crowding her mind.

• • •

Cordero leaned over the passenger's seat and told Carter what he had learned from Sergeant Emilio Amparo as they drove to the health clinic. Amparo said nothing the whole time.

"And this guy's locked up at the police station?" she asked. "You interrogated him?"

"Not yet," Cordero answered. "I want to examine the body first and get a sense of what I'm dealing with."

They pulled up at the clinic which was at the opposite end of Vila to the police station. Carter and Cordero followed Sergeant Amparo as he shuffled slowly through the front door. The relative coolness of the air inside was a relief. A nurse was attending a very pregnant woman trying to control two small children who looked to be under five years of age. The children were the first to notice the newcomers and their mouths fell open at the sight of Carter because she wasn't Timorese. They gawked at her but said nothing. The nurse recognised Amparo, apologised to the woman, and went to a desk and extracted a key. She handed it to the sergeant.

"Nothing's been touched," she said, and Amparo grunted an approval.

He led Cordero and Carter to a cool room where the body of Professor Hank Frankston lay on the floor under a sheet squeezed between stacked boxes of medical supplies.

"You went through his pockets?" Cordero asked Amparo who leaned against the doorframe.

"Of course," the sergeant said. "Everything's over there on that box of pills."

Cordero scanned what there was: a torch, a wallet containing a motor vehicle license, a library card, a ten and five one-dollar bills, and some coins.

"He wasn't carrying anything more, like a bag or a satchel?"

"Not that we could find," answered the sergeant.

"Well robbery doesn't seem to be a motive," Cordero said. "At least not robbery of the grab-the-money-and-run variety."

"I told you: the killer's crazy," said the sergeant. He pushed off the doorframe and returned to the room with the nurse and the pregnant woman to rest his leg.

"Friendly guy," Carter commented.

"Amparo? Got a badly twisted ankle," explained Cordero. "He doesn't take too kindly to rival authority figures. And he resents me coming here and taking over the case. So he's grumpy, that's all."

"That going to be a problem?" she asked.

"Nothing I can't handle," he said.

Cordero had taken a pair of latex gloves from his valise. He put one on his right hand and offered the other to Carter.

"Might as well make yourself useful," he told her.

He took the sheet off the body. The lifeless face of Professor Hank Frankston stared up at them. He had been a relatively young man, with sandy-coloured hair, a strong lean body, and the weathered complexion of someone who'd spent an active few weeks between sun and salt water. He was dressed in a T-shirt and shorts both of which were soaked in blood. The shorts had been held up by a leather belt from which hung an empty scabbard. There was an old pair of sneakers on his feet, and his arms and legs were flecked with dried blood.

"Tell me what you know about Frankston," Cordero said as he began examining the dead man's clothing.

"Thirty-two years old. Comes from a place called Eureka in northern California," Carter began, recalling what she'd gleaned from information Miller had given her at the Dili airport. "Coastal town. Did an undergraduate degree in biology at the University of San Diego followed by a PhD in marine biology at UCLA." She was shadowing Cordero as he cast an eye over each article of clothing. "That's the University of—"

"I know what UCLA stands for," he said.

"Okay. Attained his PhD eight years ago. Started teaching undergraduate science at UCLA. Met Susanna Sheridan there. The two started dating and married four years ago. He was a rising star in coastal marine biology. Lots of publications in prestigious journals followed by lots of research grants. Field work off Baja California, in Tahiti and Hawaii. That's where he obtained the grant to come here. They came for three months about ten weeks ago."

"He was about due to go home?" Cordero asked as he took each of Frankston's hands in turn in his own gloved hand.

"Yes and no," Carter replied. "He'd applied for an extension. Wanted another six months on top of the first three. He was waiting to hear the result."

Cordero moved around to examine Frankston's skull, face, and jaws. Carter leaned in to watch him.

"And the wife, or should I say widow? She a scientist too?"

"Susanna Sheridan originally. No. She studied liberal arts but at the same campus. Twenty-seven years old. Father's a prominent US senator from North Carolina. Brother died 24 years ago from leukaemia."

"If she's from North Carolina, why was she studying in California?" Cordero asked.

Carter edged away from the body and thrust her hands in the pockets of her trousers.

"It's common for American students to leave home and travel interstate for university."

"So, nothing unusual there?"

"No. Not necessarily."

"Okay," said Cordero.

"She completed her degree but after that there's nothing to suggest she worked anywhere," continued Carter. "Whirlwind romance, apparently, and they married as he was heading off to Tahiti."

"Was she pregnant?" Cordero asked.

"Maybe but there's no children."

"No children?"

Carter glanced at him. "She's only twenty-seven. Almost the same age as me," she protested.

Cordero was silent a moment.

"Happy marriage?" he asked finally.

"Nothing to suggest otherwise," said Carter.

"But no children? After four years of marriage?"

Carter glanced at him. "That's common in America too. Like I said, she's only my age, give or take."

Cordero straightened.

"I'd say he's been dead at least twelve hours," he said. "Maybe a little more. Sometime last night. Before midnight."

Carter cast an eye more closely over the body.

"Sounds about right," she agreed.

"Help me roll him on his side," Cordero said.

They pushed the body up on its right side. Cordero lifted the T-shirt which was dark and stiff with dried blood.

"Wounds in the vicinity of both kidneys," he said circling Frankston's lower back with his finger. "Nowhere else. No slashing. Not what I'd call a frenzied attack. I'd say Frankston was left to bleed out or else died fairly quickly from shock. Either way he wouldn't have lasted long."

Carter bent forward to look closely at the stab wounds. "Short blade. Very sharp. Hunting or fishing knife maybe."

They lowered the body down. Cordero took off his glove. "Seen enough?" Carter stood erect and nodded.

"What now?" she prompted.

"I'll look at the photos Amparo took. Once I've done that, I'll have a talk with the boy he's arrested. Then I'll clear the body to be taken to Dili. Mrs Frankston will have to be notified first, of course. She may want to accompany her husband's body to Beloi. I'll also call Brooks," he said, referring to Doctor Howard Brooks, the English pathologist currently in charge of the morgue in Dili. "Tell him to expect a VIP customer. I'll drop you at the place where we're staying and catch up with you a little later."

Carter held up a hand. "Wait a second," she said. "I'd like to have a look at the suspect as well."

"That won't do any good," Cordero insisted. "You don't speak Tetun."

"A *look*, I said," replied Carter firmly. "I won't get in your way." And she adopted an expression he knew from experience meant it would be useless to argue with her.

• • •

"Show me the photos you took," Cordero said to Amparo when they'd returned to the police station. The sergeant pulled out his cell and showed Cordero the dozen shots he had taken. Cordero flicked through them. There were long shots of the body lying in a ditch, close-ups of wounds, and photos of the area in which the body had been found. As he suspected, they told Cordero nothing more than what he already knew from examining the body. He handed the cell to Carter who scanned the photos quickly before returning the cell to Amparo.

"Send those to my phone," Cordero said and he wrote the number down for the sergeant. Amparo took the slip of paper without comment. "Now I'd like to talk to the suspect," Cordero added.

Justino Ferrao was crouched in a corner of the small, cement block outhouse that served as Vila's holding cell. A tiny, barred window allowed in light from the top of the far wall and a camp bed and bucket were the only furnishings. The air inside was hot and close. Cordero entered, ignoring the conditions, hands in his pockets. He took a position opposite Justino and against the wall just inside the heavy door he closed shut behind him. He could see that the boy was thin even by Timorese standards, that he was dressed in little more than rags, and that his hair was long and matted. His appearance signalled neglect and dejection. The boy brought his feet up under his buttocks and curled himself into a tighter ball as though distancing himself as far as he could from his intruder.

"*Botarde* Justino," Cordero said, meaning good afternoon. "My name's Vincintino Cordero. I'm a police investigator from Dili."

Justino said nothing, his head buried face down in his arms.

"Do you know why you're here, Justino?" Cordero asked.

Justino tried to compress himself into an even smaller bundle of misery. After a moment the head shook.

Carter was watching through a small slot cut into the door.

"Sergeant Amparo says you were found near the cemetery this morning," Cordero said, "after he thinks you killed the American."

Justino's feet shifted slightly, and his hands tightened their grip around his haunches.

He shook his head. "I don't know any American," he said.

"You don't have to know someone to kill them," Cordero said. He paused. "Did you kill someone last night? Maybe got into a fight and things got out of control?"

Justino raised his head. There were tears running down his face and mucous dripped from his nose.

"I didn't kill anyone," he whimpered. "I don't know what you're talking about."

"But it looks like you've been in a fight," Cordero said.

The head dropped and his shoulders quivered from his sobbing. Cordero waited.

"The spirits," Justino said after a short while. "They followed me. They attacked me. I didn't do anything."

"The spirits?" queried Cordero. "What spirits, Justino?"

"I don't know. Spirits of the dead. They come after me," he said and cried more loudly. "They always come after me."

"Okay. Where did these spirits attack you? In the cemetery?"

Justino snuffled once, twice, and slowly collected himself. "No. The spirits like to follow me through the forest. The forest that grows near the cemetery."

"Can you look at me, Justino?" Cordero asked, and the youth tentatively raised his head. His eyes were red from crying, his face bruised and flushed. "What were you doing in the forest this morning?"

Justino wiped a hand under his nose.

"I was coming into the village. I always do at that time of the morning. The spirits know that. That's how come they could attack me."

"And from the forest you walk past the cemetery on your way to the village?"

Justino nodded.

"Do you own a knife, Justino?" Cordero asked.

The boy stopped his crying as though the question had distracted him from his misery. "I have a machete," he said and sniffled. "To cut the coconuts. I take coconuts around the village and sell them for their water."

"I didn't ask about a machete," Cordero reminded him. "I asked about a knife."

"I don't own any knife," Justino said.

"Do you know where you could go to get a knife?"

A second time Justino rubbed a hand roughly under his nose. "My mother won't let me touch a knife," he said. "She says I'll cut myself."

Cordero pushed himself off the wall.

"Your mother is a wise woman," he said. "Would you mind standing up?"

"Why?" replied Justino.

"I just want to have a look at you," said Cordero.

"That other one hurt me," Justino complained.

"The other one? You mean Sergeant Amparo?"

"No. He just yelled at me. The other one hurt me."

"You mean the other police officer?"

"Yes. He pushed me and pulled my hair," Justino said and mimicked the actions with his hands.

"Well, he shouldn't have done that," said Cordero. "I'll have a word with him about it. But I won't touch you. Promise. I just want to have a look at your injuries. Make sure you're okay."

Justino put a hand to the bruises on his face and rubbed his fingers on his shirt.

"Don't do that!" said Cordero. "Just keep your hands by your side and I'll see that you're cleaned up later. Okay? You wouldn't want to dirty your clothes any more than they are already, or your mother might get mad with you."

"Alright," said Justino. He rose awkwardly to his feet but pressed himself tight against the wall.

Cordero came forward just a little and Justino recoiled. Cordero withdrew but cast an eye over Justino's face, his hands, and his clothes. When he was done, he went back to the far wall.

"Where were you last night?" he asked.

Justino's head jerked as though from a tic and a hand went up to the side of his head.

"Last night?"

"Yes. Last night," Cordero repeated.

"In my hole."

"Your what?"

"My hole. I like to sleep in the ground." The boy's head shook, and he brought his hand down to his side. "Up on the mountain," he said, gesturing to nowhere in particular. "I get power that way."

"Power?"

"Yes. When I can sneak out of the house without my mother knowing I climb the mountain and dig a hole to sleep in. The earth gives you power. One day I'll be strong. Stronger than the spirits and they won't attack me anymore."

• • •

"You get a look at him?" Cordero asked Carter as they walked into the main building of the police station.

"Yeah," she said. "What did he have to say for himself?"

"Said spirits attacked him in the forest as he was coming back from sleeping in a hole in the ground."

She glanced across at him.

"Troubled kid," she said.

"Yeah. But not insane and not a killer," Cordero said as he opened the door for her.

Sergeant Amparo was slumped in his chair beside the window, but he straightened himself as best he could when Carter and Cordero came in.

"I doubt he's the one," Cordero said.

The sergeant folded his arms. "You worked that out in all of five minutes, huh? What makes you think so?" he asked.

"For one thing there were no defensive wounds on Frankston and no sign on his knuckles that he'd hit anyone. Whatever fight Justino was involved in wasn't with our victim."

"The *malae* could have used a stick or a rock on him," Amparo objected. "That means nothing."

"Second," Cordero continued ignoring the objection, "the boy keeps talking about being attacked by spirits. He used the plural. That tells me it wasn't a lone American he was quarrelling with."

"*Spirits*, huh? The boy can count spirits," he said dismissively. "I told you he's crazy."

"And Frankston wasn't killed with a machete, which Justino says he owns. He was killed with a small knife. If that crazy boy, as you call him, had used a machete or a knife to attack Frankston, I'd expect to see a slashing attack not the more targeted one that the victim's injuries suggest."

"That's bullshit," Amparo said and waved a hand at nothing in particular. "You're just imagining things."

Carter was looking from one to the other, not understanding the Tetun they spoke but conscious that their exchanges were growing more heated. She also noticed the colour was rising in the sergeant's face and he had begun to sweat as their presence in the cramped room raised the temperature even further.

"You people are sent over here just to make life difficult," Amparo said, pointing an accusing finger at Cordero. "When we're under-staffed too. You've been on the island a couple of hours and already you think you know more than me. Bullshit you do! You want to complicate everything to justify your fancy title. I'm telling you: he's the one!"

Cordero ignored the outburst. "What other foreigners are here in Vila at the moment?" he asked.

"What's that got to do with it?" Amparo demanded to know.

"Well as you said, it's highly unusual for a Timorese to attack a foreigner. So, if Justino didn't do it—"

"He did!"

"Let's just say he didn't," suggested Cordero in a conciliatory tone. "What other foreigners?"

The sergeant sniffed and tugged up the front of his pants under his expansive belly.

"The widow," he snapped. "She's a foreigner. Then there's

tourists but they come and go and they've all gone now. It's the start of the wet season. They like to snorkel and dive but they don't like to get wet from the rain. There's the Australian, what's his name?" He clicked his fingers. "Evans. That's it. Robert Evans. He made a point of introducing himself when he arrived about a month ago. Comes and goes. Pays for a room where the priest lives. Historian of some sort."

"That it?"

"Well there's the African," grumbled Amparo. "But he's lived here for forty years. From Mozambique. Portuguese brought him here as a prisoner in '73 or '74. Released just before the Indonesians invaded but after they did there was nowhere he could go for the next 24 years so you might say he set down roots."

"The African got a name?"

"Yeah. *Benvindu Jezu*."

"His name's Welcome Jesus?"

"Took it when he joined the Assembly of God church. That's what he's called himself for longer than I've lived here."

"Apart from the widow did either of these two foreigners have anything to do with Frankston?" asked Cordero.

"I've enough to do without watching foreigners," Amparo complained. He tried to shrug off his annoyance. "I saw Frankston and Evans together a few times and Welcome has a boat. Frankston hired him to go diving a lot of the time." The sergeant's face hardened. "But I'm telling you it's the crazy boy we've got."

"Well, there's one way to find out," Cordero said. "I want you to send blood samples from Justino to Dili with Frankston's body. I'll take them from his face and hands and also some of the blood on his clothing. If the blood on the clothing matches Frankston's I'll give your theory more credit."

"My theory?" Amparo said in a mocking tone.

"Until we have some hard evidence it's all speculation," Cordero said. "Now where's your cadet? I'd like a word with him."

The sergeant's eyes remained fixed on Cordero but he called: "Sisko!"

The cadet officer had been outside the building fiddling with his motorcycle but he came quickly through the door. He was a young man, his uniform spotless, his hair tied neatly in a small, fashionable bun atop his head.

"*Xefe*," he said, meaning boss.

"The inspector here would like to ask you some questions," Amparo said.

Sisko twisted to face Cordero, who introduced himself. "I'm a police *investigator*," he said. "Tell me how you came to arrest Justino."

The cadet glanced at Amparo before answering. He opened his mouth to speak but noticed Carter who'd appeared from behind Cordero as she moved across the room to study the map on the wall. Sisko's face showed the beginnings of a smile. Cordero cleared his throat to focus the cadet's attention.

"Um. The arrest? Yeah. Right," spluttered Sisko as he tried his best to regain a professional composure. "Well, after the *malae's* body was taken to the health clinic, the sergeant told me to look around where he was found for anything suspicious," he said. "I saw Justino wandering down the road. I could see he'd been in some kind of fight. You know—blood, scratches, torn clothes and stuff. So I brought him in."

He smiled in Carter's direction even though she faced away from him.

"What time was that?" Cordero asked.

"Time?" Sisko fiddled with his watch. "Two, three hours ago."

"What did he say he was doing, why he was on the road, why he looked like he'd been in a fight?" Cordero asked.

Sisko raised and lowered his shoulders. "He mumbled something about spirits in the forest but nothing he was saying made any sense to me."

Cordero translated what the cadet had said for Carter's benefit. She inclined her ear to follow what Cordero was saying but continued to study the maps.

"Justino says you roughed him up," Cordero said to Sisko by way of a question.

Sisko looked over toward the sergeant. "He wouldn't come with me," he said, his voice rising as though his actions were obvious. "Resisting arrest, you know? I just had to do what I could to bring him in. I didn't hit him or anything."

Cordero didn't comment on that.

"Let's get the body off to Dili," he said. "I want you, Sisko, to inform Mrs. Frankston that her husband's body is about to be moved." He turned to Amparo. "I'll need containers of some sort for the blood samples, a pair of scissors, and something I can scrape the boy's face with. Also labels I can affix to the containers."

The sergeant waved an arm contemptuously. "Give him what he needs," he said to Sisko, "and go tell Mrs. Frankston that if she wants to come she should be at the clinic in fifteen minutes."

The cadet started rummaging through drawers on the large desk.

"But tell her if she wants to come all the way to Beloi she'll have to arrange her own return. After I've dropped the body off, I need to go check on another break-in further up the coast."

"Another *uma lulik*?" Sisko asked.

"Yeah," Amparo replied. "Could take some time. You know what these elders are like. You'll have to radio the report to Dili this evening. Seven o'clock sharp. And you'll have to do the late rounds."

He lifted his foot off the trash bin where it had rested.

"Even cell coverage goes down here," he explained to Cordero, "so we use a radio to send our reports to Dili."

4

Cordero and the police cadet Sisko loaded the body of Professor Hank Frankston into the tray of the sergeant's utility as a *tuk-tuk* putted up to the clinic's front gate leaving a trail of exhaust fumes behind it. A man jumped out, a parcel under his arm, and helped a woman down from the back of the vehicle. It was Gerard Miller and the woman was Susanna Frankston.

"What the—" Carter muttered to herself as the woman looked about uncertainly, a kerchief dabbing at her eyes as she lifted her sunglasses.

Miller escorted the woman to the utility. He un-wrapped the parcel he was carrying, unfurled a small American flag, and draped it across the body of Professor Hank Frankston. Mrs. Frankston reached a hand out to touch the body, hesitated, pulled her hand away and began to sob.

Carter approached the grieving widow, encouraged her into the health clinic with an arm placed lightly around her shoulders, and settled her into a chair. She motioned to the nurse who had given Amparo the key to the cool room earlier and signaled for her to sit with Mrs. Frankston until she had collected herself.

Carter went outside and fronted Miller, who was standing in what shade a stand of bamboo provided folding the brown paper the flag had been wrapped in.

"I thought I told you to stay at the lodge until I came," she said, annoyed.

"Ambassador Taylor wants me to offer Mrs. Frankston what support I can," he replied, focused on the folding.

"Ambassador Taylor seems to forget this is first and foremost a police investigation," Carter said. "And by approaching Mrs. Frankston you could be seen to be obstructing it."

"I don't see how," Miller countered, looking up at her.

"No, I guess you wouldn't," Carter huffed. She placed her hands in her pockets and glared at him.

"She looks so devastated," Miller was saying, gesturing after Mrs. Frankston.

"You didn't tell me her husband was a veteran," Carter said, nodding toward the folded paper Miller held in his hands.

"A veteran? He wasn't, as far as I know."

"So why the flag?" asked Carter.

"You don't have to be a veteran to have an American flag on your casket," Miller said. "You just have to be a patriot."

"I don't see a casket," Carter said.

"The Ambassador thought it would comfort Mrs. Frankston to have it placed over his body," he said.

"Did he now?" said Carter. She ran a hand through her hair. "Anyway how is she?" she asked.

"As you'd expect. Upset. Confused."

Carter nodded and began to walk away.

"The Ambassador wants an update on the investigation," Miller called after her.

Carter stopped and spun around to face him. "We've only been here since midday. What does he expect?"

"Details on the man they've arrested for a start," said Miller.

"Who told you the police have arrested someone?"

"That young police officer," Miller said, pointing toward Sisko. "When he came to tell Mrs. Frankston her husband's body was being taken to Beloi for transporting to Dili."

Carter let out a demonstrative sigh.

"Yes they've arrested someone," she said. "But we're not sure he's the one who did it."

"We?" quizzed Miller.

"See that man over there next to the young officer?" Carter said. "That's Vincintino Cordero. He's with a serious crimes unit in the Timorese police. I've worked with him before on a couple of cases. He's smart. Very smart. He and I don't think the local police have arrested the right man. Okay?"

"Why not tell Ambassador Taylor that?" argued Miller.

"You work for the Embassy—you tell him," she said, moving away once more. "We've police work to do."

Cordero had gone into the clinic and introduced himself to Mrs. Frankston. A few minutes later he returned outside, holding a hand over his eyes while he adjusted to the blinding glare of the sun. He went to the driver's side of the utility and told Sergeant Amparo that Mrs. Frankston had chosen not to accompany her husband's body to Beloi. The sergeant nodded, started the engine, and drove off.

Cordero joined Carter. "I told her we need to talk to her when she's feeling up to it," he said. "She said she'd like to get things cleared up as soon as possible so I suggested early evening, after dinner." Carter indicated that arrangement was fine with her with a quick bob of the head. Cordero turned his attention to Miller. "You're Gerard Miller? From the Embassy, I take it? Investigator Cordero of the Timorese police." He held out a hand and Miller shook it. "She wants you there too. Says you're a calming influence."

Before Carter could object, Cordero swung back to her and continued.

"Let's meet up for an early dinner. I'm just heading down to what remains of the market we passed coming here. Sometimes the locals don't reveal things to police but share what they know freely among themselves while their trading. If nothing else, it can't hurt."

· · ·

At the lodge Carter was shown the hut she would share with Estefana and went inside to freshen up. Estefana had unpacked and laid her things out on the bed but was standing over them with a vacant expression on her face when Carter came in.

"Phew, it's hot out there," Carter said and waved a hand against her face to emphasize the point.

Estefana didn't reply.

"So you've claimed your spot," Carter said. "I guess this is mine." She opened the mosquito net and threw herself down on the bed. Estefana remained atypically quiet.

Carter looked across at her.

"Is there something wrong, Estefana? You haven't been yourself since this morning," she said.

Estefana picked two items of her clothing off the bed, held onto them for a second, and put both down. She swung around and slumped down on her bed sitting opposite Carter, head down, hands clasped between her knees.

"Atauro, *mana*," Estefana said, closing her eyes. "It's where the Indonesians took my father and held him. My mother said he wasn't the same when he returned home."

Carter vaguely recalled Estefana saying something about her father when they first met, something about him being held as a prisoner and subsequently dying of heart failure. But beyond that she couldn't recall any details.

Neither spoke for a moment. The only sound was that of birds twittering outside in the oleander bushes.

"And now that I am married my husband and my mother expect babies," Estefana continued. "I'm worried that the spirits of the dead will curse me as a further punishment for the things my father did here."

Carter sat upright.

"What things?"

"He buried the ones who died here," said Estefana. "He buried them away from their origin villages on the mainland."

"So?"

"When someone is buried away from their origin village, away from their ancestors, their spirits can feel disrespected, *mana*," explained Estefana. "They are lost. There is no one to care for their graves or to conduct the ceremonies to honor them."

Carter knew Estefana was relatively well-educated by Timorese standards, she was a practising Catholic, and she was a modern woman in her outlook in many ways. But she also knew there was a core of traditional beliefs and values within Estefana that had been passed down from generation to generation over millennia. Beliefs about the dead and spirits, she also knew, were strongly held by Timorese and couldn't simply be ignored. In Estefana's case, they could compromise how effectively she worked.

"I don't know much about this island," Carter said, grabbing a pillow to place on her lap and leaning across on her forearms. "Tell me about what happened here."

Estefana looked at Carter, took a deep breath and straightened.

"The Indonesians brought the families of resistance fighters here and people from whole villages near where the fighters were active. It was so no one could offer the fighters food and information about troop movements," she explained. "They also brought people like my father who opposed their rule but were not in the resistance movement and they imprisoned them here along with some fighters they'd captured. All together thousands were brought here from the mainland." She rubbed a hand under her nose. "Many never made it home."

For a moment she seemed consumed by her thoughts.

"Some of the prisoners were tortured by the Indonesians," she continued. "Some soldiers took younger women and made them do things they didn't want to do."

She looked at Carter to make sure she understood what she meant. Carter gestured that she did.

"You said your father was given the job of burying those who died," Carter said. "Tell me about that."

Estefana wrapped herself in her arms. "Most people were made to live in huts made from tarpaulins that the Indonesians put up. The huts contained nothing, not even beds, and were very crowded. People had to find their own food, and many died of hunger, especially children, even though islanders shared what little they could with them. There were no medicines."

She sniffled and rubbed her nose.

"Hundreds died and people like my father would have to collect the bodies and bury them. Their spirits are restless and dangerous. They blamed my father for what he did. That's why he'd changed so much when he came home and why he died before his time."

Carter thought this idea absurd but kept her thoughts to herself.

"And how does that concern you? Or any children you may have?" she asked.

"If the spirits are angry they can take it out on the children of the one they are angry with," said Estefana. "Or their grandchildren. The bodies are still here, *mana*. The spirits are still upset."

Again, Carter resisted the urge to criticise what Estefana was saying.

"Where are these graves?" she asked.

"The graves?"

"Yes. Where are the graves your father had to dig?"

"Here in Vila, *mana*, but I'm not sure where. I've never been here."

"Well let's find out where the graves are and keep you away from them. How's that?"

"Spirits can travel, *mana*," Estefana said.

"Maybe but they won't have any reason to bother you if they don't see you near the graves, right?"

Estefana said nothing.

"What is it now?"

"I worry about my children, *mana*."

"You're twenty-two years old and only just married," Carter said. "Bit early to be thinking about having babies isn't it?"

"This is Timor, *mana*. It's expected."

"Well, you're not going to give birth to any children here," Carter said, trying to make light of it. She picked up a towel from the end of her bed. "But we can talk about that some other time. I need to clean up and get something to eat. Do you realise we've had no lunch?"

• • •

It was a small weekday market held on a bare patch of ground near the center of Vila. The main vendors—mostly middle-aged women dressed in jeans or skirts—occupied a dozen simple stalls made of roughly cut wooden planks. Some sat with idle expressions on their faces as they brushed flies away from bundles of fresh and dried fish hanging from poles strung across support beams. Others lingered behind neat piles of corn, sweet potatoes, tomatoes, and chilies on makeshift tables beneath the palm frond roofing.

Older women in shabby traditional *tais*—a woven sarong—squatted on the ground on their haunches. Their teeth and gums were red from years of chewing betel nut and the meagre items they offered for sale—small clumps of garlic; a few sugar bananas—indicated their near destitution. Men in shorts and flip-flops hurried back and forth from their boats with fish, octopus and shellfish for the women to sell while others sat on motorcycles smoking clove cigarettes under the shade of a large strangler fig.

Cordero's inquiries garnered little useful information. When he asked about the Frankstons he was met with blank stares; no one wanted to get involved with the affairs of foreigners. The mention of Justino Ferrao brought a different reaction: laughter from the younger men and older heads shaken in despair.

Only one old woman, her hair a silvery grey under a dirty headscarf and her front teeth missing, told him anything of interest. He repaid her by buying her small pile of four bananas.

• • •

"What have you there?" Carter asked Cordero as he joined her and Estefana for dinner.

"Dessert," said Cordero, placing the bananas on the table and seating himself.

"Hi Estefana," he said. "You must have just got back to work after your wedding. How's Josinto and how's married life treating you two?"

"Good, *maun*," was all she said and lowered her eyes.

Cordero thought the brief response unusual but the expression on Estefana's face told him not to press the issue.

"You find out anything at the market?" Carter asked.

"Only that Justino Ferrao is in the care of a *matan-dook*," replied Cordero, savoring the grilled fish that had been brought to the table along with rice and a small bowl of freshly cut chilies.

"A what?" Carter said.

"A *matan-dook*. It means 'one who sees far'. Kind of like a traditional healer," Cordero said as plates of salad were added to the table. "Name's Isahe Lengesi. But most people just call him the *matan-dook*. I was told where you lives."

"And the significance of this is what, exactly?"

"He'll know Justino's background and possibly what's wrong with him. That may help to work out what's behind his story about being attacked by spirits."

Clouds were building in the twilight on the southern horizon and a breeze was picking up. Cordero took his cell from his pants pocket, punched in a number, and shifted away from Carter and Estefana to make a call.

Carter was famished but loaded Estefana's plate before her own. Cordero closed his phone and piled rice and fish onto his own plate. Estefana picked up a fork but only pecked at what was in front of her.

"Sounds like your *matan-dook* is the same as a shaman where I work at home," Carter said. "Among the Navajo in particular, I mean. They're called a *hataalii*."

Cordero motioned her to continue.

"They're the singer at traditional ceremonies intended to heal and protect. They need good memories: those sings can go for days."

She took a bite of her dinner.

"There's a few *hataalii* around even now—a lot more fakes, of course, who make a living fleecing tourists—but most have died out. Sick younger Navajos prefer Western medicine to drums and chanting."

Cordero nodded while he chewed a helping of his dinner.

"The reverse is true here," he said. "Well, up to a point, at least." He waved his fork.

"When the Indonesians were here they only provided

healthcare to people who supported them. So most people went without and had to rely on traditional healers. Before they left, the Indonesians destroyed what medical facilities there were. So again people had to rely on the old practices. Traditional healing is now regarded as part of what it means to be Timorese."

He took another helping of fish and rice and added a spoonful of chili on the side.

"Our *matan-dook* claim to be able to communicate between the world of the living and the world of the dead," Cordero continued. "Talk to spirits, in other words."

"You've no monopoly there," Carter said. "It's the same with our *hataalii*—the genuine ones at least. They don't talk about it though. Only the fake ones do."

"Well we don't have too many fake *matan-dook* here," said Cordero.

"Timor just hasn't caught up yet," said Carter grinning.

They ate in silence for the next few minutes before Cordero sat back and tried his cell for coverage.

"I can't raise Brooks," he said, closing his phone once more and shoveling the last of the fish and some salad onto his plate. "Cell coverage—Amparo said it comes and goes."

"That reminds me," said Carter. "This is called an eco-lodge we're staying in, right? So tell me, what does the 'eco' stand for exactly?"

Cordero stifled a chuckle.

"The whole of the island is undeveloped," he said. "That includes this village and this place. So the environment here is reasonably pristine. The government is touting Atauro as an ecologically desirable tourist spot. The coral reefs, the mountains—"

"So what you're saying," Carter cut in, "is that no running water, hot showers or reliable cell coverage amounts to eco-friendly."

"Pretty much," agreed Cordero.

"I could be back on the reservation," said Carter and sighed. "Only I'm not."

Cordero turned to Estefana.

"So I need you to go to the police station this evening and ask the officer on duty to radio a message through to Brooks that we need a report on Frankston's body as soon as possible and on the blood samples I've sent with the body and whether any of them are the same as Frankston's blood. We—" he pointed his fork at Carter—"have to go see Mrs. Frankston so could you do that?"

Estefana managed a smile and nodded. Cordero checked his watch. "The police station has to radio headquarters in Dili at seven so maybe you should go as soon as you finish dinner." He cleaned up what was left on his plate. "And we should be on our way to Mrs. Frankston's now. Where's Miller?"

"Miller's nourished by duty more than food," Carter said. "He's probably already there."

5

Miller was there and he hadn't eaten. He'd stayed with Mrs Frankston after Sergeant Amparo drove off to Beloi with her husband's body almost two hours earlier. He sat now under a dim light at a table with Mrs Frankston in a room that served as a combined kitchen, dining and lounge space in a deteriorating three-room cement block house she and her husband had rented. A second room was a bedroom: the third had been used as a space for Professor Hank Frankston to keep his samples, draw his maps, compile his notes, and make entries in his journal.

A bathroom of sorts made of bamboo and tin was attached to the building as an afterthought. The only adornment in the room where Mrs Frankston sat staring at her hands was a print of the Virgin Mary on one wall, dust building up over the white dress and blue cape on the inside of the glass. Two cups of tea had been placed on the table. When Cordero and Carter entered, Mrs Frankston's cup was nearly empty, but Miller's was untouched and cold. After introducing himself and Carter a second time and offering condolences, Cordero accepted the invitation to pull two chairs up to the table opposite Mrs Frankston.

"I understand your husband was engaged in research for the University of Hawaii," he began. "Can you tell me a little more about what, exactly, he was researching?"

Mrs Frankston reached for her tea, tilted the cup slightly to peer inside, and put it down. She took a deep breath.

"Hank is—" she caught herself and paused a second "—I mean *was* a marine biologist," she began. "Coral was his specialty." She smiled grimly. "Do you know how important coral reefs are?" she asked as though the fact she was about to reveal would somehow elevate the reputation of her late husband. "The answer is enormously important. They support thousands of marine species and provide food and incomes for millions of people." She stopped, her face blank. "Sorry. I'm sounding like Hank."

She lent forward and traced a finger across the table.

"The oceans are warming and the world's corals are dying out." She eased back in the chair. "Little is known about the coral reefs here on Atauro. Hank thought he might find new species of coral reliant on unique types of microscopic algae that are more resilient to rising temperatures." She uttered a pathetic little laugh. "I sound like a textbook, don't I?"

"And did he find them?" Cordero asked. "New species and unique algae, I mean?"

Mrs. Frankston ran a hand through her hair. "I'm not sure. I think he was close. But I'm not sure. I don't know enough to follow the details of all he did."

"You seem to know quite a bit about coral nonetheless," said Carter.

Mrs. Frankston looked directly at Carter for the first time.

"It's hard not to know a bit about coral when you are married to someone obsessed by it," she said. "But I'm not a marine biologist. I only know the general stuff."

"You and your husband arrived on Atauro about eight weeks ago, I believe," said Cordero.

"Yes."

"And he went straight to work?"

She wiped her hand under an eye. "That was Hank. Yes, straight to work. I set up the house as best I could."

"Who did your husband associate with here on the island?"

"Associate with?" She considered the question. "He got in touch with that African fellow—Welcome Jesus, he calls himself. He owns a boat and speaks English. Hank hired him each week to take him out on the reef. You know, snorkelling or diving. Then there's Mister Evans. My husband and he got on well right from the start. Occasionally they dived together. Bob would also visit us often. He and Hank would go into the back room and talk for hours."

"Bob?"

"Yes. Bob. Robert Evans. That's his name."

"No one else?" asked Cordero.

The breeze outside had picked up and it shook the window and the poorly fitted front door. Cordero folded his legs back under his chair. Mrs Frankston hadn't flinched and Carter kept her eyes locked on her. Miller rose and poured a glass of water for Mrs Frankston from a bottle sitting on the kitchen bench.

She took the glass off Miller but didn't drink.

"The only other people I can think of are the police," she said. "Hank wanted to make sure they kept an eye on the place and an officer would occasionally come by. Hank didn't want anyone, you know kids mainly, fooling around with his scuba gear, the specimens he'd collected or his notes while he was out. Especially his notes."

She took a deep shuddering breath.

"They were the fruit of his work," she added. "But I wouldn't say he knew any of the police well. It was just a precaution."

"Did your husband own a knife?" Cordero asked.

"A knife?" she looked unsure. "He may have."

"There was an empty scabbard on his belt," Cordero said.

Mrs Frankston nodded. "Yes. Yes, now that you mention it Hank did carry a knife on his belt." She considered that. "Is that what—?"

Her cell buzzed. She placed her glass of water on the table and took the cell out of her pocket. She checked the caller ID and quickly cancelled the call.

"You can take that if you like," said Cordero.

"It's okay," she said, turned the cell off, and put it in her pocket.

"Do you know what kind of knife your husband owned?" Cordero asked.

"What kind?" Mrs Frankston looked at Cordero. "No. I've no idea. I'm sorry."

"What have you been doing these past few months?" Carter asked, interrupting Cordero's questioning.

Mrs Frankston waved a hand about the room.

"Keeping house has been a challenge. Cooking, cleaning—the facilities here are very basic. I do some work at the women's cooperative in the village. They make things for the tourist trade—shawls and the like mostly. I'm not much good at a foot-pedalled sewing machine but I can write brochures for tourists. Few of the local women speak English and those that do only know a few words. But I don't go often. I read, swim, go for walks…."

"Must get kind of boring," Carter said. "Having all that time on your hands, I mean."

"I've been on field trips with Hank before," Mrs. Frankston said. "I'm used to it."

"I understand your husband had applied to extend his stay here," said Carter. She tilted her head slightly. "How did you feel about that?"

Mrs. Frankston opened her hands in a gesture of indifference. "My husband was committed to his work," she said. "I was committed to my husband."

"I appreciate that but what I'm asking is how you *felt* about extending your stay on Atauro another, what, six months?"

Miller began to shift uncomfortably in his seat.

"That was fine by me," Mrs. Frankston replied. "As I said, I was committed to my husband."

"Do you know why anyone would want to harm your husband?" Cordero asked.

Mrs. Frankston wiped her nose clumsily with her hand.

"No. I have no idea at all. Hank was not a man to make enemies."

The window shook and the door rattled against its frame. The light in the room had suddenly dimmed further. A clap of thunder sounded above the house. A storm was imminent.

"What was he doing out late last night and near the cemetery?" Cordero asked.

"Hank usually went for a walk at night. He said it relaxed him and took his mind off his work. There aren't too many roads in Vila. The one going past the cemetery was a regular route of his."

"What did you do last night?" Carter asked.

"Agent Carter, really!" protested Miller.

Susanna Frankston placed a hand lightly on Miller's forearm which rested near her on the table. "I stayed in," she answered. "As I normally do. I washed the dishes after dinner, read in bed for a while and went to sleep."

"The power didn't go out last night?" Carter persisted.

"I couldn't say. We have a battery-operated lamp in the bedroom. I always use it when I read in bed."

"Did you see your husband go out?" Cordero asked.

"Of course. I told him to have an enjoyable walk."

She seemed to hold back tears at the irony of that.

"Did he say he was meeting anyone?" Cordero ventured after a short pause while she collected herself.

She shook her head. "No."

"Did he seem his usual self—I mean, not agitated or anxious?"

"He seemed perfectly normal." She wiped her eyes. "Hank wasn't one to get agitated or anxious."

"Was he carrying anything when he left?"

"No. Not that I recall," Mrs. Frankston said.

"Weren't you worried when he didn't come home?" Cordero asked.

"I told you: I was asleep. Hank often walked for hours to clear his mind," she said.

"And when you woke and found he wasn't here?" Cordero said.

"I woke quite late. I figured he'd gone to the reef."

"You didn't sleep together?" asked Carter.

Mrs. Frankston glared at her and Miller shook his head in disbelief. "Hank would sometimes come home late from his walk, go to his room in the back, dose off and stay there all night."

Carter held her stare. Cordero turned to her and Carter blinked as if to say 'finished'.

"Do you have any questions, Mrs. Frankston?" he asked.

"When can she return to Dili and when can I arrange for her husband's body to be flown to the States?" Miller interjected.

Cordero rose. "I expect the autopsy will be completed in the next couple of days," he said. "There's only one pathologist in Dili but of course this case will have priority. However Mrs. Frankston will have to remain until the investigation is completed."

"Is she a suspect?" asked Miller, his brow creased in concern.

"She may be able to assist with enquiries," Cordero phrased it more diplomatically. "Throw further light on her husband's movements, his activities—that sort of thing."

"This is a very distressing time—" Miller began.

"It's alright, Gerard," said Mrs. Frankston, touching his forearm a second time. "The police have their work to do. I fully understand."

Carter stood now as well.

"I'll need your passport, Mrs. Frankston," Cordero said.

She rose and went to the bedroom. Miller remained seated, looking annoyed. Presently Mrs. Frankston appeared with the passport and handed it to Cordero.

"I'll also need to look at your husband's study," he said. "But that can wait. Tomorrow, perhaps. Is there a way you can secure it in the meantime?"

"Hank put a lock on the door and kept the key under the tin where we keep the coffee," she said and moved toward the kitchen bench. "I'll lock it now."

Once she'd locked the door, Cordero took the key from Mrs. Frankston. He thanked her as he exited. Miller said he would stay a little longer and make his own way to the lodge later.

"A dutiful wife," quipped Carter as she and Cordero made their way toward the main road through the village.

The darkness had fallen quickly and almost completely. There were no street lights, those villagers with electricity used it sparingly, and only the public buildings—the police station, the health clinic—and the eco-lodge glowed from within. Occasionally the headlight of a motorcycle passing up ahead broke the gloom but only fleetingly.

"There are some," said Cordero.

"Even some married to an 'obsessed' husband, as she called him?"

Cordero shrugged. "Did you notice how friendly she and your Embassy fellow seem to be?" he asked.

"I think we were meant to notice," said Carter. "Just as I think we were meant to hear her call him Gerard. It doesn't hurt to look like you have the US Embassy in your corner in sticky situations."

"Even so, that relationship blossomed quickly."

"Miller is young and naive," said Carter. "And she's a fast worker, I'd say. Remember the whirlwind romance? And some of her answers came a little too fast for a grieving widow."

"Yes. I was thinking the stuff about coral might have been rehearsed," Cordero said, as the first spits of rain shot down.

"I was thinking more of her answers about the husband's movements and her own," Carter replied.

Cordero looked at the sky where heavy black clouds now blanketed the island.

"I think we'd better hurry," he said, and as they quickened their pace the wind bent the coconut palms and the rain thrashed down.

• • •

The police cadet Sisko was slumped over the large desk chewing on the end of a pencil in the police station when Estefana knocked and entered. His jaw dropped to see an attractive girl in a blue Timorese police uniform break the boredom of the paperwork he was preparing for this evening's radio report to Dili.

"So you're part of that police contingent from the mainland?" he asked after Estefana had introduced herself. "I did basic training in Dili. Would I love to work there instead of here."

Sisko had eased his chair away from the desk to get a better look at Estefana and he now leaned against the office wall on the chair's back two legs. He stretched his feet out making like it was his regular desk rather than that of Sergeant Emilio Amparo. He smiled the perfect smile that only someone brought up on a largely sugarless diet can smile.

"Seat?" he asked.

"No thanks," Estefana said. "I've been transferred to Dili from Suai on the south coast. But I was assigned temporarily as an interpreter for an American FBI agent working with INTERPOL. She doesn't speak Tetun."

"FBI huh? And INTERPOL. Wow!" said Sisko. "I'm impressed." He creased his brow and brought the front legs of his chair to the floor. "So what are you doing here?" he asked.

"She—her name is Sara Carter—was asked by her Embassy to come over while the investigation into the death of that American is carried out."

"But I thought they'd sent that police investigator over here for that," Sisko said. "That's what the sergeant told me."

"Yeah, they did. Vincintino Cordero."

There was a rumble of thunder overhead.

"But you don't translate for him, right?" he quizzed her. "I mean he's Timorese."

"I only translate for the American. *Maun* Cordero speaks Tetun and he grew up in Australia. So he also speaks English."

Sisko scoffed.

"Bet he doesn't speak Hresuk," he said. "That's my first language. I'm Humangili," he added, meaning a member of one of the small clan groups on the island. "So where's this Cordero now?"

"He and the American are talking to the dead man's widow."

Sisko placed a finger to his chin and thought. The smile re-emerged on his face. "So you're not needed to translate for this FBI agent tonight? I mean, she's with this Cordero. And that dead guy's wife is American herself, right? So they all speak English."

Estefana could guess where this was leading.

"Yeah. But I've a lot of work to do," she said.

"What work?"

"There are things I need to translate for *Mana* Carter," Estefana lied, and immediately felt a sense of guilt for having done so.

"So you're not up for a coffee?" He pointed to the radio lying on the other desk. "I just have to call through a report to Dili and I'm finished for the night."

"Sorry. I'm busy. I'm here to ask you to add a message for the pathologist in Dili. Dr Howard Brooks. *Maun* Cordero wants him to perform an autopsy on the body when it arrives. As soon as possible. Also he needs him to test some blood samples that went with the body to see if any match the dead man's blood."

Sisko sighed with disappointment.

"Yeah. I can do that," he said. "Sure you don't have twenty minutes? Ten even? I make a great coffee."

He took a coffee mug off the desk that held the radio and held it out to her. The mug was imprinted with the white crest and gold crown of the Real Madrid soccer team.

"Aren't you a girl who likes to play?" he asked, grinning.

She frowned in a way that told him he'd gone too far.

He wrote a short note of the instructions for Brooks on a slip of paper. "I'll get this off first thing," he said. "You can count on me."

"Thanks," she said and made to leave when she noticed the map on the wall.

"Where did they bury the people who died after the Indonesians brought them here?" she asked, inspecting the map.

"The prisoners?" Sisko asked. He rose and joined her in front of the map. "The Portuguese had their prison here," he said and pointed to a spot on the southern fringe of Vila. "It was an underground prison—easier to keep them secure that way I guess. You can still see the depressions where the cells were dug."

He checked to see if he had her attention. Her gaze was fixed to the map.

"The Indonesians used it for serious prisoners. But most people they dumped here were left to fend for themselves so long as they didn't move around. If they died, they buried them here."

He reached a hand out and circled a finger around a place on the map.

"At the main cemetery," he said. "There's a couple of mass graves there somewhere but I'm not sure where. It was before my time."

He stepped back from the map and glanced sideways at her.

"Atauro was closed as a prison in 1988. I'm only 24. You?"

Estefana didn't answer. She surveyed the map for half a minute longer before wheeling around to go.

"I'd sure like to be working in Dili," Sisko repeated, eyeing her figure as she made for the door.

"You'll get a transfer in time," she said over her shoulder. "What's your rush?"

He sat down by the radio.

"This place," he said. "It has a way of crushing dreams."

Suddenly raindrops started hammering on the tin roof of the building and Estefana made a dash for the lodge hoping she could make it without getting soaked.

6

"She has access to information I might need," said Cordero into his cell, "and she's an experienced investigator."

"That's all immaterial," said the voice at the other end. It was Cordero's superior Chief Inspector Francisco Jada and the two had had their disagreements before. "Her country is about to consider a replenishment grant for the Timorese justice system. That means millions of dollars for police training and equipment."

Jada's voice was rising.

"It could mean your salary Cordero and mine!" he continued. "They'll be watching this case closely because the victim's one of their own. If we can't show them we can solve it ourselves, quickly and efficiently, they might start asking questions about whether their aid is doing any good or is just a waste of money. You have your orders: keep the American at arms length and wrap this case up yourself."

With that Jada ended the call. Cordero swore under his breath just as Carter appeared and joined him for breakfast.

"Hi," she said. "What was that about?"

"Nothing. Just Dili checking in," he replied vaguely. "You sleep well?"

"Yeah but Estefana didn't."

"She okay? Something wrong?" he asked.

"She kept talking this morning about the gecko in our hut."

"The gecko?"

"Yeah. Asked me if I'd heard it. Said it only clucked three times not ten or twelve as she says it should. She thinks it could be an omen."

The coffee arrived and Carter grabbed hers with both hands.

"What do you mean, an omen?" Cordero asked as he sugared his own coffee.

"Her father was imprisoned here by the Indonesians. He was made to bury people who died here in exile. Estefana thinks the spirits of the dead are restless because the bodies are not in their origin villages and they might be inclined to take their anger out on her or, worse, her children."

Cordero tapped his spoon on the rim of his coffee cup, placed it on the saucer and tested his espresso. Satisfied he put the cup down to enjoy the anticipation of drinking it before he actually did.

"You should have a talk to her about it," Carter said, quickly downing her own coffee.

"Estefana holds a lot of traditional ideas," Cordero said eyeing the kitchen for someone to bring the food. "I grew up in Australia so to her I'd be an outsider. She wouldn't take any notice of anything I told her about spirits."

A woman from the kitchen brought two plates with omelets and a basket holding fresh bread rolls. Cordero drained his coffee and asked the woman for more. The day was hot already but freshened after the previous night's drenching. The scent of lantana hung in the air.

"You don't sound overly sympathetic," Carter said.

"You're closer to her than I am," he said. "If she won't listen to you, she's unlikely to listen to me."

Carter eyed him for a moment before taking up her knife and fork.

"So what's the plan today?" she asked.

"I want to talk to Evans. The church is next door and the room where he's staying is in a building next to that. I walked past it this morning. There's a jeep parked outside with a slouch hat on the dashboard. Australians love slouch hats. So he's there. I'll pay him a visit after breakfast."

"Okay," said Carter, as she worked through her omelet. "After that?"

"After that I'll go see Isahe Lengesi—the *matan-dook* I was telling you about. See what he can tell me about Justino." Cordero pulled apart a bread roll and loaded a piece with some of the omelet.

"What about Frankston's study? You told the widow you wanted to go back there and take a look today," Carter pointed out.

"That can wait for now," said Cordero. "I'll go later."

"You're using the singular pronoun a lot," she commented.

Cordero stopped chewing and threw her a quizzical eye.

"'I', 'me'. What about 'we'?" she said.

"I can work faster on my own," he answered.

"Bullshit," she replied. "Is that the best you can do?"

He popped more of the omelet into his mouth, rubbed his thighs, and looked away.

"Something wrong?" she asked.

He shifted to face her and hesitated. "I've been told to carry out this investigation by myself."

"You mean not with the grumpy sergeant?"

"I mean not with you," he said.

"That so?" she said, showing no surprise. "Why?"

More coffee was brought to the table in a small jug and Cordero welcomed the distraction. The woman lingered and asked if there was anything else they needed. He said 'No' and thanked her while he considered his reply.

"Well?" Carter persisted, picking a bread roll out of the basket.

"They don't want you taking any credit for solving the case," he said.

"I didn't know we're in a competition for credit," Carter said and bit into the roll.

"They say it would reflect badly on the effectiveness of the Timorese police if an FBI agent was involved," he explained. "And that could impact on your government's aid program to our judicial system."

"Who's 'they'?" she asked.

"My superiors," he said.

Carter considered that while she ate the rest of the roll.

"How would your superiors know if we were working together?" she asked.

"I'd say Sergeant Amparo is on to them," said Cordero, refilling his coffee cup. "He doesn't like me meddling in this case, like I told you. Seems to think it's his murder case to solve. He could have called Dili when he reached Beloi yesterday or when he returned last night. You'd have noticed that cell coverage resumed while we were talking to Susanna Frankston. Her cell buzzed, remember?"

Carter nodded and helped herself to the coffee from the jug.

"I'll be having a word with Sergeant Amparo," Cordero added.

Carter drank from her cup. "I'm under instructions too," she said.

Cordero had been about to sugar his second cup of coffee but held the spoon aloft.

"Instructions?" he repeated. "What do you mean?"

"Ambassador Taylor wants me to ensure what he calls an 'acceptable' outcome is achieved in the case."

"Meaning?"

"Meaning Mrs. Frankston goes home as quickly as possible and nothing scandalous is discovered about her or her late husband."

"But what—?" he began.

"Daughter of a US senator, remember?" Carter said.

Cordero sugared his coffee and relaxed.

"So special treatment for Americans," he said.

Carter shrugged.

"What are you going to do about those instructions?" he asked.

She drained her cup and scrunched up her napkin.

"Ignore them," she said in a matter-of-fact tone. "And you?"

He lent forward. "You don't like taking orders do you?"

"Not when they conflict with what it is we're supposed to do as police officers," she said. "And that's to solve cases properly and bring the bad guys to account." She eased away from the table. "Or girls, as the case may be."

He studied her. "You think Mrs. Franskton killed her husband?"

"A pretty young girl in a place like this with few entertainments and a husband devoted night and day to rocks. What do you think?"

"Coral isn't a rock," he said. "It's a living organism."

"I know that," she said. "I was making a point. You saw how quickly she cut off that call last night."

"You're thinking a suitor?"

"Suitor, lover, accomplice. Who knows?" She came forward and jabbed at the table with her finger. "Ever heard the saying 'Still waters run deep'?"

She relaxed.

"So what are you going to do about your instructions?" she asked.

He folded his arms on the table and smiled. "You about ready to go talk to Robert Evans?"

"Just need to brush my teeth," she said, grinning.

As she rose from the table, he held up a hand. "Could you ask Estefana to find out where the African who calls himself Welcome Jesus lives? I don't want her to approach him, just to find out where we can locate him."

He rose from the table.

"Oh, and tell her that the number of 'clucks' that a gecko makes depends on whether it's a mating call or a warning to another gecko about something. She may take my word for it on that subject."

• • •

Carter encountered Miller as she walked to her hut.

"Morning Gerard," she said.

"Morning ma'am," Miller replied. He was dressed casually this morning in jeans and a garish yellow T-shirt that read: 'Put A Smile On Your Dial'.

"What are you up to?" Carter asked.

"I thought I'd help Susanna pack."

Carter stopped, blocking his path.

"So Susanna, is it?" she said not trying to hide her sarcasm.

The boy in the 'Batman' T-shirt was eyeing them from the side of the kitchen.

Miller blushed.

"Mrs. Frankston told me to call her Susanna," he explained.

"I bet she did," said Carter. "What exactly are you two going to pack?"

"Her personal things," Miller said and the colour in his cheeks deepened just a little. "But we won't touch Professor Frankston's study," he quickly added. "I promise you."

"You'd better not, Gerard, or you'd be interfering in a police investigation. Think how that would look at your next performance review." She decided to ease up a little and moved to the side to let him pass. "Look, just take care of yourself, okay? Be sensible. There's a lot about Mrs. Frankston...there's a lot about this case which needs looking into."

Miller nodded.

"By the way, ma'am," he said. "Ambassador Taylor was trying to get you about five minutes ago but you didn't answer your cell."

"I left my cell in my hut when I went for breakfast," Carter said. "I don't like to be disturbed when I'm eating. Upsets my stomach."

"Do you think you could give him a call, ma'am? He's calling me all the time for an update," Miller said.

"I will if you stop calling me 'ma'am,'" Carter said. "I'm not much older than you, you know. Just call me 'Carter'. Everybody else does."

Miller smiled uncertainly and went off to the dining area. The boy followed him and loitered by his table as the woman from the kitchen served Miller his coffee.

"*Bondia*," Miller tried with the boy.

"Benni," the boy said.

"Benni? That's your name?" asked Miller, smiling.

The boy blinked but didn't answer.

"Well, why aren't you in school, Benni? What are you doing here?" Miller asked in Tetun.

The boy scratched his backside with one hand and pointed with the other to a soccer ball lying by the side wall of the kitchen.

The woman appeared with Miller's omelet. She took the basket of bread rolls from Cordero's table, placed it on the side of Miller's plate, and left without speaking.

"Football? You're playing football?" Miller said, tasting his coffee. "You like football?"

The boy nodded. He asked Miller if he wanted to play.

"Not today, Benni. I have some things I must do," Miller replied. He held the basket out to the boy. "Want a bread roll?" he asked.

The boy ignored the basket of rolls and remained fixed on Miller for a moment before running off to kick his ball.

• • •

As Carter entered her hut she heard Estefana in the washroom conducting what sounded like a poor excuse for a shower. She picked up her phone, went outside, and sat down on a step. She punched in the ambassador's personal number. He picked up on the second ring.

"Agent Carter," he said avoiding pleasantries. "I've been trying to get you. Gerard tells me the police have arrested someone for the murder of Professor Frankston. Can we put this tragedy to rest and get Mrs. Frankston over here to Dili today?"

"*We* can't do anything," Carter said. "This is a Timorese police investigation and it's up to them to say when the case is closed and Mrs. Frankston can leave."

"Alright but surely if they've arrested someone—"

"There are doubts about whether they have the right person," Carter said.

"Doubts? What doubts? Who has them?"

"Investigator Cordero".

"Investigator Cordero! But surely you…you're an FBI agent, attached to INTERPOL, representing the United States Embassy—" Taylor spluttered.

"None of that carries any jurisdictional clout here—sir," she said, already tiring of trying to explain things to Taylor.

"Do I need to remind you—?"

"No sir, you don't," Carter interrupted. "We may know more by the end of the day. Hold on a minute." She put her hand over the cell for several seconds and admired the birds skipping through the oleander bushes. "I'm sorry," she said, re-engaging Taylor. "Something urgent has come up and I have to go."

With that she ended the call, stretched, and went inside to brush her teeth.

7

A straggly stream of young children had taken over the main road through Vila, each of them in a neat blue and white uniform with a backpack hanging off their shoulders. Some were in pairs, singing and laughing, others in groups of three or four kicking coconut husks between them, some walking solo as though deep in thought. On the opposite side of the road, sitting on the low stone wall that bordered the Catholic church compound, sat Robert Evans, his chin resting on a heavy wooden walking stick under his unmistakable slouch hat.

He was a solidly built man who looked to be in his early sixties, a flurry of greying hair poking out below the brim of the hat, a matching grey goatee beard below a parched, sunburnt face. The underarms of his khaki shirt, sleeves rolled up, were circled with sweat. Cordero and Carter walked up and joined him.

"*Senyor* Robert Evans?" Cordero said.

"Call me Bob," said Evans, his eyes trained on the children across the road. "And you are?"

"Timorese police investigator Vincintino Cordero and this is—" he hesitated "—my colleague *Mana* Carter."

"G'day. I thought you'd want to talk to me," Evans said. He hadn't looked up. "About Hank, I mean. That's why I stayed here today. In Vila. How can I help?"

"When did you hear about Professor Frankston's death?" asked Cordero.

"Yesterday. News travels fast around here. The priest told me."

Cordero looked across at the jeep.

"That your vehicle?" he asked.

"The priest's," said Evans. "I pay him to use it when he doesn't need it."

"What brings you to Atauro?" Cordero asked. "And for such a long time? You've been here, what, a month, I believe?"

"Yeah, 'bout that. You see I'm—hold on! Shit, look!"

They followed Evans' gaze across the road. A boy of about ten had spotted something on the road. He was pointing with one hand while gathering two friends around with the other. He bent down, picked it up, wiped the thing on his shorts, and held it up to the sun. A cry of excitement went up from each of the three. It was a fifty-centavo coin and they would all have a treat at the kiosk going home.

"Ha ha," Evans burst out, letting his walking stick drop as he slapped his thigh. "Don't you love it? I put coins on the road every morning I'm here in the village. Sometimes here, sometimes further up or further down. It's usually a ten-centavo coin but today I felt generous, so I put that fifty. I love to sit and watch the kids find them. See the expression on their faces. The joy of discovery—it's the thing that makes us truly human, wouldn't you say?"

He looked up at the bemused expression on the faces of Cordero and Carter.

"Sorry, what did you ask?"

Cordero refocused his attention from the excitement of the children on to the excited Australian. "I was asking what brought you to Atauro, *senyor*?"

"Bob. Just call me Bob, mate. What brought me here? Well history. My passion is history. Southeast Asian history in general and Portuguese colonial history in particular." Evans waved his arms around. "This place is full of it going back five hundred years. And very little has been studied." He looked up at Cordero. "You know what the Portuguese called this place?"

"Goat island," Cordero replied.

"No," corrected Evans. "That came later. Much later, when the goat population was out of control. The Portuguese called it '*Ilha dos Condenados*' which loosely translates as 'Island of the Damned'. See they sent their prisoners here from Portugal, Angola, Mozambique, Goa, Macau, and Timor, of course. And no one bothered to research what went on here because, well, it was the island of the damned! Isolated and forgotten. Eventually the Portuguese pulled out, but the Indonesians managed their own hellhole here and no one was allowed to enter or leave. It's only now with independence—"

"That's very interesting," Cordero interrupted, "but what's it to do with you?"

"I taught history in three different universities in Australia," Evans explained, taking his hat off to scratch his head. "But history's not in great demand these days unless it's about something big, you know? Islamic studies after 9/11 or the rise of China. Apart from that it's all finance or digital shit and computing stuff these days. So, I retired and that gives me time to come and study things properly." He put the hat on his head. "There's a lot of old Portuguese relics here just rotting away. The underground prison," he said pointing down the road, "and what's left of old colonial buildings."

Cordero settled himself down on the wall next to Evans and Evans shifted along slightly to give him more room. Carter remained standing, arms folded, in the freckled shade of a large pink hibiscus.

"You knew Professor Frankston well I believe," said Cordero.

"Hank? Shit yeah. We got on well," replied Evans.

"How did the two of you meet?"

"Hank and his missus were here before me but there're few foreigners in Vila as you can see—or rather can't see now," he said and laughed. "So we stood out like sore thumbs. When I started talking to Hank we realized we had a lot in common. Academic backgrounds for a start. You speak good English, by the way. Where did you learn it?"

"I grew up in Australia," said Cordero.

"Melbourne?"

"That's right."

"Thought so. Lot of Timorese there. But I'm from Sydney."

He brushed a fly away.

"What about you, love?" he asked Carter.

"Missouri," she said.

"Never been there," said Evans, before taking up Cordero's question again. "Anyway, as I was saying, mostly Hank and I just hit it off, enjoyed each other's company. Can get lonely here, you know? Along with Susanna we were kinda like the three misfits of Vila?"

"Were you interested in Professor Frankston's research into the reefs?"

"Yeah, nah. Well, sort of. When it comes to the sea, colonial navigation and shipwrecks are more my thing, as I said." Evans picked up a handful of pebbles and began tossing them casually onto the road. "But you see you folks haven't mapped the reefs properly yet. You Timorese I mean. Neither did the Portuguese. Isolated and forgotten, remember? Plus coral spreads and dies, so things change over time."

A screeching *teer-teer-teer* call of a small bird in the trees next to the presbytery distracted Evans. He looked across but couldn't make the bird out through the heavy foliage.

"Hear that?" he asked of no one in particular. "That's the call of an orange-sided thrush. A threatened species, even here. I can't make it out but I know the call." He looked Cordero. "I do a bit of bird watching too," he said.

A fluttering of wings and the bird was gone, its flight shielded by the tree.

"Anyhow, as I was saying, Hank was compiling his own charts and they interested me. Often I'd head over to his place at night and we'd discuss them. Sometimes we'd just have a meal together and sit around and chat."

He dropped the pebbles and raised a knee between his hands.

"Sometimes I'd go diving with him. But he was a lot younger than me. He could go deeper and for longer." He pointed a finger toward the sea. "Do you know how deep that Wetar Straight is out there?" he asked. "At its center almost two miles down. Two miles! Whales use it to swim from the Indian Ocean to the Pacific. So do your country's nuclear submarines, love," he added, tilting his head toward Carter. "It's deep, mysterious. Fascinating."

Cordero ignored the day dreaming. "You know the African?"

"Welcome Jesus," he laughed. "Some name, huh? Yeah, I know him. Hank hired him and his boat. I know Welcome speaks some English. I know he was brought here in the 1970s as a prisoner by the Portuguese."

Evans leaned slightly toward Cordero.

"He was a rebel with FRELIMO. The Mozambique Liberation Front. A real hero to some." He cleared his throat. "Anyway, I've talked a little about those early days on Atauro with him. But that's as much as I know about Welcome."

"What can you tell me about Mrs. Frankston and what she did in Vila?" asked Cordero.

"Susanna? Nice kid, mate," he said nodding. "You bet. Talkative too, you know? What did she do?" He folded one arm under the elbow of the other and cupped his chin. "I'm not sure, to tell you the truth. There are plenty of books in the house and they're not about marine biology, I can tell you that. And sometimes I'd see her at the women's co-op. Oh, and she swam, of course. That's so common in Vila you forget. Everyone swims."

"Did she appear happy?"

Evans shrugged.

"Happy enough, I guess."

"Did you see Professor Frankston the night of his death?" Cordero asked.

"No. Sometimes I'd see him out on his nightly walks. Sometimes I joined him. But no, I didn't see him two nights ago. No."

"His body was found near the cemetery. Was that on his usual route?"

"Search me," replied Evans. "I've done that walk with him, yes. But sometimes he'd walk along the beach. So 'usual route'? I couldn't say."

"What were you doing the night he was killed?"

Evans pursed his lips. "Bloody hell, I didn't kill him, if that's what you're getting at, mate. I was here," he said and flicked a thumb over his shoulder. "Talking to Father Robeiro, actually, at least until the power went out."

"What time was that?"

"Dunno. About nine, ten o'clock I guess," Evans said. "I'm usually in bed by then."

"You speak Tetun, I gather."

"*Uitoan*," said Evans, meaning a little, and he smiled. "I've been learning it in Australia. And I speak a little Portuguese and Father Robeiro speaks a little English. You might say our conversations are a bit like the talk at the United Nations."

The last of the children were running to the school and a crackling recording of the Timorese national anthem seemed to herald the beginning of the day's classes.

"Do you know why anyone would want to kill Professor Frankston?" Cordero asked.

"Shit no!" insisted Evans. "Hank was a nice guy. A real nice guy. And he kept to himself, you know? He didn't buy into anyone else's business. Just focused on his research work."

"Did his research pose a threat to anyone?"

"Coral reefs and algae?" Evans said and laughed. "Are you kidding me, mate? Course not."

"Did Mrs. Frankston have any friends here?" Carter interjected.

Evans looked up at her. He picked up his walking stick in one hand and raised the other to shield his eyes from the glare.

"Friends, love?"

"Yeah, friends."

"If you mean *friends*," he said emphasizing the word, "the answer's no. Certainly not that I'm aware of anyhow. Theirs was a strong marriage so far as I could see. As for *friend* friends, no one special stands out to me."

"We'd appreciate it if you stayed here in Vila until further notice *senyor*," Cordero said, pushing himself up off the wall. "And give me your passport for the time being."

"Blimey. You are serious," Evans said. He unzipped a belly bag on his belt and handed the passport over. "Here. No worries, mate. What about Susanna? When will she be leaving?" Evans asked.

"When our investigation has concluded," Cordero told him.

"I haven't been to see her yet," Evans said, staring blankly across the road. "Not quite sure what to say, you know? And I thought I'd give her some time to herself. Maybe that wasn't such a great idea."

• • •

Carter and Cordero left Evans and walked off toward their lodge. Cordero would go on alone to speak with the *matan-dook*. "A lot of people on this island are reluctant to involve themselves in the affairs of outsiders," he'd explained. "Especially the more traditional types. This *matan-dook* is more likely to open up if it's just another Timorese man asking questions."

Cordero suggested Carter locate Estefana and find out what she'd learned about Welcome Jesus and his whereabouts. They had just parted company when Cordero's cell began to vibrate in his pocket. He retrieved it.

"Cordero," he said.

"Tino!" came the familiar voice of Dr Howard Brooks. "Howard here across the waters in Dili."

"*Bondia*, Howard," said Cordero. "How's your morning?"

"I'm sleep deprived," Brooks complained. "Your body arrived early evening with instructions to give it priority. American, you see, so everything else has to be put to one side. I was just starting to work on it when your urgent message came through about the blood samples. I've been up all night."

"Have you learned anything?"

"Must you really ask a consummate professional that, dear boy?"

Cordero stopped walking and waited. Brooks was yawning, demonstratively.

"He was found about 6am, I believe, and soon after put in a cool room. I checked the weather on Atauro on Tuesday night and noticed heavy cloud cover. That would have kept the ground temperature somewhat warmer than usual. I won't bore you with the science of it as much as I'd like to, but I'd say he was killed no more than eight hours before he was found. So, between ten and twelve the previous night."

"No earlier?" asked Cordero.

"Not unless he'd eaten a substantial meal mid-afternoon and nothing after that."

As far as Cordero knew, he hadn't: Susanna Frankston had mentioned washing the dishes after dinner and that her husband had eaten and gone for his walk. But no one could corroborate where she was after that, and Robert Evans said he had finished talking to Father Robeiro around 9 o'clock.

"The clothes told me nothing," Brooks continued, "but the scabbard on the belt would have housed a knife of about the length I'm thinking caused the fatal injuries. Short and sharp is all I can tell you until I've had a closer look."

Cordero traced the toe of his shoe across the dirt. "What about the blood samples?"

"Well, that's the main thing you wanted to know right away, isn't it?" Another, longer, yawn this time. Brooks was not one to hide how he felt about things. "All the samples you sent are B positive. It's fairly common in this part of the world. Our victim was A-positive, but I found none of that type in any of the samples."

"Just as I thought," said Cordero. "Great. Thanks Howard."

"There's one other thing, dear boy."

Cordero heard what he thought was Brooks pouring himself a cup of tea.

"I'd say our victim was grabbed from behind and constrained by an arm around his neck. The deepest stab wound is to his right kidney and so I'd be confident in saying it was a right-handed assailant who held him by the left arm. On Frankston's right collar bone, I found a small abrasion. A scratch barely visible except to a trained eye, namely mine. It was fresh. It could be nothing but on the other hand it may have been caused by an article of jewellery the assailant was wearing—a watch, bracelet or a ring, something of the kind. But as I said it was superficial—barely visible, no blood—and so it would be nigh on impossible to match with anything."

Cordero couldn't recall if Mrs. Frankston was wearing jewelry. He had spoken to her after a long and tiring day. But he assumed she wore a wedding ring on her left hand: he knew most married Western women did. As for Evans, he should have stayed standing, facing the man. By sitting down next to him, he hadn't been in a position to notice a ring on his left hand or a watch on his left wrist. He was annoyed with himself for his carelessness and hoped that Carter might have been more alert than he'd been.

"But I would say," Brooks was continuing, "that he was grabbed around the neck from behind, stabbed in the right kidney, turned abruptly in shock and pain causing the abrasion to his right collarbone and angling his body for the second stab to his left kidney, and was dead within a matter of seconds, a minute or two at most."

8

Carter expected Estefana to return sooner rather than later and so instead of chasing after her in the clammy heat she decided to take a seat at a table in the lodge's dining area, have another coffee, and wait. Presently, Estefana appeared. Carter noticed her friend's police shirt was slightly untucked which wasn't like the tidy and presentable Estefana at all. The look on her face confirmed that something wasn't quite right.

"How did you go?" Carter asked.

"Well thank you, *mana*. The African is working at the church today but I found out where he lives," Estefana said, joining Carter at the table. "It's not far."

"Cordero and I just came from the church," Carter said. "Well, the small rooms the priest rents out in the grounds. We didn't see anyone at the church when we walked by."

"That's the Catholic church, *mana*. The African belongs to the Assembly of God church. It's near the cemetery."

"Oh, right. You want a coffee?"

"No thank you, *mana*," Estefana said. "I've had breakfast."

Carter studied her friend's sombre expression. "Missing your husband?" she asked, and edged toward her over the table. Estefana had been married less than a month. She wiped a hand under her nose.

"Yes. But it isn't that." She cast her eyes down at the table top. "It was something the police officer I saw last night said."

Carter waited. Estefana's head remained bent and she seemed lost in a thought.

"Which was?" Carter asked.

After a brief hesitation Estefana looked up. Her eyes were moist. "He said this island crushes dreams."

Carter sat upright.

"Okay…so?"

"Don't you see, *mana*?" Estefana asked, her voice strained. "It all comes down to what I was telling you."

"About your father burying people on this island?"

Estefana grew visibly more upset.

"About me and the children I will bring into this world," she said.

She wiped away tears with the palm of one hand.

"What the spirits might do." Estefana lifted her head and looked at Carter directly. "I might already be pregnant."

Carter placed her hand lightly on Estefana's. There was the sound of a thump and a thwack against the side of one of the huts as the young boy in the courtyard kicked at his soccer ball repeatedly. A woman in the kitchen burst into song and someone else—a male perhaps—could be heard laughing at her.

"Are you sure you're pregnant?" Carter asked, lowering her voice.

Estefana inhaled fitfully. "No," she said and shook her head. "But I could be."

"Do you have any reason to think you are?" Carter pressed her.

Estefana's eyes dropped.

"No."

"So why worry?" asked Carter.

"Because things could happen when I do have children, *mana*," Estefana almost cried out.

Carter hushed her, even though workers in the lodge could not speak English as far as she knew.

"As I've told you, Estefana, you're only young," she said. "And you've only just married. You have plenty of time to think about children."

Estefana sniffed and rubbed at her nose. "It's what's expected when you marry, *mana*."

Carter sat upright.

"I know family's very important in Timor," she said. "But things are changing. You have a life of your own, whether you're married or not. And that life includes your career. You're a promising policewoman, Estefana. Better than a lot of policemen I've had to deal with here and in the States. You should allow your career to take you as far as it can."

"What you call my career in Timor is to submit to my husband," Estefana said.

Carter resisted the urge to say 'Nonsense'. She appreciated she was in Timor now, not the US.

"Well, that's what you've been encouraged to believe."

"*Mana*, it is part of my culture. If I don't follow the rules of my culture I embarrass my husband and I bring dishonor to my parents."

"But your culture is changing. How many women police officers would there have been in Timor twenty years ago?"

"Twenty years ago the Indonesians were here, *mana*."

"You know what I mean," said Carter suppressing her annoyance. "Women in Timor are taking on new roles all the time. I've seen that in the short time I've been here."

Estefana's shoulders quivered. She rubbed at her face and ran her hand over the ponytail she'd made with her hair. She took a deep, faltering breath.

"*Mana*, you are looking at things like a *malae*. Not a Timorese. In my culture a woman who marries is known as *moris nia hun*. That means source of life. It is an important role. It brings respect. Not your kind of *malae* respect. That kind says you can do things, say things, go anywhere you want. It's all about allowing you to behave the way you want. Our kind of respect, Timorese respect, is not like that. It values who you are not what you do."

"So long as you bear children," scoffed Carter.

"That's what a woman is born to be, *mana*." Estefana looked up. "A mother. It's not just my culture that says that. Even the Church tells us the same thing."

"Don't get me started on the Church," Carter said. "Everything the Church says, remember, comes out of the mouths of men! Celibate men, I might add!"

She took to her feet and paced the dining area.

"Some Timorese women have chosen careers—your type of careers—but most haven't," Estefana said, following Carter as she strode back and forth.

"But marriage is very important to us. It's not just an occasion for a party as I've seen in American movies. Marriage here weaves two families together—parents, grandparents, uncles, aunties, cousins, even our ancestors. My children will belong to my husband's people. It is how his people, his family line, will go on. But because of our marriage his people will help my people go on, too. Without us joining together our social life would fall apart. We would fall apart. Perhaps it's already happening because of outside influences. But I won't let it happen to me and the ones I love."

Carter held a hand up to indicate she followed the drift. "Okay, I understand that. In every country people have to join together to help each other out from time to time." She sat down opposite Estefana and spread her hands. "But there are different ways of joining together, right? In my country women used to be told to stay at home, raise the kids, cook and clean for their husbands. They were told they shouldn't upset things—men's things, typically. But women started to challenge that and break down barriers to being whatever they wanted to be. Now women are free."

Estefana stared at her.

"Free from what, *mana*?" she asked.

"Free *from* the roles men confined them to," said Carter. "And free *to* be anything they choose."

"You mean free to be like men?"

"I mean free to be equal to men," insisted Carter.

"*Mana*, in Timor a woman is already equal to a man but we have different roles. Men and women have rights and respect because of those roles."

"That may be so, but your life is not the life your mother or grandmother had, Estefana. You're educated, you have a career. You live in a country that is modernizing, not in a tribal society." She leaned in. "All I'm saying is that things change and evolve if we help things along by not always doing what we're told to do because someone says that's the way it's always been."

She paused.

"Why can't you be both a mother and a woman with a career, Estefana? Why are you making it out to be one or the other?"

"This is Timor, *mana*, not America. We don't have all the things you have in your country to make that possible. But why would I want to have both but not have the time and energy to do one or the other well?"

Estefana faced Carter, her eyes red-rimmed.

"Not everyone wants to be like that, *mana*. Not everyone wants to have everything, to be like an American. Look at you. You are thirty years old and you don't have a husband or a boyfriend. You may never have children, never be a mother. What good is your freedom then? You'll have your career but couldn't someone else do your job? What does your life *mean* apart from the work you do? What do you *mean* apart from what you do?"

Carter took a deep breath. She fiddled with her empty coffee cup and remained silent, lips tight. A breeze was spreading droplets of sea spray across the road, through the dining area and out into the courtyard. She could taste the salt.

"Let's continue this some other time," Carter said. "There's work to do now."

9

Cordero had learned that the *matan-dook* lived on the outskirts of Vila just to the west of the cemetery. It was one of the broadest areas of flat land on this part of the island and huts were scattered among small gardens and the few surviving stands of sandalwood, the scent of which freshened the air. He found the hut he was looking for without difficulty as it was the only one situated at the end of a long dirt track he'd been told to take beside a narrow channel dug to control stormwater flows in the wet season.

The hut was a small, traditional plank and thatch construction set off the track behind a tumble-down fence made of the spines of palm fronds. A wooden gate had fallen down and Cordero, who had walked from outside the church where he and Carter had spoken to Robert Evans, entered the property without breaking his stride.

The yard had been cleared to bare earth to keep scorpions and snakes at bay and a large tamarind tree grew off to one side. Clothes had been strung atop a bright purple bougainvillea to dry. Cordero made for the front entrance to the hut but heard clanging and scraping at the rear. He moved away from the hut a respectable distance so as not to frighten whoever was making the noise and walked around the side to where an old man was cutting and pounding something on a rough wooden bench under a shade canopy of palm fronds.

"*Tiu* Isahei?" Cordero asked, using the title for a respected older man.

Slowly the old man righted himself and swung face-on. He was short and thin, perhaps seventy, maybe eighty years of age but Cordero couldn't tell. The skin on the man's face was brown and winkled but tough like leather. His hair, moustache and long beard were white, his eyes soft and dark like a cow's.

Around the man's neck hung a necklace made of small shells. He wore a faded yellow T-shirt, a decorative red and blue *tais* over his left shoulder, and a head scarf with feathers coming out of the top. Another, drab *tais-mane*—or long woven cloth worn by men—covered him from the waist down to his calves. There were sandals on his feet, his toenails popping out hard and brittle, and bangles on his wrist. He moved his body as silently as an owl and he made no attempt to reply.

"Isahe Lengesi?" Cordero asked once more. Silence. "Are you the *matan-dook*?"

The old man looked Cordero over. "Who's asking?" he said in a dry, hoarse voice.

"My name is Vincintino Cordero. I'm a police investigator. I'd like to ask you some questions."

"What've I done?" the old man asked and coughed to clear his throat.

"Nothing *tiu*," Cordero said.

"If I've done nothing, why do you want to ask me questions?"

"It's about Justino Ferrao," said Cordero. "I understand you are his healer."

"I've never seen you before," the man said and coughed once more.

"I'm from Dili," said Cordero.

"I don't care where you're from. I've never seen you before. You're not from here. You're not one of us. So there is nothing I can tell you."

The old man bent over his bench and re-started his pounding. Cordero held out a conciliatory hand. "They have arrested Justino Ferrao for the murder of a *malae*," he said. "I think he's innocent. But I need to know more about him to be sure."

The old man didn't respond.

"And to convince the police to let him go," Cordero added.

The man straightened but with his face turned away from

Cordero. He took his time to answer. "Justino is my patient," he conceded at last, tilting his head only slightly to the side. "What I know of him is not for sharing with people like you. I am a *matan-dook* not a *bufa-nain*," he said, meaning a police informer.

"I appreciate that," said Cordero. "But surely you want to help Justino."

"He doesn't need the kind of help you speak of. I will not tell you anything about him. You are not one of his people and so what I know is none of your business."

Cordero ran a hand through his hair while he tried to think of another approach. He knew that to assert his police authority would be useless. The old man was not only a traditional Timorese but a *matan-dook*—someone of far greater standing among the people on the island than a police investigator. He would suffer whatever punishment Cordero might choose to threaten him with before he would violate his cultural norms and social responsibilities by revealing confidential information about someone given into his care.

The man seemed to be preparing a paste of some sort in a large metal dish from ingredients arranged in smaller metal tins and straw baskets on the bench.

Cordero peered over his shoulder. "What are you mixing up there?" he asked.

The man stopped what he was doing. Without looking at Cordero he pointed a pestle in his hand toward the garden.

"See my herbs?" he said. "That's what I'm mixing."

"For a patient?" Cordero asked.

"Yes. But I'm not going to tell you who, if that's what you're thinking of asking. As I said before, it's none of your business."

He resumed his mixing.

"I'm just curious," said Cordero. He lifted his head and sniffed. "Is that lavender I can smell? You mix lavender in there?"

"Lavender, kava kava and a few other herbs. Combined in this way they have a calming effect."

"Interesting," Cordero said. "So you mainly deal in herbal mixtures?"

The man stopped what he was doing and faced Cordero. He seemed to examine Cordero's face as though he could see through it and read his thoughts.

"You need a mixture?" he asked, a note of mistrust in his voice.

"No," said Cordero. "I'm just curious, like I said."

"Police are curious about a lot of things but I've never met one who was curious about my herbal mixtures," the man replied.

Cordero shrugged and smiled.

"I use what I think the situation requires," the man said and emitted a rasping cough. He caught his breath. "The knowledge has been handed down. I don't make it up. Sometimes what's required are healing ceremonies at the sacred house when what I seek requires changes in the behaviour of many people. Sometimes I need to assign tasks to those I work with."

"Tasks?" Cordero repeated.

"Sometimes an illness makes people invisible," the man waved his pestle to emphasize his words. "I don't mean you *can't* see them, I mean you *never* see them. They hide inside their huts. Day and night. Their families think they bring shame upon them and keep them inside. So nobody sees them or talks to them. People think the tasks I set are merely about getting a job done and so what I say to do is done without question. But the tasks are really to make the sick person get out among other people."

Like Justino's job of selling coconut water in the village, Cordero thought.

The man swung away.

"Tell me something, *tiu*," said Cordero thinking about Justino's explanation for his injuries. "Can spirits attack you? You know, beat you up when nobody's around?"

The old man shuffled ever-so quietly to a stool next to his bench. He motioned to Cordero to pull up a plastic chair nearby. He picked up a rolled cigarette, a match which he struck along the bench, and lit the paper. He took a puff, coughed out smoke, and puffed some more. Cordero couldn't smell tobacco or cloves and he wondered what the *matan-dook* was smoking.

"Hops," the man said, reading the question on Cordero's face. He held up the cigarette. "It's for my throat."

Cordero thrust his hands in his pockets and waited.

"The spirits know everything," the man said. "They know what we do. They know why we do what we do. They may help us if we deserve it but if they harm us it's because of something we've done, not them. They don't do evil. People do evil."

"So what you're saying is—?"

"What I'm saying is the knowledge handed down to us. That knowledge tells us that the spirits don't beat up anyone. That's a thing bad people do—in this village, mostly young people who have lost their way."

The *matan-dook* sucked on his hop cigarette. The smoke drifted out from his nose and into the yard and disappeared in the sunlight. Two warblers landed on a branch of the tamarind tree and began to trill so fast the notes blurred together. Cordero just made out the yellow chest of one when the old man began speaking again. The birds seemed to recognize his voice, flew closer, examined the man and his companion, and were gone.

"Spirits may throw stones at you from a distance if you frighten them," he said. "They may curse you with illness, put thoughts in your head that lead you to harm yourself, even die. But that's because of something you've done that was wrong. And the harm comes from inside you, not from outside. Spirits don't beat people up like you mean. People do that to people. Especially people who've lost their way."

"Tell me more about the young people here who have lost their way," said Cordero.

The man shifted on his stool. "You want a lot," he said.

"As you said, I'm not from here," Cordero replied. "I'm from the mainland. I only want to know a little about how things work here so I can do my job."

"Your job," the man repeated, in a tone that seemed a little dismissive. He stubbed his cigarette out in a hollowed-out coconut shell that lay on the bench. He'd stopped coughing now and the trace of a smile played on his lips as the last of the smoke he'd inhaled drifted between them.

"That amuses you?" Cordero asked.

"Your job is to find people guilty of a crime and put them in a prison," the man scoffed. "'Guilt', 'crime', 'prison'—these are all foreign words for foreign ideas. They're not part of our culture."

He placed his hands on his thighs.

"There were no prisons on this island before the Portuguese came. They made the whole island a prison and all of us its prisoners. We've had enough of that. My job as a healer is to restore harmony. That means bringing people together, not dividing them and setting them apart. It's what our ancestors taught us to do."

"I respect that," said Cordero, "but—"

"Do you understand *lisan*?" the man asked.

"Yes," replied Cordero. "It's the set of rules and beliefs that govern a particular clan or social group."

The man nodded.

"We are mostly Humangili in this part of the island," he said, reaching out and outlining the shape of the island on the bench with his finger. "Humangili have twelve major *lisan* groups each with their own particular variations called *rumanan*. Sometimes there are twenty *rumanan* for each *lisan*. So more than a hundred variations in this small area," he said and circled his imaginary map. "People move around, like coming to Vila from Maquili when the Indonesians made the road. When they move around, they get confused as to what their *lisan* is. And the elders grow old and their teeth fall out, so many have trouble pronouncing names properly and that adds to the confusion."

He sat upright on his stool and folded his arms across his chest.

"Are you following what I am saying?"

Cordero signaled that he was.

"Have you heard of Menunu?" the man asked.

"No," answered Cordero. "What is that?"

"Who, not what," the man said. "Menunu was what we call a *Haha Opun* or keeper of stories. When he was a young man,

Menunu had an accident and died. But when they went to bury him he came to life again. No one knows how. He had been dead for several days and during that time he lived in the spirit world. He returned from the dead with supernatural powers and everyone respected him, whatever their *lisan*. So he was able to clear up confusion and decide which elders spoke the right way about what practices people should follow. He did this for nearly one hundred years until he died for good four years ago, in 2010. No one has had the same respect among the people to be able to take his place. So now many in Vila and Maquili, especially young people, do what they want or copy what they learn from the *malae* tourists who have started coming here. There's no one who commands respect to point out the correct way."

He unfolded his arms, peered out from under the thatch at the position of the sun, and reached for his healing paste.

"That's why I say many have lost their way," he said and made to leave.

"That tells me a lot, *tiu*," Cordero said. "Thank you."

"Don't tell me lies like many others do here. I haven't told you much because you are not one of us and so you wouldn't understand," the man said. "But it is time I went. I have to work with someone on the other side of the village. I've been going there most days this past week. I'm gone a long time. I don't get home until late."

He stood and collected his things into a canvass bag as Cordero also rose to leave.

"Justino is *pontu*," the man said, meaning only a little bit crazy, "not *bulak* like the other one."

He ran an index finger over his forehead which was an indication of a serious illness.

"Which other one?" asked Cordero.

"The one who talks a lot but knows nothing," the *matan-dook* said and with that he walked out into his yard and through what was left of his gate.

· · ·

"Let's take a break, Gerard," Susanna Frankston said, brushing a strand of hair from her forehead.

He'd come in from outside, his jeans now spotted with dirt and his T-shirt soaked in sweat. In the full glare of the sun he'd raked the yard, collected the primitive tools with which Mrs Frankston had tried unsuccessfully to grow herbs and flowering plants as a pastime, sorted Professor Frankston's diving gear into a neat pile, and repaired a sheet of tin on the roof which had blown free in a recent wild wind.

She'd packed kitchen utensils and unused groceries into one cardboard box and gathered her books into three others. She'd also swept the floor and cleaned what benches there were. She wore shorts and a loosely fastened blouse without a bra. When she leaned forward, as she was doing know to indicate a chair for him she'd pulled up next to her own, her breasts were exposed. Miller averted his eyes and edged his chair a little away from hers when he sat.

"I want to thank you for the help you've been, Gerard," she said. "If it wasn't for you, I don't know how I would have coped."

"Well, the Ambassador told me to offer you all the assistance I can, ma'am," Miller said.

"But he's not here and you are," she replied. "You've done all the work. So, thank you." She touched his knee lightly. "But it's Susanna, okay?"

"Yes ma'am—I mean Susanna."

She smiled at him and flicked hair off her face.

"Where are you from Gerard?" she asked.

"North Dakota," he said.

"Do you miss the cold now you're here in East Timor?" she asked giggling.

"No—well yes, actually. Sometimes." He suppressed a laugh. "You know, snow, wood fires, chestnuts—that sort of thing."

"I'm from North Carolina via California," she said. "California is where I met Hank. It seems a long time ago now."

Her smile appeared to contradict the pain in her eyes. Miller stared at the floor. After a long moment she stretched her shapely legs into his field of vision. He lifted his gaze.

They were silent and the ticking of a clock was the only sound in the room.

"Would you like some tea?" she asked. "I'll eat at your lodge until they let me go. I only need what gas I have left in that canister for making tea and coffee."

"No, I'm fine, thanks." He fluffed his T-shirt which had stuck to his body. "Maybe a little water."

She rose and bent in front of him to retrieve a glass from the cardboard box. Her rump, scarcely covered by the shorts, was at his eye level. He turned his head away in embarrassment. She straightened, opened a bottle of water, poured some into a glass, and handed it to him. She licked up a little water she'd spilled onto her fingers.

"When will they let me go?" she asked, resuming her seat.

"I'm not sure. That policeman from Dili seems pretty determined to keep you here until he's finished his investigation. He seems thorough, or maybe just rigid."

"Yes, seems so," she agreed, her eyes on Miller.

Miller was in two minds. He wanted to stay and help but felt things were getting a little too familiar and he should leave. He felt nervous. He sipped the water awkwardly.

"I should be going," he said. "I have to speak with Agent Carter and prepare a report for the Ambassador."

"Of course," said Mrs. Frankston. "But could you just help me with one other thing first? In the bedroom."

She sprang up and slid into the room before he could answer.

"When I was living in North Carolina my brother died of leukemia," she was saying aloud from the bedroom. "He suffered terribly. We all did. Of course, all the attention had to focus on him and for years after my parents seemed to be preoccupied with grief. So I was left alone a lot of the time. That's when I started reading books and I haven't stopped."

He placed the glass she'd given him on the table and wiped his mouth with the back of his hand. He followed her into the bedroom. She'd placed her cell on the nearside of the bed and gone to the other side to poke around inside a drawer in a chipboard cabinet.

"Hank kept his personal things in that old trunk," she said pointing. "I could never open it. I've a Hessian bag here somewhere. Could you try to lift the lid and I'll pack up his clothes?"

Miller fiddled with the lock on the trunk. It was broken and offered no resistance but the lid was out of shape and had jammed shut. On the third attempt he managed to pry it free when Mrs. Frankston's cell buzzed.

He looked away as she bent across the bed, her breasts again clearly visible down the wide-open top of her blouse. He cast his eyes on the cell as her hand reached out to end the call.

10

The utility was parked at the side of the police station, the dog lay asleep in its shade, and Sergeant Emilio Amparo was slouched in a chair by the window with his foot resting on the bin when Cordero entered the police station mid-afternoon. He'd come from the *matan-dook's* hut, and his feet hurt from all the walking on the hard-packed roads and rocky tracks in shoes rather than boots.

"*Botarde maun*," he said to Amparo.

"'*Tarde*," the sergeant allowed without looking up from what looked like the same magazine he had been reading the day before.

It was hot inside the room, the air conditioner obviously still not working. Cordero took a kerchief from his pocket and wiped his brow.

"The other one not here?" he asked referring to the cadet officer.

"Sent him out to buy some reef fish for my dinner," Amparo said.

"I want Justino released," Cordero said.

The sergeant slapped his magazine shut, tossed it on the floor, and sat up in his chair.

"You crazy, *maun*?" he said. "What do you want to let him go for? I keep telling you he killed the American!"

Cordero put his kerchief in his pocket.

"I took a call this morning from the pathologist in Dili. The blood samples we took from Justino and from his clothing all match and none of them are the same type as Professor Frankston's."

"That doesn't mean he didn't kill him," protested Amparo.

"No, but it means we have no evidence that he did."

"What evidence you need? He was found in the same area as the body. He'd obviously been in a fight of some kind. And he's crazy!" complained Amparo.

"I've just been speaking to the *matan-dook* who's treating Justino and he says the boy's ill but not crazy," Cordero said.

"Oh, so now you're taking advice from quacks?"

Cordero ignored the slur.

"After talking to the *matan-dook* I think it likely that Justino was attacked by some young people with little to do, who regard him as an object of ridicule because he's not right in the head," Cordero explained calmly. "I take it you've had a few problems with some of the teenagers in this village?"

The sergeant hoisted himself from the chair and limped toward Cordero.

"Every place has problems with teenagers," he said. "You've no proof that boy was attacked by anyone other than the American."

"True, but it's the most likely explanation for the marks on his face and the blood on his clothes and an attack Justino couldn't fight off would be consistent with the blood samples all being of his type."

The sergeant lurched closer to Cordero.

"You people think you're so superior to us local police, don't you? You come here to show us up. That's what this is about, isn't it?" he said.

"It's about releasing someone who's innocent and concentrating our efforts on finding whoever killed the American," Cordero said, his voice firm and insistent. "Where're the keys to the room you've locked him in?"

"What if we let him go and afterwards we find whatever evidence you need to be convinced that he did kill the American?" Amparo asked. "How are we going to look? Huh? And I know who'll take the blame. It won't be you!"

"I'll take full responsibility," said Cordero. "Now where are the keys?"

Amparo's fists were tightening and he held Cordero's stare.

"There," he said and thrust a hand toward a key rack on the wall behind the desk. "Last on the right."

Cordero took down the key. "I want to borrow your vehicle too," he said. "I want to make sure that boy gets home safely. You won't need it for a while if your cadet officer is out buying your dinner." He held out his hand and Amparo produce the car keys from his pocket and shoved them into Cordero's hand.

"Thank you," Cordero said and he walked out to where Justino was being held.

• • •

After he'd dropped Justino to his mother and apologized for his arrest, Cordero called Estefana to ask if she'd found the location of the African who called himself Welcome Jesus. She had and they agreed to meet on a barren patch of land that masqueraded as Vila's soccer field midway between the police station and their lodge. He asked Estefana to let Carter know about the report from Brooks on the blood samples and that he'd consequently had Justino released and had taken him home. After ending the call he returned the utility to Sergeant Amparo and walked to the field. When he arrived he was surprised to find Carter sitting on the trunk of a fallen pawpaw tree behind a goal post made from bamboo culms. Four small boys, all barefoot and smeared with dirt, encircled her. One was holding a deflated soccer ball under his arm.

Carter had put aside the remarks Estefana had made about her lacking a boyfriend, being absorbed in her work, and possibly denying herself a chance at motherhood. She had composed herself from that critique and had chatted normally to Estefana as they walked to the rendezvous with Cordero. Now she was smiling but saying nothing as she held the children transfixed with something she was demonstrating.

As he approached Cordero watched as Carter pretended to pull a strand of hair from her head, lick it straight, and make as if to balance it end up on the tip of her index finger. None of the children would be able to see a single strand of hair in the harsh light but the theatrics—a credible 'ouch' as she made to pull the hair from her head, the jiggling to supposedly keep it upright on her finger, and the concentration on her face with her tongue poking out between her lips—were enough to beguile the boys. They all giggled at the small feat of acrobatics. With their urging she repeated the trick a third time before rising from the tree trunk to indicate the show was over.

"What?" she said to Cordero's look of amazement as she brushed her hands on the sides of her jeans. "You could do it too if you learned to put a bit of feeling into it."

Estefana led them down to the beach where fishing nets were laid out drying in the sun. They plodded along the sand to a reedy verge where she'd been told the African lived. It had once been a bright green cement block house but was now dilapidated and what paint had not peeled away was the colour of bruised avocado. The roof was rusted tin and a small addition of rough planks erected behind the main building had collapsed. An outrigger boat had been hauled off the sand and onto a side yard, its motor raised, the propeller blades bent and broken.

Behind the main building stood a man dressed only in a pair of ripped shorts scattering food scraps among chickens. His body was taut, his hair a shade of silver on his head and on his chest. His hands were calloused and he was barefoot, the soles of his feet a lighter shade than the rest of him which was a dark chocolate. "*Koko rai!*" he called, mimicking a rooster's cry, and chickens pecked and clucked on the ground around him. "*Koko rai!*"

"*Botarde tiu*," Cordero called and the man swung around squinting in the sunlight.

"*Botarde maun*," he replied, emptying the rest of his scraps over the chickens. He came toward Cordero and the women, smiling a smile of perfect white teeth.

"Are you the one they call Welcome Jesus?" asked Cordero in English.

"That be me, brother," the man said. "How can I help you and these fine ladies wit' you?"

"My name is Vincintino Cordero. I'm a police investigator from Dili. These are my colleagues. We'd like to ask you some questions about the American who was killed."

"My, my," the man said. "An important 'ting to be doin', yes. Let me get chairs for the sisters here and we can talk, brother. Come."

He went into the house and brought out two yellow plastic chairs for Estefana and Carter. He placed them in the shade of a tamarind tree. He fetched another chair for Cordero.

"Please," he said, motioning Cordero to sit. "That's all the chairs I got." And he crossed his legs under him and sat down on the ground.

"That's an interesting name you have," remarked Cordero.

"All names are interestin', brother, if you 'tink about them long enough."

"But I'm guessing you have another name," said Cordero. "An African name."

"Yes, brother, I do," said the man. "My heathen name is Eduardo Selewesi. But I'm no longer a savage. I'm *sarani* now," he said, meaning a baptized Christian. "And when I became *sarani* I took the name of my Lord Jesus because he welcomed me into His holy fold."

He flashed his perfect white teeth at Carter and Estefana.

"When was that?" Cordero asked.

The man directed his smile to Cordero.

"You want the whole story, huh?" he said. "Okay."

He tugged a blade of grass from the ground.

"The Portuguese brought me here in 1973. They called me a rebel, you know? I was a sinner, brother, yes indeed. They put me in that hole in the ground they call a prison. When they ran away, we all popped out like sand worms. But soon the *bapa* came," he said using the colloquial term for Indonesians.

"No one could leave this island for the next 24 years, you know what I'm sayin'? I figure I had to fit in somehow. I married a local girl here. Natalia."

He dropped his gaze and shook his head.

"Beautiful she was, my Natalia."
He lifted his head.

"There was this pastor here. Pastor Gomes. He was a real Jesus man, you know? Pastor Gomes persuade a lot of people to accept Jesus after the big earthquake in 1979. Lot of people die then, you know, so a lot of them that was left say 'Okay' to Jesus. My wife say 'Okay' so I do too. Why not? But Natalia got sick and Jesus call her to heaven. What I gonna do? By the time the *bapa* go, I'm 42 years old. Where I'm gonna go, huh? So I stay and make my life here."

He'd spread his arms wide.

"So you belong to the Assembly of God church?" Cordero asked.

"Only true church, brother," Welcome Jesus said. "I'm a minister of prayer and devotions now, praise the Lord!" He smiled at Carter and Estefana.

"You knew the American—Professor Hank Frankston?"

"Yes brother. But he not an Assembly man. I don't know what he was."

"No, I figured he wasn't a member of your church but it's not what I'm asking," said Cordero. "He hired you, right?"

"Yes brother he did hire me and I did know him. He hire me because I speak English. Need to speak this language for the foreigners who come to see the reef, you now? I speak their language, they pay me to go in my boat. But the American pay me to take him over the reef lots of times and further out too. In my boat," he said and pointed in the direction of the outrigger. "He dive under the water, you know?"

"How often would you take him out?" Cordero asked.

"How often?" the man considered, rubbing his chin. "Two, maybe three times a week. Big job for me, brother."

He tossed away the blade of grass he'd been fiddling with.

"Other boat people don't like me after that. They say I get money too easy, you know? Not like them havin' to go out and fish every day. But I don't get paid that much, brother. Not enough to anger nobody like that. You know what I'm sayin'?"

Cordero didn't answer.

"Did you know his wife?" he asked.

"Miss Susanna? Fine lookin' woman, brother, like these two sisters here. Fine lookin'."

He grinned this time toward Carter and Estefana.

"Yes brother, I know her but not much, you know? Never talk to her much. Most times Mister Hank and I would leave early in the mornin' before she woke and not come home 'til late in the day. That Mister Hank work real hard, you know? Long days." He shook his head. "Nobody 'tink about long days for me when they say I got money easy."

"Do you know Robert Evans—the Australian?"

"Mister Bob? Sure I knows him. He come with us sometimes. Funny man. Always laughin' 'bout somethin' or other. He dive too but not like Mister Hank. He was better."

He leaned in as though sharing a secret.

"And I never got more money when I take Mister Bob too, you know? I take him for free."

"How did the two of them get on?" asked Cordero.

"Mister Bob and Mister Hank? Them two get on real good, brother. Yes, real good. Never hear one raise his voice agin' the other."

"Did *you* ever argue with Professor Frankston?"

"Me?" he asked in mock horror. "I never argue with no one, brother. Jesus say show the other cheek, you know?"

"Did you ever have to show the other cheek with Professor Frankston?"

Welcome Jesus hesitated a second.

"Even Blessed Jesus must show the other check, brother. No sin in that."

"What did you have to show the other cheek about?"

The man looked off and raised his chin toward the outrigger.

"That Mister Hank want to go all over, you know? Close-by reefs and far-out reefs. He want to go in low tide and high tide—don't matter to him. He say, 'I don't have much time and there's lots of work to do'. I say, 'It's not safe, brother!' and he say, 'I'm payin' you, go here, go there!'"

He ripped up another clump of grass.

"I break my propeller out there on that coral reef 'cos of him and he don't want to pay no compensation. Where I'm gonna get a new propeller out on this island, brother? You tell me that. How I'm gonna work now?"

"So you argued about that?" Cordero asked.

"Not argue, brother. I tell him it's not fair but like I say, I show the other cheek."

"When did you break the propeller?" Carter injected.

"Week ago maybe," the man said, and tossed the grass away.

"You didn't get another boat to take him out?" Cordero asked.

"No. No one will give me one boat more for work with him. No one will even take me out now. Like I say, they all jealous of me 'cos of the money they 'tink I make."

"Was that the last time you saw Professor Frankston?"

"I seen him around here and there but we don't speak after that," Welcome Jesus said.

"Did Professor Frankston go out with anyone else?" Cordero asked.

"I believe he did. Said he had work need finishin'."

"Who'd he go with?"

"That be Zeka. He lives down by the school," he said, pointing. "Used to be a blue house but the sand blow the colour away same as it blew mine."

"What's this Zeka like?" Cordero asked.

"He's a fisherman. Not a bad one, brother. But his boat's not good like mine when I can put it in the water. Even so Mister Hank pay him and he go out couple of times with Zeka after the fish catch unloaded in the mornin'."

"How did Zeka get on with the American?"

Welcome Jesus shrugged. "Zeka not speakin' to me neither. He's jealous too. So I don't know. Zeka don't speak English. He just be drivin' the boat, you know?"

Cordero paused to consider that.

"Do you know why anyone would want to kill the American?" he asked.

Welcome Jesus shook his head. "No. I figure the devil tempted someone real bad, you know? Satan does that, brother. I saw it when I was in that prison in the ground. He gets into a lot of people and bad 'tings happen."

"Where were you the night Professor Frankston was killed?" Cordero asked.

"At the church, brother," Welcome Jesus said. "Prayin' to the good Lord Almighty. Like I do most nights."

"Anyone else there with you?"

"Most Assembly people have families. I'm on my own. Maybe someone come to pray. I'm not sure. I was workin' with my Bible and gettin' 'tings right with the Lord."

• • •

"What do you make of that holier-than-thou routine?" Carter asked as they made for the main road.

"What, you're a skeptic? I thought you were brought up Catholic," replied Cordero.

"Brought up," said Carter. "Then woke up. Answer my question."

"Could be sincere," Cordero answered.

"Yeah, and could be a load of bullshit," said Carter. "He had reason to be pissed off with Frankston for ruining his livelihood and not paying compensation. And it wouldn't surprise me if he's a bit of a pants man and fancied Mrs. Frankston."

"Pants man? What makes you say that?"

"Your saw the way he was smiling at Estefana and me. Women get to know that look," Carter said. "It's a necessary part of our survival strategy."

They reached the road, stopped and Cordero looked left to where he knew the school to be after watching the children in uniform walk that way in the morning. A strong wind suddenly whipped up grit along the road and they had to shield their eyes. The sky was hidden behind heavy, dark cloud.

"There's something else Brooks told me this morning," he said. "He found a small scratch on Frankston's right collar bone. Said it could have been caused by something on the assailant's left hand or wrist when Frankston was grabbed from behind and jerked with the impact of the first blow to his right kidney. Couldn't be sure but it's worth considering. You notice any bracelets or rings on Mrs. Frankston?"

"You mean you didn't?" Carter asked.

"No."

"Attractive woman that widow Frankston," Carter teased him.

"I wasn't noticing," said Cordero.

"Yeah, right," said Carter. "She wore a small gold wedding ring. Nothing more. It was flat and featureless—unlike the woman herself. I doubt it could have caused a scratch." She waited. "That doesn't mean she can't twist things around her finger."

"You don't like her?" he asked.

"Nothing to do with *like*. She's a flirt. Look at Miller. Didn't take her long to work him over."

"I think you're exaggerating," said Cordero.

"Am I?"

"I doubt your State Department would assign someone to an embassy if he was that gullible," he said.

"I hate to tell you this, Tino, but East Timor rates pretty low in the State Department's scheme of things. Look at Hudson Taylor. Or look at me. Assigned here because I was considered a problem by my resident agent. See the connection? It's a dumping ground. Miller fits right in."

Cordero didn't react. "What about Evans? Did you notice a ring or a watch?"

"Another one you missed?" said Carter enjoying Cordero's discomfort.

"I was sitting on his right side," Cordero said.

"Well had you been standing in front of him, as I was, you would have noticed that on a tanned left arm was the pale outline of a wristwatch." She paused. "But no actual watch."

Cordero rubbed at his face. "That's interesting," he said. "I wonder where it is and why." He checked his cell. Coverage had gone. He consulted his own watch and addressed Estefana.

"There's an hour or so before dinner time, Estefana," he said. "I'd like you to go to the Assembly of God church and see if anyone there can verify the African's alibi. The church is out past the police station so on your way back could you go and ask that another report be sent to Dili on the radio tonight in case our phones are down?"

Estefana was taking in the instructions.

"Keep it simple: Tell them cell coverage is *mosu-lakon*," Cordero said meaning intermittent. "Report the initial suspect has been released on the basis of pathologist's report and local investigations. Tell them I'm still interviewing people of interest. Don't mention anything about *Mana* Carter. She and I will go down to the school and find this Zeka. Let's meet up at the lodge in an hour or so and talk about what we know so far over dinner."

He started walking but swung around to Estefana.

"Oh, and ask Dili to contact the Australian Embassy and dig up anything they can on Robert Evans. Tell them to send it over as soon as they can."

11

Estefana found the police cadet Sisko slouched behind the main desk with his feet raised when she called into the police station after her visit to the Assembly of God church. Sisko's eyes widened and he broke into a grin when he saw who it was. He removed his feet from the desk and tried his best to look professional.

"*Bonoiti, mana*," he said, meaning good evening. "You're back."

"Yes," Estefana replied. "We need another report radioed to Dili. Cell coverage is down tonight as well."

"That happens," Sisko said and he rose and made for where the radio was positioned but only to get nearer Estefana. "The sergeant's not here. He went home. Went to cook a nice fish I picked up for him for his dinner."

He folded his arms.

"I used to be a fisherman myself, you know? Most people where I come from in Maquili are fishermen," he said and laughed. "And fisherwomen too." He moved a little closer. "You like fish? I can tell today's catch from yesterday's when I see them and I know how to cook fresh fish too. Maybe I can cook for you, what do you say?"

"I'm just here to get the report sent to Dili," Estefana said as she sidled away from him toward the map on the wall.

The window shook as the wind picked up, the room darkened, and the scent of rain infused the air.

"Another downpour's coming," said Sisko, reading Estefana's mind. "They come fast this time of year."

He unfolded his arms and grabbed the back of a chair.

"Where're your two friends?" he asked.

"They've gone to talk to someone who might know something connected with the death of the American," Estefana said, keeping things vague.

"This policing business is all work, huh?" Sisko said as he settled himself down by the radio. "Want to see how this thing works?" he asked, indicating the radio with a flick of his thumb. "There's lots of dials and things here but it's real easy if you know how. I can show you."

"No," Estefana said. "Thanks. I just want to make sure you get the message sent."

She told him what Cordero had said and Sisko scribbled it down on a piece of paper. She noticed his writing was little more than a scrawl.

"You sure you can read that?" she asked.

Sisko looked down at what he'd written and up at her.

"Sure. No problem," he said. He read back from his notes.

"I'm impressed," said Estefana.

The young cadet seemed pleased with that.

"I can do a lot more than people think I can," he said. "Sure you don't want that fish cooked later? Or I could make a coffee for you now, if you like."

"I must go," Estefana said and moved toward the door. "We are having a meeting over dinner."

"Must be important," he said. "What's it all about?"

"The case," she said to keep it simple.

"Any developments?" he asked.

"Maybe. I'm not sure. That's what we have to talk about."

"I'd sure like to make you that coffee sometime," Sisko said, his eyes trailing after her as she was leaving.

"Maybe another time," she said over her shoulder and hurried off into the street.

• • •

Zeka, the fisherman, was in his late thirties, thin, and balding. He wore shorts, a greasy T-shirt, and was barefooted. He stood under a coconut palm as Cordero questioned him, clearly uncomfortable in the company of the two strangers.

"I took him out twice, down off Maquili," he said of Professor Frankston. "He dived both times but what he did under the water I don't know. I wasn't interested."

"How long was he in the water for each time?" Cordero asked.

Zeka took a loose cigarette from his pocket, cupped his hands and lit it. He took in a lungful of smoke before answering.

"I don't have a watch," he said. He took the cigarette out of his mouth and held it out to Cordero. "But I smoked two of these both times."

By the way Zeka tugged on his cigarette, Cordero guessed that was about fifteen minutes, maybe a little longer, on each occasion.

"Did you two talk about anything?" he asked.

"I don't speak English," Zeka said, looking slightly abashed at Carter, who Cordero was translating for. "He didn't speak Tetun or Bahasa."

"When he came out of the water did he bring anything up into the boat?"

Zeka took another drag and stared at the cigarette as he rolled it between his fingers.

"He had a bag," he said but he had no idea what was in it. "It wasn't a string bag you could look through and anyhow I was busy watching the tide."

A young girl of about eight or nine in pigtails came running from the house. She threw her arms around Zeka's legs and held on tight as she goggled at the strangers. Zeka took another puff and then another while he stroked her hair.

Cordero smiled at the child and asked Zeka: "What can you tell me about the African?"

The man dropped his cigarette to the ground and glanced down at the girl. He was slow to answer.

"Well?" urged Cordero.

"He's a good boatman," Zeka said.

"That's all?"

Zeka eased some dirt with his bare foot onto the smoldering cigarette butt.

Cordero titled his head to indicate he wanted an answer.

"The American paid me well for the two boat rides," Zeka said. "Imagine how much that African got paid all the weeks he worked for the American. He could have given more of that work to me. Shared it out, you know. That's how we do things here. But he didn't."

"You said yourself you don't speak English," Cordero reminded him. "He can. Maybe the American only wanted to hire him, at least until his boat was damaged."

Zeka made no comment.

"Do you know the American's wife?"

"I've seen her in the village but I've never spoken to her," Zeka said.

"What about the Australian—Robert Evans? You have anything to do with him?"

The man shook his head.

"He didn't come out on the boat with you and the American?"

Another shake of the head.

"*Papa, mai atu haan*," the little girl said, meaning come and eat, dad.

Zeka put his hand on the girl's shoulder and stared at Cordero.

"Thanks for your help," Cordero said and wiggled his fingers at the girl. "Have a good night."

• • •

Back at the lodge Carter and Cordero freshened up and waited for Estefana. Miller appeared from the road and went straight to his hut. A little while later Mrs. Frankston showed up in a modest cotton summer dress and sandals. She sat at a table by herself and thumbed through a book she'd brought with her. Cordero suggested to Carter that they hold off on dinner until she had eaten and left so they could then talk more freely. They sat on stumps in the yard and exchanged smalltalk. Soon Miller emerged from his hut and joined Mrs. Frankston. The two shared a pizza, ate quickly, and chatted quietly.

When Estefana returned Carter stood, brushed the rear of her jeans, and went into the hut with Estefana while she too freshened up. Cordero remained seated on his stump, swatting mosquitos. After a short time Mrs. Frankston left the lodge to walk home before it rained and Miller paid for their pizza and retired to his hut.

"Ah, my favourite," Cordero said as they took their table and plates of chili-fried chicken, sweet potato fries and salad were laid in front of them.

"Everything here seems to be your favourite," said Carter.

"Salt air gives me a good appetite," said Cordero.

"You didn't examine Frankston's study today as you said you would," Carter said.

"Tomorrow," Cordero said. "Things outside the house are looking more interesting today." He turned to Estefana. "Find out anything at the church?"

"There weren't many people there," Estefana said, "but I managed to speak to three of them. Two had not gone to the church the night Professor Frankston was killed so they had no idea if the African was there."

Carter encouraged Estefana to start eating.

"But they both said he only came occasionally during the week," she said, picking up her fork. "The third person was an old woman. She said she was there Tuesday night from about eight o'clock until after nine. She lives down by the school. She said she didn't see him that night either. Not in the church or when she walked home."

Cordero faced Carter and raised an eyebrow.

"See what I mean?"

"That's not all," said Estefana. "The old woman seemed upset when I mentioned Welcome Jesus to her. She denied it at first but I sensed something and asked her outside the church. She seemed—" she looked across to Cordero "—*laran-moruk, maun*. I don't remember the word in English."

"Bitter," Cordero said, cutting strips off his chicken.

"Yes, that's it. Bitter," said Estefana. "Like she disapproved of something strongly. Eventually she told me she thought Welcome Jesus was *finjidu*."

"*Finjidu*?" Carter said looking from one to the other. "What does that mean?"

"It means a pretender, *mana*. It means he makes out he's innocent when he's not," Estefana explained.

"Did she say why?" Carter asked.

"She said I should talk to the ones who wear the black veil, *mana*. That means the widows. She said I should start with a woman called Lazara. She lives out beyond the cemetery and the old woman told me where."

"Well, well," said Carter, and she winked at Cordero. "What did I tell you about a pants man *and* a religious fraud?"

"Right," Cordero said, ignoring the bait from Carter. He waved a fork at Estefana. "Can you go and talk to this *Mana* Lazara after dinner?" he said before attacking the chicken.

"Why don't we all go?" asked Carter pecking at her fries.

"I want to talk to the priest," Cordero said. "Evans has been staying with him and says he and the priest talk from time to time. Let's see what they talk about and what the priest knows of his guest's movements. After all, Evans is in the habit of using the priest's vehicle."

He loaded salad onto his plate.

"Come on, eat before it goes cold," he said, urging on Estefana in particular. He peeked out from under the thatch roof of the dining area. The sky was roiling with heavy clouds. "If we hurry up, we might just get things done tonight before the rain."

12

Father Robeiro lived behind the building where he rented accommodation to visitors. They approached his quarters careful not to be seen from Evans' room. The priest opened the door as though interruptions were a regular feature of his life and invited them in after Cordero had introduced himself and Carter, and explained the reason for their visit.

The priest was Timorese—though from the mainland—middle-aged, and well presented. His hair was slicked down as though he had just showered and his white business shirt and navy-blue trousers were clean and uncrushed. He wore spectacles in the style of someone who read a great deal, a cord attached to the temple tips to allow the lenses to hang from his neck when not needed. A trail of smoke curled upwards from a cigarette he'd stubbed out in an ashtray next to his easy chair. He indicated a couch to Carter and Cordero, smiled a practiced smile, and asked how he could help.

"Did you know the American who was killed, *amu*?" asked Cordero using the polite colloquial term for a priest.

"Not well," said Father Robeiro in his limited English. "He wasn't Catholic. I doubt he belonged to any religion. You know what these Americans are like." He glanced at Carter, embarrassed. "What I mean, *mana*, is they keep their beliefs to themselves."

"What about his wife?" Carter asked.

"Same," said the priest. "I would see her on the road on occasion but we didn't speak." Cordero had to translate for Carter when the priest slipped into Tetun as he did when what he had to say grew more complex.

"You didn't comfort her after she'd learned of her husband's death?" Cordero asked.

"No," the priest replied. "There was no suggestion she wanted or needed me."

"No need?" repeated Carter. "Curious."

"What about the Australian?" asked Cordero. "*Senyor* Evans? What can you tell us about him?"

The priest reached for another cigarette, offered the package to Carter and Cordero, and, when they declined the offer, placed a cigarette in his mouth and lit it. He drew in a lung full of smoke before answering.

"I have two rooms I rent to visitors," he said, the smoke drifting from his lips. "You know, mainly tourists traveling on their own or volunteers who come occasionally to help in the health clinic or the school. It's no secret. It brings in a little money to help maintain the church." He looked across at Carter. "The roof," he said. "There's always a need to repair the roof."

He took another drag on his cigarette.

"*Senyor* Evans came about four weeks ago. He asked for a room and I gave him the one he's staying in. He pays each week and is no trouble."

Thunder rippled overhead.

"You also lend him your vehicle, I understand," said Cordero.

"I rent that to him as well. When I have no need of it. He likes the jeep because he can fit his diving gear in." A second time he looked at Carter. "More money for the roof, you understand."

"Do you know where he goes in the jeep?" she asked.

The priest shrugged.

"I am my brother's keeper," he said smiling, "but not my tenant's."

More thunder boomed, closer this time. Carter glared at the ceiling: Cordero and the priest were more familiar with violent tropical storms and didn't react.

"You get on well with *Senyor* Evans?" asked Cordero.

"Yes, he is a friendly man," said the priest. "All the Australians I have met seem to be like that."

"What do you and *Senyor* Evans talk about?"

Before he could answer the rain began—a sudden torrent hammering on the tin roof of the presbytery and blanketing the village outside.

"What does anyone talk about?" asked the priest in English, raising his voice above the noise. "The weather. The village." He looked up and across to Carter a fourth time.

"The roof?" she guessed.

"Yes. And the roof."

"You spoke to *Senyor* Evans on Tuesday night," Cordero said. "What time was that, *amu*?"

The priest looked at the cigarette in his hand, took another drag and stubbed it out. "Let me think," he said. "I had just finished saying the rosary in the church. So it must have been close on nine o'clock."

"How long did you speak to him for?" asked Cordero.

"Oh, just a few seconds. 'Good evening', 'How are you?'—that sort of thing."

"And that was it?"

"Yes. That was it."

"Do you know what *Senyor* Evans is doing here on Atauro?"

"He told me he was interested in history when he rented the room. That was all. I told him he'd come to the right place because the Portuguese came here five hundred years ago. He seemed very interested in the Portuguese history of Atauro."

"Did *Senyor* Evans know other people in the village?"

"He knew the Americans but he would, wouldn't he? They are all *malae* and they all speak English."

"Anyone else?" asked Cordero. "Anyone local?"

"You'd have to ask him, I'm afraid."

The priest reached for another cigarette, his brow furrowed.

"Is he in any trouble?"

"No, no, *amu*," Cordero reassured him. "We just have to ask these questions."

The priest played the unlit cigarette through his fingers.

"There was a young man," he said. "It's probably nothing but he came to see *Senyor* Evans one day. I just caught sight of the two of them as I was off to say Mass."

"Yes?" encouraged Cordero.

"I don't know what they were talking about or what they were doing. I only saw them for a second or two as I walked past."

"Do you know this young man, *amu*?"

The priest laughed.

"Everyone knows everyone in this village, *senyor*."

"So who was this young man?"

"His name is Antonio Gomes. I promised his mother I would encourage him to attend Mass, but so far I have not been successful. Like some other of the young ones here, he's gone his own way for a while. But he'll come back to his roots. They all do."

"Where does Antonio live?" asked Cordero.

"That I don't know," the priest said. "It's one reason I haven't been able to persuade him to come to Mass: I can never find him! His mother lives just outside the village on the road going south. She comes to Mass three times a week. A very devout woman. But Antonio left home about six months ago and he stays with different friends." He laughed some more. "Some of the young ones are hard to keep track of these days."

• • •

Dogs were howling and snarling at each other on the short track off the road beyond the cemetery where Estefana had been told by a man digging in his garden that she would find the hut of *Mana* Lazara. She gave the dogs a wide berth and hurried along thinking that perhaps the coming storm with its peals of thunder was unsettling them.

A woman of generous proportions with her hair tied atop her head was cooking on an outdoor fire next to a simple plank and thatch hut at the end of the track. A cloud of smoke coiled into the yard carrying the aroma of barbecued chicken with it. Two small boys, each naked, squealed and hollered as they chased each other around a sago palm. The woman ignored them as she tossed the roughly cut chicken pieces over the flames and brushed the few flies braving the gusts of wind away from a green salad sitting in a bowl on a stool next to the fire.

Estefana approached the woman, introduced herself and apologized for interrupting what appeared to be the preparation of dinner.

"My children have kept me busy all day," the woman complained. "I've just had time to cook and I need to get it done before the storm comes. What is it you want?"

"Do you belong to the Assembly of God church?" Estefana asked.

"If that's a crime you'll have to arrest half of Vila," the woman said. She lifted a piece of chicken onto a metal tray and began raking the meat off the bone with a knife so the children could eat it easily.

"I was wondering if you knew a member of the church called Welcome Jesus," said Estefana. "He's from Africa originally."

The woman stopped what she was doing immediately and faced Estefana.

"Why are you asking me that?"

"He's helping us with our investigation into the death of the American and I just wanted to check something he told us, that's all," said Estefana.

"Sounds like you want to check up on *him*," the woman huffed.

Estefana didn't respond.

"Welcome is a decent man," the woman said, hands on hips now, the knife pointing out from one. "He hasn't done anything wrong."

"I'm sure that's true, *mana*," Estefana said. "But I need to check something."

"Pedro! Fernando!" the woman called over her shoulder without looking. The boys ignored her.

"How well do you know this man?" Estefana asked.

The woman puffed out her chest and stared at Estefana. "Pedro! Fernando!" she called and this time the boys stampeded in. She turned and with the knife jabbed pieces of chicken onto a plastic plate for each and handed one the bowl of salad. She told them to sit under the palm and eat up. The boys rushed off, giggling to each other.

"*Mana*?" Estefana persisted.

The woman rested the knife on the stool and wiped her hands on her skirt.

"You're a pretty young woman," she said. "Are you married?"

"Yes, *mana*," Estefana replied.

"Consider yourself lucky and take care of your husband," the woman said.

She looked away at the boys eating their dinner on the ground under the palm.

"I was married once. Long time ago now. My husband Francisco drowned, out there," she said and raised her chin toward the sea. "In a big storm. He was a fisherman. It's not easy being a *feto-faluk* here," she said, meaning widow. "No other man wants you and you have to fend for yourself."

She picked the knife up, moved the carcass of the chicken off the flames and onto the side of the makeshift grill, then sat down on the stool.

"That African lost his wife too. He's kind to me. He brings me things to eat," she said. "So I know him well, yeah. And that's no sin."

"Was he here with you on Tuesday night?" asked Estefana.

The woman considered the question.

"He's one of the leaders in our church," she said. "Can't be a leader if you get up to mischief, you understand?"

"I understand," said Estefana. "But was he here that night?"

The woman rubbed a hand under her nose. "But I don't call it mischief," she said. "I call it taking care of each other."

Her expression suggested she was looking for a little sympathy for what she meant.

"What you tell me doesn't have to go beyond me and my police colleagues, *mana*. No one at the church needs to know."

The woman inclined her head slightly toward the darkness engulfing the yard and lowered her eyes.

"Some of the other women at the church already suspect Welcome Jesus is up to the Devil's work," the woman said. "That's because they're all dried up inside and jealous." She fixed Estefana with a look of bravado. "The sap still flows through me."

"So he was here?" Estefana repeated.

The woman nodded.

"Came around sundown. Brought that chicken. I rung its neck and plucked it today."

"Was he here the whole time after dinner?"

The woman hesitated.

"Pretty much, yeah," she nodded.

"What do you mean by that?" Estefana asked. "Was he gone at any time?"

The woman waved a hand.

"One time he saw someone pass down the road. Saw him waving a torch. Said he knew the man. Went down and talked to him some."

"What time was this?"

"You see any clocks around here?"

The woman appeared annoyed but her appearance quickly softened.

"About the time we got ready for bed. I was just settling Pedro in. Fernando kicks him in his sleep. Wakes him up all the time."

"How long was the African gone?"

"Not long," the woman said. "I was getting undressed for bed when he came in."

"How did he seem?"

The woman made a face.

"*Raan-sa'e*," she said. It meant angry.

"Did he say why?"

"No. He just grumbled some and climbed into bed."

"How long did he stay?"

"Long as it took him to finish the job," the woman said.

"The job?"

"If you're married you know what I mean," the woman said and smiled for the first time. "Welcome's not young anymore. Takes him a while, you know?"

"So he stayed all night?"

"He left as the roosters started crowing. The sun was coming up. He doesn't like to be seen coming and going. People talk."

The woman rose and hovered over the fire, poking at the chicken as though about to serve herself.

"He's a decent man," she said, not bothering to look at Estefana. "Decent leader in the church too. He doesn't want to lose that role. Says he's nothing without the Lord."

• • •

Cordero's cell came to life. He stared at it, surprised to have coverage during a storm. The caller was Howard Brooks.

"Howard!" said Cordero. "We're in the middle of a thunder storm."

"I'll make it brief," said Brooks.

Cordero heard what he took to be the sound of surgical implements being tossed into a metal tray.

"I've had a close look at those knife wounds," Brooks began, "and can give you some more information on the weapon used. From—" but a roll of thunder broke up what came next.

"Could you repeat that, Howard?" pleaded Cordero. "Like I said we are in the middle of a storm."

"I was saying I measured the distance between the angles on each of the wounds. That's the tips of the wound at each end, dear boy. They suggest a small-bladed instrument. I can only posit a guess as to the length of the blade because, as you would know, the skin shrinks when a weapon is withdrawn from an incision. Also it is rare for a knife to enter and leave at the same angle and this distorts measurements from the wound."

Cordero was trying to follow the technical detail. He walked into the center of the dining area in an attempt to hear Brooks more clearly but that didn't make any difference. He pressed a finger more firmly in the ear opposite where he held the cell. That helped a little.

"But both margins of each wound have pointed edges." Brooks paused. "Are you getting all of this, dear boy? I'm hearing a lot of static on the call."

"Yes, go on," said Cordero.

"That's the sides of the wound, you understand. A single-edge knife causes pointing along only one margin. A double-edge blade causes pointing on both margins. So I'm confident in saying we're not looking at something like a kitchen knife but more a hunting or diving knife."

Thunder sounded overhead.

"—and hope that helps, dear boy," Brooks was saying.

"Thanks Howard," said Cordero. "Yes it does."

• • •

As Estefana made her way from the hut of *Mana* Lazara the clapping of palm fronds in the wind unnerved her. She glanced up only to be distracted by the dogs which were still aggressive up ahead. Three were menacing a fourth dog which was yelping, its ears flat and its tail drawn tight between its legs. The rain had already created deep puddles in the track and to avoid them Estefana found herself having to advance too close to the pack. One of the dogs noticed her and snarled, saliva dripping from its jaws. The other two ignored the fourth dog and started barking at her as well. Estefana tried a retreat but that only encouraged the dogs to creep closer.

She sensed that one of the dogs was trying to position itself behind her. Her breathing quickened. She twisted to keep the dog face-on, knowing that if the pack managed to surround her, the dogs would almost certainly attack. As she moved, the two dogs in front shifted too, low to the ground, primed to strike. A thunder clap overhead set one of the dogs to howl. The one angling to get around her began a continuous baying. The largest one in front flattened its ears, its eyes yellow and fierce, and it snapped at Estefana's legs.

"*Lakon tiha!*" a voice ordered, meaning 'Be gone!'

"*Lakon tiha!*" a second time but closer now.

The big dog raised its ears and swung toward the voice. Another stopped its howling and did likewise. The third dog began to whimper.

"*Lakon tiha!*" the cry repeated and the three dogs tore off into the undergrowth. The fourth dog which the others had been taunting earlier scrambled after them.

"Are you all right, *mana*?" a person asked, but Estefana couldn't make out a figure, only a voice, through the murky dark.

"Yes, thank you," Estefana said, wondering who this could be.

Out of the gloom a man appeared. He was old, short and thin. The man's hair and beard were matted damp against his skin. He wore a *tais* over his shoulder, a necklace of shells around his neck, and a head scarf from which water droplets channeled down his face. His appearance somehow calmed her.

"I live over there," he said pointing. "I was coming home when I heard the commotion. No one takes care of them," he said lifting his chin after the dogs. "So they become wild and savage and like to fight."

He chuckled.

"But they listen to me. You see, I'm a *matan-dook*."

13

There are no permanent rivers or lakes on Atauro and apart from the few cement block houses and government buildings that have acquired run-off tanks, most people rely on water piped from springs on the main mountain—Manucoco. Perhaps that's why the first inhabitants of the island believed their god dwelt in Manucoco which towers 3,000 feet over the southern part of Atauro. When water flowed freely from the springs it was a blessing from the god: when the springs dried up, it was a hex from the demons who were also believed to dwell on the mountain.

In recent years culverts had been dug to protect Vila and direct heavy stormwater around buildings, under roads and out to sea. They were full now, the night's rain collecting, swelling and finally driving discarded plastic bottles, cigarette stubs, and empty two-minute noodle containers onto the reef. Trees and bushes drooped with moisture from the heavy storm. Roads were puddled and household gardens sodden. At dawn dampness had hung over the village like a dirge but by mid-morning the sky was clear and blue, the air crisp and fresh once more.

Miller had left the lodge early to offer more comfort to Mrs. Frankston in any way he could. Carter and Estefana had decided to use the break in the weather to their advantage. The clothes they'd been wearing the night before were soaked through and it looked like they'd be staying on Atauro longer than the two days they'd packed for. Washing and drying were in order. There was no laundry service at the lodge. They'd need to do it themselves.

Cordero considered washing to be women's work: he'd given them two shirts to wash and a pair of socks. He told them he would do his shorts himself.

"You should have seen their eyes, *mana*," Estefana was saying as they wrung and hung out the clothes. "They were not the eyes of a dog. They were demons' eyes."

"We went through this last night, Estefana," Carter said as she draped a T-shirt across an oleander branch. There were no clothesline or pegs, so they had to hang the clothes where and how best they could. The oleander was soon sagging under the weight. "You're talking yourself into believing it."

"But you weren't there, *mana*. You didn't see the dogs. I saw them and I know what it means."

"Mangy dogs are mangy dogs and nothing more," said Carter, wringing out one of Cordero's shirts. "Maybe the ones that attacked you were rabid. Are there rabies on Atauro?"

Estefana didn't answer. She held a wet sock in her hand and a worried expression on her face.

Carter tossed Cordero's shirt over a branch without bothering to spread it out. "Look, you weren't injured, okay? Stray dogs are a real problem on a lot of Native American reservations where I work, believe me. I've been attacked several times. They're a fact of life in some places and nothing to do with demons or devils."

"I don't know, *mana*," said Estefana. "I feel it was a warning. Spirits can take the shape of dogs, snakes, anything they want." She looked at the sock as though seeing it for the first time. "That's how they warn you. I've felt it ever since we came here. I should never have come."

Carter ignored the comment and lifted Cordero's second shirt from the pile.

"*Mana?*" Estefana said.

"What?"

"Could I ask you something?"

Carter was squeezing water from the shirt.

"Sure. What is it?"

"Can I go back? To Dili, I mean," said Estefana, eyes downcast.

"Today."

Carter stopped what she was doing.

"Look Estefana. We're police officers. We can't let fears about—"

"It's not fears, *mana*," Estefana interrupted. "It's the harm the spirits on the island may do to my children."

Carter held her frustration in check.

"Well it's for Cordero to decide not me," she said.

"But I'm her as *your* translator, *mana*," Estefana countered. "And I haven't had to do much translating with *maun* here to work with you."

Carter tossed Cordero's shirt roughly over the oleander. She let out a deep sigh.

"Okay, I'll talk to him, all right? Later. He's been told by Brooks that Frankston was killed by a sharp double-edged knife. Where it is, nobody knows. That's all he's focused on at the moment."

Sisko drew up on a motorcycle outside the lodge. He noticed he'd stopped in a pool of water, revved the engine and moved the bike a little further along the road. From where he dismounted, he could see Carter and Estefana in the yard. He took a folder from his pannier, propped it under his arm, and strolled over.

"*Bondia, mana*," he said to Carter before slinking closer to Estefana. "*Bondia, mana*," he repeated to her. "That was a big storm last night."

Estefana translated for Carter's benefit and they both agreed it had been a big storm for want of anything better to say.

"I have something for the investigator, *Senyor* Cordero," Sisko said to Estefana.

"You passed him coming in," she told him. "He's over in the dining area having coffee."

She stepped away from him and reached for more washing to hang.

"Oh, umm, right," Sisko said but he didn't move. He was staring a little too long at the bras and panties that were hanging from the branches until Estefana caught his eye.

"The dining area," she repeated and pointed.

"Yes, yes, of course, yes," Sisko stammered. "Maybe I'll see you later. I'm on an important job now but I'll get it done before too long."

He walked across to the dining area, almost tripping as he kept his eyes glued to Estefana and her washing. Cordero was sitting at a table at the rear in full shade. He was hunched over an empty coffee cup he was about to refill from a small jug resting on the table. A plate with the remains of a serving of scrambled eggs and tomato lay off to the side.

"*Senyor*," Sisko said approaching the table. "*Bondia*. The internet is working this morning. This came for you from Dili ten minutes ago. I printed it all out and rushed over here with it because I knew it was important."

He handed the folder to Cordero. It contained three printouts concerning Robert Evans.

"Well done, thanks," Cordero said. He placed the folder on the table and finished refilling his coffee cup. "Coffee?" he offered.

"No thanks," said Sisko. "Been sent out on a job. It's important."

"Okay, thanks," repeated Cordero and the young cadet took off to his motorcycle. Cordero reached for the sugar to sweeten his coffee and opened the folder when he had.

Carter and Estefana finished hanging out the washing. Estefana went inside their hut, saying she'd pack up her things to go if Cordero approved her leaving. Carter walked over to the dining area. Cordero was stirring his coffee.

"Interesting reading?" Carter asked as she settled opposite him.

"Yeah," he said absently.

Carter tested the coffee jug. It contained a little coffee. She signalled to the woman in the kitchen to bring her a cup.

"I'm waiting," she said to Cordero. "Or is it confidential?"

"What? No," he said. "Dili managed to get some printouts on Robert Evans from the Australian Embassy. I'm surprised they came so fast."

Carter's coffee cup arrived. She thanked the woman and poured herself the dregs from the jug.

"The first one's an old bio from the last university where he worked. Lists a book he wrote: *Viagens no Éden*. I've enough Portuguese to be able to translate that as *Voyages in Eden*."

He looked up.

"So?"

"He told us he spoke a *little* Portuguese," Cordero said. "So how come he writes an entire book in the language?"

"Maybe there's an English original and a publisher in Portugal had it translated," suggested Carter, sampling her coffee.

"Maybe," grunted Cordero as he consulted the printout. "But it doesn't say anything about an English original. Says he was born in 1956. That makes him 58 years old."

He drank some coffee.

"A little early for retirement for an academic, wouldn't you say?"

She shrugged and drained her own cup.

"Maybe he was burnt out."

"At 58? I had lecturers in their seventies," Cordero said.

"You're a little suspicious this morning, Tino," Carter said to tease him. "Coffee too bitter for you?"

"Coffee's fine," he said. "Look at this."

He handed her a printout of a short newspaper article dated almost exactly one year earlier—October, 2013. The article was entitled: 'Disgraced academic fired for fraud'. It said Robert Evans had been sacked after an investigation into his unauthorised use of university funds had uncovered he had falsely claimed to hold a PhD in history.

"Well, well," said Carter. "What's the other printout?"

"Just another newspaper article on the same subject," Cordero said. "Says the funds amounted to $15,000."

His cell buzzed. He checked the caller ID, mouthed a silent 'sorry' to Carter, and walked out into the full glare of the sun.

She could hear a loud voice on the other end of the call but couldn't make out the Tetun that was being spoken.

"It's not—" Cordero began but he was shouted down.

"I don't—" he started to say but the other caller talked over him.

Cordero paced up and down, waving his free hand around at nothing in particular.

"If I wanted to bait authority," he said finally, shouting into the cell, "I'd pick someone with a lot more of it than you!"

With that he closed the phone, stormed into the dining area, and picked up the folder.

"There's someone I must see," he grumbled.

He finished the rest of his coffee, replaced the cup in its saucer a little too forcefully, and was gone before she had a chance to ask who.

• • •

Sergeant Amparo was propped gingerly on his one good leg, his eyes fixed on the map on the wall of his office when Cordero burst through the door.

"What's your game, Amparo?" he snapped at the sergeant.

Amparo hopped around and put a hand on the desk to steady himself.

"What are you talking about, *maun*?" he said.

"You've been telling my superior in Dili that I'm working with the American FBI agent! Now he's threatening to have me suspended for disobeying orders! I didn't take you to be one for *lori lia dór!*" he said, meaning tittle-tattle.

"What're you talking about, *maun*?" the sergeant said shuffling over to slump into a chair. He picked up his magazine and started fanning himself. Cordero noticed the electric fan on the windowsill was not working, its plug having slipped away from its socket.

"You weren't happy I was sent here to investigate this murder in the first place," Cordero said. "Called it interference. Said Dili police have a high opinion of themselves and a low one of the likes of you. And you certainly objected to me ordering the release your prime suspect."

He was now standing over Amparo.

"You figured a little payback was in order, eh? And so you've twice now told Dili I'm including the American in my inquiries.

You're an *asu*," he said, meaning a dog—one of the worst things one Timorese can call another.

Amparo dropped his magazine on the floor and lifted himself awkwardly out of the chair to confront Cordero. His face was red with anger.

"Fuck off out of my office!" he yelled and waved an arm at the door.

"So you can sit there, read magazines and arrest innocent people?" Cordero shouted in reply.

"Fuck you!" snapped Amparo.

"No fuck you!" Cordero shot back.

"I didn't tell Dili nothing!" Amparo protested. "You think I'd do that? I haven't been a police officer all these years causing trouble for fellow officers. And I haven't spoken to Dili since that American's body was found. You don't believe me, you ask them!"

"If it wasn't you, who else would it've been?" demanded Cordero.

Amparo slumped back down to think. Cordero waited.

"Sisko's been doing the radio reports to Dili the last two nights," the sergeant said, his voice lowered now. "Always gossips, that boy. Can never do one thing the way he's been told."

He looked up.

"Did he know you two were working together?"

Cordero considered that. Estefana had taken the messages to be sent to Dili to the police station each night. She certainly knew Cordero was including Carter in his interrogations. She could have let something slip.

"Well?" Amparo pressed him.

"Maybe," conceded Cordero. He drew back from the sergeant. "He brought that folder for me with printouts from Dili this morning," he said. "Where is he now?"

Amparo rose and hobbled over to the map. "I've sent him to Maquili. The sacred house there was broken into last night."

He traced a finger down the right-hand side of the map.

"That means every sacred house on the east coast has been

broken into," he continued. "Except for the one here. Maybe too close to home."

He rubbed the back of his neck.

"There's something going on but I can't figure out what," said the sergeant.

Cordero joined him but his mind was on Sisko.

"I want to talk to him when he shows up," he said.

"What?" asked Amparo, his eyes still fixed on the map. "Oh, okay. I'll let him know."

"Thanks," Cordero said and made for the door. "Good luck with the break-ins," he added.

Amparo peered over his shoulder.

"What did you say?" he asked.

"I said good luck with your sacred house break-ins," said Cordero.

Amparo hobbled back to his chair and slumped down into it.

"Aren't you forgetting something?" he asked.

Cordero paused. He approached the sergeant, dropped to one knee, and inserted the plug of the fan into its socket. Immediately the blades of the fan started swirling.

"I apologize," Cordero said. "It's just that my boss gives me the shits sometimes."

Amparo regarded Cordero, the fan, and Cordero again.

"Don't they all?" he said. "Apology accepted."

• • •

Cordero was grumpy when he returned to the lodge. He noticed Carter collecting some items of clothing which had already dried in the heat.

"You ready to talk to Evans?" he called to her.

"Sure," she said. "But I need to talk to you about something first."

"Can't it wait?"

"No."

He thrust his hands in his pockets and waited as she wandered over.

"Okay, what is it?"

"Estefana wants to leave. Today. For Dili."

Cordero frowned in annoyance.

"She can't get it out of her head that the people her father was forced to bury here have it in for her," Carter continued. "Last night she was almost attacked by some wild dogs. She says they were spirits warning her."

"Did she find out what the African was up to?"

"Yeah. He was visiting a lady friend. Out near the cemetery. The lady friend told Estefana he left her for a short time to talk to someone walking along the road to the cemetery. Returned angry and upset about something but didn't say what."

"I didn't think he was being entirely honest with us," Cordero said.

"No you didn't. Neither of us did."

"Well I'll certainly be having another talk with him."

He made to leave.

"Hold on," she said. "What about Estefana?"

"What about her?"

"Have you listened to what I've been telling you?"

He cast his eyes to the ground.

"Look, I know that kind of stuff bothers her and I'm sorry she feels that way. But she can't go," he said. "Not now."

"Cordero, she's terrified," Carter said, raising her arms into the air. "I've tried to talk sense to her but I'm not getting very far."

"We need her here," he said.

Carter's expression hardened.

"Technically she's my translator," she pointed out.

He met her eyes.

"Officially she is an officer in the Timorese police and I have authority over her," Cordero said.

"What's wrong with you?"

"Look," Cordero said, sweeping a hand through his hair and trying to adopt a more reasonable tone. "If Evans doesn't tell us who and where this Antonio Gomes is, I'll need Estefana to ask around the village. That's a job you can't do because you don't speak Tetun. It's a job I can't do because I'll be asking the African what he was doing the night Frankston was killed out on the road near the cemetery and why he didn't bother to mention he was there."

He took his hands out of his pockets and presented them as though pleading with her to understand.

"So I need her here to help us out. I'm sorry. I really am. But the sooner we get to the bottom of everything people are hiding from us, the sooner we can all go home."

He dropped his eyes.

"Tell her 'no' and to stay put until we return."

14

Robert Evans was not in the room he rented from the priest. Nor was the priest's jeep parked anywhere outside the building. Cordero found Father Robeiro joking with some children by the side of the church and asked him if he knew where Evans had gone. The priest said he hadn't seen him that morning and didn't know where he was. Cordero asked about the jeep. The priest said he hadn't needed it and assumed Evans had taken it as a result. There was no option but to wait until Evans returned.

"So what's bugging you this morning?" Carter asked as they sat on the fence in the shade of the hibiscus.

Cordero rubbed his hands on the sides of his pants and sniffed.

"Jada," he said. "My boss. Someone told him I was working with you and he's had another go at me over it. Threatened to suspend me."

"Join the club," she said.

He looked at her. "What do you mean?"

"Hudson Taylor called this morning while you were out." She picked up a pebble and tossed it out onto the road. "Complained that Mrs. Frankston hadn't yet been allowed to go to Dili. Complained it was taking too long to find her husband's killer."

An old man walked past carrying freshly caught fish that were hanging off a pole across his shoulders. They exchanged greetings.

"Complained that I wasn't keeping him informed with regular briefings." She huffed softly. "Complained I wasn't doing the job I was sent here to do. Complained, complained and complained. I think he'd suspend me too if he could."

"What did you tell him?"

"I wanted to tell him to put a sock in it," she said. "That means—"

"I grew up in Australia, remember. I know what these expressions mean. Well, most of them."

She picked up another pebble and rolled it between her fingers.

"I distracted him by telling him what a great job Miller was doing," she said and laughed this time. "Miller's like his little puppy."

"Where is he by the way?" asked Cordero.

"I'll give you two guesses," she said. "No, make that one."

"Do you think he's having an affair with Mrs. Frankston?"

"I think Miller would need to consult a user's manual first," she said. She tossed the second pebble onto the road. "It's not my concern what he does with his dick just so long as it doesn't interfere with the police investigation."

Cordero coughed to hide his embarrassment at the way she talked and nodded.

"I thought it was Sergeant Amparo who was telling tales to my superior in Dili. You know, because he's been so resentful that I'm here. So I gave him a mouthful. But it seems more likely it was that cadet of his. He's the one who's sent the reports to Dili the last two nights and each time I'd sent Estefana there with a message. She might have told him we were in this together."

They sat in silence.

"I'm sorry if I appeared a little hot under the collar this morning," Cordero said.

Carter glanced at him. "You didn't *appear* hot under the collar, Cordero," she said, "You *were* hot under the collar."

He shifted nervously. "Well, I'm sorry anyway. How did Estefana take my instructions?"

"You mean your orders? Well, she's not happy, I can tell you that much."

He plucked a flower off the hibiscus, careful not to damage the soft pink petals.

"Like I said, I'm sorry," he said. He held out the hibiscus flower to her. "Peace offering?"

She took the flower, smiled, and twirled it in her hand. He

checked his watch.

"I'll accept your peace offering if you go easy on Estefana," she said. "It might be a crock of shit but she believes it." She studied him. "You do know what the expression a crock of—"

"Yes," he said. "I like Estefana. You know that."

"What I know and what she perceives is not the same thing," said Carter. "And it's not about liking her, although you could be a bit more demonstrative about it. Why don't you tell her she's a good police woman from time to time? Reinforce that professional ambition she has locked away insider her. She looks up to you."

He chewed over that and nodded.

"Got it?" she asked.

"Got it," he said.

"Do you think Evans is our man?" she put to him.

"Well he lied to us about a few things and kept a few more hidden," Cordero said. "He's whole purpose here sounds more than a bit strange to me. This was a place where the Portuguese dumped prisoners and just ignored them. There aren't a lot of old colonial structures here to examine or to justify the time he's spent on the island. And there's the wristwatch." He checked his own. "What say we get some lunch? We can keep an eye on movements in and out of the church yard from the lodge."

• • •

Estefana joined them for lunch. She had a downcast expression on her face and only picked at her meal of vegetarian pasta and *rujak*—the Timorese fruit salad of oranges, mango, watermelon and banana in a lime and chili dressing. It was another of Cordero's favourites and buoyed by its offering on the table he tried to explain why he needed her on the island as gently as he could. He also threw in some comments on how valuable her work was and how well she was coming along as a police officer.

It seemed to make little difference to her composure.

As time drew on, Carter and Estefana checked the washing, read, and drank mineral water. Cordero's mood brightened a little more. He even collared some children who strolled past the lodge on their way home from school and tried Carter's trick with the balancing strand of hair. He managed only doubtful looks from the children and criticism from Carter for not putting enough expression into the act.

They packed away the washing, read some more, and drank more mineral water. Cordero's cell buzzed. He took the call as he walked out into the garden.

"Yeah…. Uh-huh…. Waiting to talk to the Australian but he's not in his room and no one knows where he's gone." More chatter followed from the other end. "Let me think about it. I'll call you."

Carter threw him a questioning look as he re-entered the shade of the dining area.

"That was Sergeant Amparo," he said. "He asked me to go with him to inspect the *uma lulik*, you know, the sacred house, here in Vila." He placed his cell on the table. "Could be he's reaching out somehow."

"Reaching out?" Carter asked.

"Yeah. I fixed his fan," said Cordero. "He couldn't bend down to do it with that ankle of his. So maybe this is his way of, you know, repaying the gesture."

"So what are you going to do?" she asked.

"I'm not here to investigate break-ins," he said.

"It wouldn't hurt to have him on side," Carter said. "Besides, it's better than just killing time here. Call him."

Cordero tossed the idea around.

"I guess I owe him something after I lost my temper with him this morning," he said, and he picked up his cell. "This won't take long. Keep your eyes on Evans' room. If he appears before me, just wait, okay? But make sure he doesn't leave this time. Maybe let down the tyres on that jeep," he added only half jokingly.

15

"Haven't been inside this place in a while," Amparo was saying as he drove toward Vila's sacred house, the utility splashing mud onto the verge either side of the road as it jolted through the puddles. "I'm not from here and anyhow I don't go in for that kind of thing. Like I told you, I'm not Catholic, Protestant...traditional or anything in between." He swerved suddenly to avoid a goat that was trotting across the road and let out a groan as the jerking movement shot a pain from his injured ankle up through his leg. He corrected the vehicle and drove along straight ahead.

"How about you?"

"Well certainly not traditional," said Cordero. "My family fled to Australia after the Indonesians invaded. My father was a reporter. He wouldn't have lasted long if he'd stayed."

He steadied himself from the jostling by clutching the grab handle above the passenger's door.

"I grew up in Australia. School, university. I've been back in Timor about ten years, but I wasn't here long enough to absorb the traditional thing and I haven't felt drawn to it since."

Amparo nodded, his elbow resting on the base of the driver's open window.

"Why'd you return?" he asked. "Given the chance, most wouldn't."

"It wasn't my idea to leave," Cordero said, and rubbed his free hand under his nose. "I was too young to have a say. My brother stayed. He was in the seminary, training to become a priest. He was shot and killed at the Santa Cruz massacre."

Amparo glanced across. Over two hundred Timorese were

gunned down by Indonesian soldiers in 1991 at the central cemetery in Dili during a funeral for a young Timorese killed a few days earlier protesting Indonesia's occupation. Amparo had an uncle fatally shot and an aunty wounded on the same occasion. He felt something of a connection.

"A lot of us suffered that day," he said vaguely. "So, you came home for your brother's sake?"

Cordero inclined his head and thought about that.

"In part, I guess I did, yeah," he admitted. "We'd been close. But I never really fitted in over there. In Australia I mean. In those days few people even knew where Timor was on a map. And when the country became independent, I wanted to be part of it."

"Part of what?" asked Amparo, his tone a little cynical.

"Good question," Cordero said. "Part of making this a better place, I guess." He paused. "You think that's a silly idea?"

"I've heard sillier," was all Amparo said.

The sergeant pulled the vehicle onto an even more pot-holed track. Cordero glanced sideways out the passenger's window.

"Look, again I'm sorry for this morning," he said, turning forward. "I shouldn't have accused you and come at you like I did."

Amparo laughed and swivelled toward him. "Well, I guess I shouldn't have told you to fuck off."

Cordero smiled.

"I'm guilty of that one too," he said.

Amparo brought the utility to a juddering stop on the side of the track. He cut the engine and engaged the park brake. Through the trees in the distance could be seen the distinctive roof of the sacred house. It was adorned with the carved images of the rare Timor green pigeon and the skulls of goats (there being few buffalo—their skulls the usual adornment atop an *uma lulik*—on the island).

"I've had to visit each place that's been broken into. Keep the elders happy like I said. Not Maquili. Rough road. My foot wouldn't take that drive. That's why I sent Sisko. He's from there. He's Humangili. Did I tell you that?"

He opened the driver's door and shifted sideways to free his injured ankle from the floor controls.

"The reason I asked you to come along is I figure a fresh pair of eyes just may see something I'm missing. This *uma lulik* hasn't been broken into. All the others were full of the usual stuff only the elders would value—old spears, weavings, carvings. I'm thinking there might be something here a thief is after, and the other break-ins are designed to hide the fact by having us think it's all just a prank."

"That the only reason you brought me?" asked Cordero.

"Well, we're both police officers. We should be working together," said Amparo as he slid out of the utility.

He looked back grinning.

"Besides," he said, "a smart investigator like you might just come up with another theory beyond the reach of a simple police officer like me."

"Whatever you say," Cordero said as he opened the passenger's door and got out.

• • •

Estefana was playing absently with the food on her plate. Carter reached over and covered the hand that held the fork to make her stop.

"We're just going to have to make the best of it, Estefana," she said. "I tried my best but he needs you here. He needs your skills as a police officer. Concentrate on that and try to put your other concerns aside."

Estefana withdrew her hand.

"How do I put things aside, *mana*? Healthy children are all I've ever wanted."

"You also wanted to pursue a career as a police officer, remember? And sometimes that means putting personal issues aside," said Carter.

Estefana wasn't persuaded.

"Look, let's try to concentrate on the case, okay?" Carter said. "And if Cordero asks you to go someplace you don't feel comfortable going, I'll come with you."

"You can't protect me from the spirits, *mana*," Estefana said.

Carter smiled.

"Maybe not," she conceded. "But you've never seen me take on a pack of rabid dogs!"

• • •

Amparo placed his hands on his lower back, stretched, and leaned a hand on the side of the utility.

"I called the *uma hein* this morning," he said. "You know who that is?"

"Person who guards the sacred house?" Cordero said.

"See. I knew you were smart. He lives nearby. Would have heard us drive up. Should be here any minute."

Amparo took a packet of cigarettes from his shirt pocket and offered it to Cordero, who declined. He extracted one, lit it, and took in a lungful of smoke.

"The Indonesians destroyed most *uma lulik* in Timor," he said as the smoke drifted out of his nostrils. "They didn't want people to congregate in case that led to organized resistance."

"Yeah, I've heard that," said Cordero.

"Except here," Amparo continued. "They couldn't give a shit about Atauro so sacred houses on the island were left alone. There were no missionaries here to tear them down either, or to demand people bring out their contents and burn them as happened on the mainland. Even the Church thought nothing of this island until fairly recently."

He took another lungful of smoke.

"So, things were left pretty much intact here. One word of advice though," he said. "Don't mention anything about dead Americans inside. Certain things are forbidden to be spoken about in there and that could be one of them."

"There's no connection I can imagine with the dead American," Cordero said.

"All the same—" said Amparo and abruptly cut short the rest of the statement. "Ah, here's our man now."

Two elderly men, one in shorts the other in a grubby sarong, came through the waste-high grass beside the track and up to

Amparo and Cordero. Amparo ground his cigarette under his boot and introduced Cordero as a police colleague from Dili.

The man in the sarong appeared to be a ritual leader. He wore sunglasses and carried a switch with which he kept flies at bay.

"I give you permission to come inside," he said in a croaky voice. "But don't ask me anything. The knowledge belongs to our ancestors. It is not mine to share with outsiders."

With that curt greeting the man took off and he and the one in shorts led them through a stand of coconut palms to a small rectangular building made of Timor pine and bamboo held together by twine. It sat on hardwood stumps a few feet off the ground and was capped with thatch. No nails, screws or man-made materials could be used in the construction of a sacred house and this one, though old, remained intact and sturdy.

The man in shorts retrieved a ladder from the undergrowth and positioned it so they could enter the structure through the door on the eastern side. This was the door through which all males entered. The door on the opposite side was for females only. The man in the sarong mounted the ladder first, followed by Amparo, Cordero, and lastly the man in shorts.

The interior was dark—there were no windows—and the air was cool despite the heat that choked the air outside. Cordero let his eyes adjust and when they had he scanned the room slowly.

A center pole holding up the roof was adorned with the skulls of goats and pigs, and at its base were woven baskets containing betel leaves, areca nuts and lime for use in rituals. Sanctums for heirlooms such as swords, long knives and half-moon head-dresses believed to have belonged to the ancestors were cordoned off by woven throws hanging from cross beams. Other shelves around the walls held a variety of lesser objects: necklaces, bracelets and cloth. A large pot, blackened by years of use, dangled above a hearth of stones. Dried herbs lay in small clumps nearby.

In the corner of one sanctum was a bust of a carved ancestor figure with an elongated face. The figure was dusty, but Cordero gently blew some of the dust away and thought it was made of red cedar and very old. In an adjacent reliquary, propped up against the wall, was a face mask carved from a white hardwood. Open sockets made for eyes and a mouth and a long thin nose ended in a chiseled moustache that covered the bottom of the mask.

Amparo was checking a collection of metallic spear tips, the shafts long since rotted and discarded. The collection was bound in an old wrap, the original blue colour fading from the fabric. Like the sculpture and the mask, these objects would be viewed as tangible connections between the living and the dead. They were essential markers of the community and would be revered accordingly.

"Anything?" Amparo asked.

"Not yet," said Cordero as he moved around the room, careful not to touch or disturb any of the objects.

A rolled-up straw covering was propped against the wall in the far corner. This was the *biti*—a ceremonial mat used in rituals to sit two warring members of the community on a shared covering to resolve their differences. Cordero noticed something protruding from beneath it.

He took a closer look. It was the edge of a piece of frayed fabric. It seemed to have no connection to the *biti*.

"Can you ask if we could examine what's under this mat?" he said to Amparo.

The keeper of the *uma lulik* and the ritual leader had waited patiently off to one side watching the two policemen in silence. Amparo moved closer to Cordero see what he was talking about and then turned to the two men.

"*Senyor, husu lisensa ba haree objetu nee,*" he said, asking the ritual leader for permission to view the object.

The two men exchanged glances and the ritual leader approached. Amparo pointed.

The man carefully moved the *biti* aside.

"*La keta kona,*" he said, meaning don't touch.

Cordero bent down to view the object. He took his cell from his pocket, engaged the flashlight, and waved it slowly over what had taken his interest.

"What is it?" Amparo asked.

"Wait a minute," Cordero said, and held the flashlight steady. He studied the fabric. "It's part of a flag. A very old flag." He focused the flashlight on one spot in particular. "You can see here the edge of a red cross pattée," he added and pointed.

"A what?"

Cordero straightened.

"Heraldic cross," he explained. "It's a particular design used by the Order of Christ."

Amparo scratched his head.

"Under Prince Henry the Navigator it came to be used on Portuguese caravels," Cordero said. "You know, ships. "

"How do you know that?" Amparo asked.

Cordero pocketed his cell.

"I spent a few months in Portugal undergoing training for the police unit I work for. They didn't give as much of an allowance so I spent a lot of time in museums to entertain myself."

He looked up at Amparo.

"Admission was free for Timorese, you see."

Amparo seemed neither enlightened nor amused.

"Okay, so it's an old flag," he said.

"It's a very old flag," Cordero corrected him. "*Very* old. At a guess, I'd say it's four, maybe five hundred years old."

Amparo shifted slightly.

"Okay. So what does that tell you?"

"How do you reckon it ended up here?" Cordero countered.

Amparo merely shrugged.

"Did you see any old Portuguese artifacts in the *uma lulik* that were broken into?" Cordero asked.

"No. None."

"Maybe whoever did the break-ins was looking for something like this," said Cordero.

"Why? It's not even the whole flag," said Amparo. "What possible value could it have outside a ritual house? For that matter, what value could it have inside one? It's not Timorese and it doesn't belong to this island or anyone who lives here."

"I have no idea of its value," said Cordero. "Maybe it wasn't this particular object our intruder was after but something akin to it."

"Well that doesn't make a lot of sense to me," complained Amparo.

Cordero took a kerchief from his pocket and wiped his hands.

"Doesn't make a lot of sense to me either at the moment," he said. "But it does raise some interesting questions."

16

"I told you not to leave Vila, *Senyor* Evans," Cordero said. He had returned from the visit to the *uma lulik* with Sergeant Amparo, collected Carter, and the two of them were now standing at the open door of the room Evans rented from the priest. Evans had his back to them. He was taking off a soiled T-shirt and replacing it with a clean one. Once done, he swung around and smiled.

"Yeah, I know," he said. "Sorry about that, mate. Made a lightening trip to Maquili on a little bird watching expedition. I told you that was also an interest of mine."

Evans took a seat and motioned for them to come inside. His demeanour suggested he considered himself irreproachable.

"If this monsoonal weather continues, which looks likely now, the road could get cut. I'm told it's happened before. And I haven't much time left here but a lot to get done. I was looking for the Timor Bush Warbler. Know it? It's quite rare."

He could see Cordero wasn't impressed.

"Had no luck," he added. "But I wasn't gone long."

"You've been gone since at least late morning," Cordero pointed out.

"Yeah, well, they don't have many gas stations, mate. I ran out about three miles from the village. Had to walk in, find someone with a little gasoline, walk back to the jeep and arrange more gasoline to get here. Which—" he spread his hands wide "—you can see I've done. I wasn't doing a runner if that's what you're thinking."

They hadn't taken his offer to come inside. He rose, went to the doorway, and waved them to some chairs outside his room.

"Please," he said. "Let's sit. It's been a hard drive plus a bit of bush-bashing and my back's killing me."

All three sat but Cordero pulled his chair up to face Evans. He was recalling Carter's quip about sitting beside him the first time they spoke and missing the detail about the pale skin indicating where a watch had been affixed on Evans' otherwise tanned wrist. This time Carter took to the side of Evans.

"I've been doing some checking up on you," Cordero began.

Evans leaned his forearms on his knees.

"Thought you might," he said.

"You said you'd retired from your university but that's not exactly true is it? You were sacked, weren't you?"

Evans' face registered no surprise or sense of guilt.

"Hardly a hanging offence, mate," he replied.

"Like to tell us about your falsified academic qualifications?"

Evans laughed and sat erect.

"I do have an undergraduate degree in history," he said and swatted at a mosquito on his forearm. "First class Honours in fact. But you're right: I don't have a PhD."

He looked at Carter.

"You don't need all that academic hoo-ha to teach, love," he said to her. "You need passion. And to research things, curiosity and elbow grease will take you further than academic credentials. Much further."

"You're not explaining yourself," Cordero said.

Evans slouched again.

"I was working at a different university. In the academic records section. I knew what a lot of bullshit most academics traded in. And most couldn't teach to save themselves. Just used big words to keep students guessing instead of complaining."

He sat up.

"I wanted to teach. I knew I could do a much better job of it. But academia is a closed shop. Like the bloody priesthood," he said and threw a thumb over his shoulder toward where Father Robeiro lived. "Need this qualification and that qualification. All bullshit. Anyhow I had access to academic transcripts. Part of my job was to send them to graduates. So, I made one up for myself. Why not? Gave myself a PhD in colonial history."

He broke into a self-satisfied grin.

"Also took some letterhead and wrote myself a glowing reference. In someone else's name, of course. Managed to get other letterhead from other universities by writing to them and doing a little cutting and pasting with the replies. Not hard. Wrote more references for myself. I was quite the scholar before long. After a time, I applied for a lecturing job at another university."

Again, he turned to Carter.

"They say they check references but in those days I knew they were too bloody lazy to spend time on that. And if they did, what did I have to lose? I was jack of the job anyway."

Evans sniggered.

"But I didn't lose, did I? Got the job and it took the buggers twenty years to catch on. Bloody joke the lot of them."

"They caught on because you embezzled funds?" Carter asked.

"Oh, that's a bit rich, love. I didn't exactly *embezzle* anything. I merely *redirected* some research funds from one departmental account to another for my own purposes. Happens all the time. It's just that my efforts weren't authorized, as they say."

"You published a book in Portuguese. *Viagens no Éden*. Is that what you used the funds for? What I believe they call a vanity publication?" asked Cordero.

"You pronounce that title beautifully, mate," said Evans. "Yes and no. I write passable Portuguese, but I don't speak it well and certainly can't understand it spoken. I'm strictly book-taught you see and there aren't too many Portuguese where I live to practice with. So I can't communicate with anyone in the language beyond simple sentences. Bit like my Tetun. Part of the money paid a native speaker to correct the language in the manuscript. The rest went to subsidizing publication. *Subsidizing*," he emphasized and held up a finger. "Not quite a vanity publication."

"Why in Portuguese?" asked Carter.

"Because, love, no one would publish it in Australia, the US, or the UK. The subject was too esoteric and its treatment was mainly of interest to a select group of Portuguese historians."

"Why hide all of this from us?" Cordero asked.

Evans looked out toward the road. "I don't know. Maybe I'd just convinced myself that all the bullshit I told about myself was true."

"But you also lied about how much time you spent talking to Father Robeiro last Tuesday night," Cordero said.

Evans folded his hands behind his head.

"Well, that was a bit different, wasn't it?"

"How so?"

"I saw Frankston that night. I knew it was him because he always walked at night waving a torch around like a bloody blind man with a cane. He walked past as I was entering my room after exchanging a few pleasantries with Robeiro. We spoke. I'll admit it," he said and gestured down the road beyond the lodge. "There. But not for long. Bloody mosquitos were getting to me, and I didn't want to join him for one of his hour-and-more long lectures about bloody coral. Besides I was tired. I went to bed. I didn't tell you because I figured you might put me in the frame for killing him."

"What made you think we'd do that?" Carter asked.

"Who else is there to blame, love?" Evans replied. "I know how copper's think."

"So, you insist you didn't argue with him, follow him, kill him?" said Cordero.

"Of course bloody not!"

"What did you speak about?" asked Carter.

"His latest dive out on the reef," said Evans. "Like I said, we only talked for a minute or two. He was excited. He'd found something. But he wouldn't tell me what it was."

"I imagine that annoyed you," Cordero said.

"Sure," said Evans. "But I was used to Hank. It didn't annoy me enough to kill him."

"Did you notice if Frankston had a knife on his belt?" Cordero asked.

"A knife?" Evans thought about the question. "Couldn't tell you, mate. It was dark. No bloody streetlights in Vila in case you haven't noticed."

"What time was this?" Cordero asked.

"Can't say exactly," said Evans. "Quarter, maybe twenty after nine. My watch is on the blink."

"I was going to ask you about that," said Cordero.

"About my watch? Shit! What else are you curious about?"

"Where is your watch?" Cordero asked, ignoring the sarcasm.

"It cost me all of ten dollars, if you must know. Water-logged from my last dive. You want it, you can have it."

"I want to examine it, yes," said Cordero.

Evans pushed himself up, walked into his room, and came out with the watch. He handed it to Cordero who gave it a quick examination. He could see no sign of skin or blood or scrapping of any kind on any of the edges or the band. As Evans said, moisture had built up inside the crystal of the watch obscuring the face entirely.

"What can you tell me about Antonio Gomes?" Cordero asked, placing the watch in his shirt pocket.

"Who?" said Evans.

"Antonio Gomes. Local youth. You were seen talking to him."

"Antonio? Antonio?" repeated Evans. He clicked his fingers. "Oh, you must mean that kid who speaks a bit of English. He wanted to practice, that's all. He's just popped around here a couple of times and I chatted with him for a few minutes. I don't know any more about him."

"Where does he live?"

"Search me. We didn't get much beyond 'My name's Antonio' and 'I'm from Vila.'"

"You know anything about Portuguese flags?" Cordero asked.

"Well, I did write a book on Portugal's colonial expeditions. Why? You come across one you want to sell?" he joked.

"You have any interest in *sacra*?" Cordero asked.

"*Sacra*?"

"You know, the sacred objects stored in *uma lulik*," Cordero said.

"You've got me there, mate," Evans said. "Even if I did, there's no way I could get inside a bloody sacred house. They're off limits to foreigners."

Cordero glanced at Carter and they both made to leave.

"I'll take the keys to the jeep," Cordero said and held out his hand.

"Bloody hell! Where am I going to go without it?"

"You're not going to go anywhere," insisted Cordero. "You're going to stay put like I told you to do the first time. We haven't finished with you yet."

Evans handed over the keys and Cordero took them to Father Robeiro in case he needed to use the jeep for his own purposes. He asked the priest not to give the keys to Evans until further notice.

As they walked to the lodge Carter asked him: "Mind telling me what that was about flags?"

"In the *uma lulik* I visited with Amparo I found a section of an old flag the Portuguese used to fly on their ships in the sixteenth century."

"You think Evans is after an old flag?"

"I don't know what he's after. There's nothing to connect him to any of the break-ins and for all we know he wasn't anywhere near the sacred houses when they were broken into. Also, as he said, a foreigner would normally not be given permission to enter one so if he was seen trying, you'd figure someone would have reported it. There's always someone nearby who keeps an eye on a sacred house."

He stopped at the entrance to the lodge.

"So, what's eating you?" Carter asked.

"You peel away one layer of Robert Evans only to find there's another to contend with," said Cordero. "I wonder how many layers there are."

• • •

Sisko was pacing up and down outside the dining area. He'd been trying to talk to Estefana but she'd rebuffed him, took off inside her hut, and closed the door.

Cordero stopped to talk to the cadet while Carter went to the kitchen to ask for a menu.

"Sergeant Amparo said you wanted to see me about something," Sisko said, staring down at the hut Estefana had entered.

"I do," replied Cordero. "Over here."

He led Sisko away from the dining area so they could speak without being seen or heard from the kitchen. Cordero didn't want to undermine the young cadet's authority by dressing him down in earshot of anyone who worked at the lodge.

"I believe you've been gossiping about me to Dili when you've made those nightly radio reports," Cordero said.

"What are you talking about, *maun*?" Sisko asked.

"You heard me," said Cordero. "When I've asked for reports to be sent to Dili, you've seen fit to add some comments of your own about what I'm doing and who I'm doing it with."

"That's bullshit, *maun*!" Sisko said, but he was averting Cordero's glare.

"I want it to stop. Hear me? You're a cadet officer. I'm a senior investigator. It's not your job to report on what I do or how I do it and if I hear that you've done it again, I'll have you disciplined."

"Get off my back, *maun*!" Sisko told him. "That's shit!"

Cordero was taken aback by the young man's petulance.

"What did you just say?"

Sisko's cheeks were red and his eyes flared. He took two deep breaths before answering.

"I said *sin*," he said, meaning 'yes' but anger remained in his tone. "Whatever you say."

And with that he strode out to his motorcycle and revved the bike more loudly than usual.

• • •

Cordero asked Estefana to spend the next day tracking down Antonio Gomes.

"Can't tell you much about him," Cordero was telling Estefana. "His mother lives on the road to Beloi. Father Robeiro may be able to tell you where. Antonio speaks a little English. Stays with friends. It shouldn't be hard to find some young local who knows him and knows where to find him. Do your best, okay?"

Estefana signaled her agreement.

They were sitting in the dining area mulling over the dinner options. There were only two—chicken or fish—and Cordero was leaning toward the latter.

Gerard Miller appeared, looked out onto the road and over to his hut, and approached their table. Cordero grabbed another chair and invited him to join them.

"Looking for someone?" Carter asked.

"No ma'am," Miller said. "I mean Agent Carter."

"How's the *widow*?" Carter asked, emphasizing Mrs. Frankston's status.

"She's coping well, I think," said Miller. "Well, as well as could be expected."

"You spent the day with her?" Carter asked.

"Not the whole day, no. The roof I thought I'd repaired yesterday needed more work after last night's storm. After that we went over the procedures for her to have her husband's body repatriated to the States. It's a complicated process as I'm sure you'd appreciate. After that I went for a walk along the beach. She didn't want to come. Said she didn't feel well. I just checked with her and she's feeling better now but wasn't hungry and thought she'd skip dinner."

"So are you hungry?" Cordero asked.

"What? Um, yes."

Cordero stood to go to the kitchen. "I'll get someone to bring you some dinner. We're having the fish," he said, deciding for the others. "It's fresh. Relax."

Miller looked sheepish.

"You feeling all right, Gerard?" Carter asked.

"Yes, ma'am. I mean—"

"You don't look too well," said Carter interrupting him.

"It's just that I'm worried about Mrs. Frankston. That's all."

"Of course you are," said Carter.

"She's lost her husband, ma'am. And there's no one she can talk to now in Vila. She's had a difficult life, you know?"

"I'm sure life is difficult for a senator's daughter," said Carter.

"You don't understand," Miller insisted. "I think she's grieving the death of her brother. Her husband's killing has brought all that up again magnifying the trauma for her."

Cordero resumed his seat.

"Won't be long," he said to no one in particular.

"She was three or four when her brother died, Gerard," Carter was pointing out. "I know you can grieve for a long time, believe me, but even so."

"Yes but it's a matter of how her brother died. She doesn't talk about it much. She just started telling me yesterday when her cell rang. She hasn't raised the matter again. I think it is too much for her to deal with."

Cordero held his fork up.

"Who called her?" he asked.

Miller shook his head. "I don't know. She ended the call as soon as the cell started to buzz."

"She has a habit of doing that," Carter said and caught Cordero's eye.

"I saw the caller ID before she cancelled the call," said Miller. "It was MAF. You know, the people who flew us here."

"Well, well," said Carter. "I wonder why she's getting calls from MAF. You think they want her to rate their services?" she asked sarcastically.

Cordero checked his watch. "Their office will be closed now. I'll ring them first thing in the morning."

"Why? What's going on?" asked Miller.

"That's what we'd like to know," said Carter as their meals began to arrive.

17

Cordero was stretching and tugging his clean shirt at the breakfast table when Carter and Estefana joined him.

"Something wrong, Tino?" Carter asked, as a woman from the kitchen brought coffee and fresh bread rolls to the table.

"This shirt's creased," he said, trying now to flatten it out over his chest.

"Well maybe you should have washed it yourself," said Carter as she took her seat.

He stopped fiddling with his shirt and filled each of their cups with coffee. Miller emerged from his hut and was immediately accosted by the boy Benni. The two talked for a minute and Miller scooped the soccer ball from Benni, pretended to run with it, and allowed the boy to rake it back with his foot. He ruffled Benni's hair before joining their table. Cordero held the jug of coffee up to him and he nodded to have his cup filled as well.

"I spoke to MAF this morning," Cordero began as the woman approached with omelettes.

He waited until she had put a plate before each of them and left.

"They said Mrs Frankston rang the morning her husband's body was found and asked for a seat on the next available flight. Said it was urgent she get to Dili."

He took a mouthful of omelette.

"They told her the next available flight was the one you three came on. Told her it was a special flight returning around midday with no passengers and she could have a seat."

He glanced across at Carter, put his knife and fork on the table, and pulled his bread roll apart.

"She didn't show up, obviously, so they rang twice to see if she was okay and if she wanted to reschedule. You know, because she'd said it was urgent. One call was made while we were questioning her the first time. The second was made while Gerard was helping her pack. When she didn't answer either time, they gave up."

"Well now," said Carter, easing back in her chair with her coffee cradled in both hands. "That is interesting."

Cordero worked on the rest of his breakfast.

"But shouldn't the Jesus freak be our first priority?" Carter asked. "He lied about where he was the night Frankston was killed and thanks to Estefana, we know he was right there with him with a grudge to settle about a broken propeller."

"Don't worry," Cordero said. "He's not going anywhere. He doesn't have a vehicle. His boat's damaged, remember? And that boatman Zeka confirmed what he'd told us about other fishermen not having anything to do with him because they were jealous of the money they imagined he'd earned from Frankston."

He took a bite of his bread roll.

"So, he's stuck here," he said, chewing. "But Mrs Frankston has already made one attempt to leave the island and I wouldn't put it past her to try her luck a second time."

"You're not implying—" Miller began but Carter held up a hand and cut him off.

"I guess she could have figured the body wouldn't be found until much later that day or the next," Carter said, ignoring Miller. "And by the time it was she could be on her way home to the protective arms of daddy—the senator."

"That's what I'm thinking," said Cordero. "She certainly didn't venture the fact that she'd planned to go. There's no one to vouch for where she was the night her husband was killed. And she's shut down two calls from MAF when one of us might overhear the conversation."

"Inspector Cordero, really!" snapped Miller, and he threw his napkin on the table.

"I'm an investigator, *maun*, not an inspector. Is there a more innocent way you can explain her behavior?"

"All I know, Mister Cordero, is that she is an upstanding woman and incapable of… of—"

"Stabbing her husband?" Carter offered.

"It's preposterous!" Miller protested and stood, knocking his chair over as he did.

"Well, we'll soon find out. After breakfast, Carter and I will visit Mrs. Frankston and let her explain herself," said Cordero.

"I insist on being there," said Miller.

"You'll stay put, Gerard," Carter said. "This is a police matter. Nothing to do with you."

"She's right," said Cordero. "This is not something that concerns you or the Embassy. You stay here and don't try to contact her." He pointed his knife at Estefana. "As I was saying last night, could you ask around about Antonio Gomes, Estefana? We need to talk to him about his relationship with Evans and the sooner the better."

• • •

They'd almost reached the house the Frankstons had rented when Carter's cell came to life. She whipped it out and answered without first checking the caller ID.

"Carter," she said.

"What on earth are you up to?" boomed the voice at the other end.

She suppressed the urge to swear.

"Ambassador Taylor?" she asked instead.

"You're damn right it's me."

He was shouting so loudly she had to hold the phone away from her ear.

"Gerard tells me you're on your way to arrest Mrs. Frankston for her husband's murder. Have you gone mad?"

Carter took a deep breath.

"News travels fast but fast news can be wrong, sir," she replied. "Mrs. Frankston—"

"I don't want to hear your excuses, Agent Carter," Taylor broke in. "You were sent there to arrange her return to Dili. Now you're going to arrest her! My God woman!"

"I'm not going to arrest anyone...sir," she said, her impatience about to boil over. "Investigator Cordero and I are merely going to question Mrs. Frankston about some plans she had around the time of her husband's death that have just come—"

"I want you to put a stop this very minute to her persecution, Agent Carter!"

"Excuse me? What persecution?"

"That's what it sounds like from what Gerard has told me just now."

"As I was trying to say...sir...some plans of hers that have just come to our attention raise questions that need to be answered as part of this investigation. The *Timorese* police investigation," she added by way of emphasis.

"I don't care about that. And I don't care what this Codato wants—"

"It's Cordero, not Codato, and he is the police investigator in charge of this case."

"You were sent—"

"I have no authority here. I was sent, on your instructions, as an interested party to observe the investigation because an American citizen was killed under suspicious circumstances. I wasn't sent to rescue a senator's daughter because that would benefit your reputation!"

"You'll take that back, Agent Carter! I can see why you're here in East Timor and not doing proper FBI work in the States. You're out of line, hear me, out of line!"

"I'm here because you pressured me into extending my secondment with INTERPOL...sir!" she said, trying to hold her voice in check.

But Taylor wasn't listening.

"I have a responsibility toward American citizens visiting this country and I don't play favorites," he said. "Now you arrange to get that woman off the island and to Dili. Today, you hear me! I want no more of this Timorese police nonsense, goddamnit! And let me know as soon as you've made the arrangements."

The call went dead. "You have a nice day too," Carter said

glaring down at the cell in her hand. She'd fallen behind Cordero and had to run to catch up.

"Problem?" Cordero asked.

"Constipation is a problem, Tino. Hemorrhoids are a pain in the ass. Ambassador Taylor is more the latter. He wants Mrs. Frankston on her merry way to Dili today."

"That's not going to happen," said Cordero.

"I know," said Carter. "And he'll blame me."

She stopped walking and clicked her fingers.

"Hey, you're good on expressions. Ever heard the one about every cloud having a silver lining? Maybe Taylor will have me shipped home to Arizona before my current contract with INTERPOL expires as punishment for ignoring his demands."

"That wouldn't be a silver lining for me," he said. "I'd miss you."

She watched him as he strode up to Mrs. Frankston's front door.

"Really?" she asked.

But he'd knocked without further comment.

• • •

After breakfast Estefana visited Father Robeiro to ask him if he knew where the mother of Antonio Gomes lived. The priest had told her *Senyora* Gomes lived in a red cement block house on the southern edge of Vila where the road to Maquili took the first of many twists snaking up the hill and over the range. Estefana found the woman in her garden. She was middle age, skinny, dressed in trousers and a worn T-shirt, and was head down, weeding.

Senyora Gomes said her son didn't live with her anymore.

"He's a '*baruk-teen*' that one," she said, meaning lay-about. "He hasn't had a regular job since he came home from a year in Dili."

"What was he doing in Dili?" Estefana asked.

"What was he doing?" the woman repeated, straightening with a bundle of weeds in one hand. "Hustling tourists for a living."

The woman shook her head.

"That's how he bought that red motorcycle," she said. "I'm sure of it. How else would he have got that much money?"

"What red motorcycle?" Estefana asked.

"The one he rides everywhere," the woman said. "Except back home here to help me!"

"Do you know where I can find him?"

The woman gave Estefana the names of two youths—also unemployed, she said—and directions to where they lived. Estefana thanked her and headed for the home of the first of the two names.

It was Arturo Sousa. He and his family lived a short distance from the Gomes home but Arturo wasn't there and his sister, who was the only one home, didn't know where he was.

The second person *Senyora* Gomes had mentioned was a girl—Eskolastika Suarez or Esky for short. She lived with her mother and two younger brothers on the beachfront near the health clinic. Estefana found Esky hanging a large load of washing on a length of rope strung out between two avocado trees in the yard.

The girl looked to be about sixteen years of age. She wore ripped shorts and a white T-shirt that carried the signature Bob Marley logo *One Love* in faded red, yellow and green print across the front. She appeared furtive when Estefana introduced herself as a police officer and her answers to Estefana's questions were brusque and evasive.

"But you do you know Antonio," Estefana was trying to clarify.

"Sort of," the girl answered.

"Does that mean 'yes' you do know him or 'no' you don't?" Estefana asked.

The girl hesitated.

"Well?" said Estefana.

"Yeah I know him. So what? Everyone knows everyone in Vila."

"Do you know where I can find him?"

"No."

"When was the last time you saw him?"

The girl bit her lip. She put her hands on her hips and gazed out to the sea.

"When Eskolastika? Antonio is not in trouble, we just need to talk to him."

"We?" the girl asked, turning back to face Estefana.

"I'm here with two other police officers. We're investigating the death of the American. You must have heard about that."

"What's that got to do with Antonio?"

"Probably nothing," said Estefana. "But he may be able to help us with our inquiries."

"How could he help you? He doesn't know any Americans."

A wind blew in from the sea carrying fine particles of sand from the beach. Estefana had to shield her eyes while the girl caught the washing she was hanging and swore. When the wind had eased, the two faced each other again.

"So when was the last time you saw him?" Estefana repeated.

The girl bit her lip.

"When, Eskolastika?"

The girl hesitated.

"Come on, Eskolastika. Help me," pleaded Estefana. "Better you talk to me than the other police officers I came over here from Dili with."

Eskolastika picked up some wet clothes from the basket at her feet and kneaded them while she studied Estefana and weighed her options.

"Saw him yesterday," she said.

"Morning or afternoon?"

"Morning," the girl mumbled.

"Okay. Do you know where he was going?"

The girl threw the damp clothes back into the basket. She seemed to be struggling to hold back tears.

"Maquili," she said. "That's all I know."

"You don't know why he went there?" Estefana pressed her.

"I told you: that's all I know!" Esky said through gritted teeth.

"Do you know when he came back? Where he went when he did?"

"Isn't back yet," the girl said and sniffled.

"Did he say when he'd be back?"

"Antonio doesn't tell me when he's coming or going!" the girl said in a suddenly harsh, irate tone. "But he said he'd help me do the washing and I've had to do it all myself! If he's been with Rosa Monteiro again I'll cut off his balls!"

• • •

Mrs. Frankston invited Carter and Cordero in and they sat around the table in her front room. She offered them tea but they declined.

"Where's Gerard?" she asked.

"He's at the lodge," said Carter. "Embassy work to do today."

"Oh," uttered Mrs. Frankston as she slumped into her chair. "Of course."

"We'd like to know why you booked a flight to Dili the day after your husband was killed," said Cordero.

"Flight?"

"With MAF," Cordero added. "I spoke to their office this morning."

Mrs. Frankston crossed her legs and jiggled a foot.

"Well?" Cordero pressed her.

She bit at a fingernail.

"It's not what you think," she said.

"Okay. Tell us what it is," Cordero said.

She ran a hand roughly through her hair, stood and folded her arms tightly across her chest. When they'd first met, she'd affected the look of an injured animal. It had worked on Miller but not on Carter. That façade had gone. The Mrs. Frankston confronting them now was self-possessed and angry.

She waved her arms around.

"Look at this place!" she snapped. "They call this a kitchen. What kitchen? It's supposed to be a dining and a living room as well. Really? What a joke!"

They waited. She pointed toward the rear of the hut.

"There's a rat living in my toilet," she said. "I don't mean in what they loosely call the washroom," she said, shaking her head dismissively at the term. "I mean in the drain itself. Do you know what it's like to take a dump knowing there's a rat there right under you!"

She began pacing the room in front of them.

"Centipedes crawl out of the sink when I'm brushing my teeth. The power goes out. Cell coverage comes and goes. The gas bottles—" she slung a hand toward the far wall "—sometimes they have them in the kiosk and sometimes they tell you the boat didn't come and so it's a diet of bananas and water."

She lifted her arms.

"And what am I supposed to do all day? It was okay for him: he had his damn coral! What about me? There's no one to talk to, nothing to do. I was going crazy!"

"So I take it you argued about being here?" Cordero asked.

"You bet we did!" she shouted, face flushed.

"But you'd been on research trips with him before," said Carter. "You must have known what you were in for."

"Oh, I've been on research trips before alright!" she said, nodding her head furiously. "First Mexico, then Hawaii, after that the Pacific islands. Always remote, always impossible living conditions. Not to mention sharks, crocodiles, scorpions, snakes. You name it, I've seen it all. Ants, mosquitoes, sand flies—God how I hate sand flies!"

"Why did this come to a head now?" asked Cordero.

"It was building for a long time. I told him I'd had enough. I told him I wanted to go home. And what did he do?" She laughed grimly. "He applied for funding to stay even longer!"

"So you were angry," Cordero offered.

"Yes, I was angry! He wouldn't listen. He never listened. It was all about him and his damned research. 'My contribution to marine biology', he'd say as if he was on some kind of sacred mission. I was well and truly pissed!"

"So you argued and things got out of hand," Carter suggested.

"What? No!" she said, indignant now. "I loved Hank. I just didn't like coming second to his obsessions all the time. I was going home. That's all. I told him I would but he just ignored me. When he didn't wake up next to me that day I figured he'd left early for another goddamn dive. I was furious. I rang and arranged the flight in a fit of anger."

"Why didn't you tell us this before?" said Cordero.

She glared at him.

"How would it have looked when his body showed up?"

"If you had nothing to do with his death—" Cordero began.

"I'm a senator's daughter for God's sake!" she said. "Do you know what the media back home would have done with that? I can see the headlines now: 'Senator's daughter flees dead husband'. I could explain the need to go home for some reason or another if he was alive but when he was found dead, I'd be accused of all sorts of things I can only imagine. My father would never have lived it down."

The gust of wind blew in under the tin roof and dislodged a fine layer of dust that fell onto the table.

"Lovely. Just lovely," complained Mrs Frankston, watching the dust fall.

Cordero glanced at Carter. The story seemed credible enough but could easily have been concocted. Carter's expression said she felt the same. His cell rang. He rose, walked outside and took the call.

Mrs Frankston sat down, arms tightly folded around her chest, expression blank.

Cordero re-entered the room.

"My friend here will now take a look at your late husband's study," he said to Mrs Frankston before turning to Carter. "I've got to go. That was Amparo. He's re-arrested Justino. Says this time it's an open-and-shut case."

Mrs Frankston stared at him.

"The boy's been found with the knife," Cordero added.

18

"Welcome back," Sergeant Amparo said as Cordero came through the door of the police station. He was standing over his desk, hands spread out on the top to support himself on his injured ankle.

"I was questioning Mrs Frankston," Cordero said.

Cordero closed the door to keep what heat he could out. Amparo straightened.

"Why more questions for the widow?" he asked.

"She'd booked a flight with MAF to Dili the day her husband's body was found," explained Cordero. "I wanted to know why."

Amparo titled his head to the side.

"And what did she say?"

"Said she'd had enough of living rough and wanted to go home. Said Frankston wouldn't listen and when she found out he'd applied for funding to stay on longer, she'd had enough."

"You believe her?"

Cordero shrugged one hand.

"Not sure," he said.

Amparo raised an eyebrow.

"She wouldn't be the first person who wanted off this island. Where's your American friend?"

"I left her with Mrs Frankston. Gave her the key to Frankston's study and asked her to take a look over his things."

"You trust her to do that properly?"

"She knows what she's doing, and she might get a better sense of whether Mrs Frankston's telling the truth without me there. The woman knows Carter doesn't have any police authority here so she might open up a little more. Where's Justino?"

Amparo indicated with a flick of his head.

"Out back. Sisko's settling him down." The sergeant smirked. "Told you he did it."

"What happened for you to bring him in?"

Amparo raised a hand and flicked his fingers to indicate something vaguely outside.

"There was a commotion near the kiosk," he said. "The owner said a boy rushed in yelling that Justino stole his soccer ball. Kept yelling and screaming for the owner to do something."

He pushed off the desk and gazed out the front window.

"Justino was out front wheeling his barrow of coconuts around. The kiosk owner went out, challenged him, but Justino claimed he'd done nothing wrong. The boy kept hollering for his ball. He points into the barrow. The ball was sitting among the coconuts. All the noise brought both of us out to take a look at what was going on. The boy started yelling again and pointing into the barrow. I sent Sisko over to take a look. Under the soccer ball he found the knife wrapped in a rag."

Amparo signalled down to the desk.

"Want to take a look?"

Cordero drew closer. Amparo took the knife, wrapped in a grimy rag, from a drawer and placed it on top of the desk. He flicked one side of the rag off the knife. It was a small, sharp knife and specks of blood could be seen along the blade.

Cordero examined the knife closely.

"You had time to test for prints?" he asked.

The sergeant laughed.

"With what? This is Atauro, *maun*. There's nothing here for that sort of thing."

"You or anyone else touch this since it was found?" asked Cordero.

"We're not that stupid. I lifted the rag to see what we had, replaced it and covered it before I picked it up. Sisko had done the same. I figured they'd want to test for prints in Dili. You know what *malae* are like: they'd rather rely on technical shit than common sense. They'd expect the knife to be tested for prints in Dili even if it proves nothing."

Sisko re-entered from locking up Justino. He acknowledged Cordero with a flick of his head.

"He's crying and carrying on like a baby but he won't be going anywhere," Sisko said to Amparo. The cadet replaced the key to the secure room on its hook on the wall.

Cordero gave the knife a second examination. He straightened and told Sisko to go to the kiosk for a packet of corn starch and a small brush like a basting brush. Sisko looked at the sergeant who simply shrugged.

"They have both there?" Cordero asked Amparo.

"Should have. Why?"

"I've a hunch," was all Cordero said and, tugging only on the rag, he repositioned the knife to allow him better access to it on the desk.

A few minutes later the cadet re-appeared with the items Cordero had asked for.

He handed them over. "Cost me almost a dollar, *maun*," he said.

Cordero sighed, reached into his pocket and extracted some coins.

"Keep the change," he said, handing the coins to Sisko.

Sergeant Amparo steadied himself on his good leg and watched on over Cordero's shoulder as the investigator sprinkled a little of the starch on the handle of the knife. Gently he whisked excess powder off with the brush. He did the same to the blade. He twirled the knife over with his fingers pressed against the tip of the blade and the butt of the handle and repeated the process on the other side.

Cordero straightened and wiped a little starch off his hands.

"It's been wiped clean," he said.

Sergeant Amparo smiled. "Well it wouldn't have told us anything if I'd done that, would it?" he said. Sisko was grinning in agreement.

"This isn't the murder weapon," Cordero said. "The pathologist in Dili told me Frankston had been killed with a double-edge knife not a single-edge like this one."

Amparo snorted. "How were we supposed to know that?" he demanded to know.

"Sorry. I should have told you. I've had other things on my mind," said Cordero.

"Why test it for prints if it isn't the knife?" the sergeant asked.

"How many people on this island know about fingerprints?" Cordero asked. "And among any who do know, how many would think to wipe clean a weapon they'd used on another person?"

Amparo's expression went blank.

"But foreigners watch a lot of television shows about how police solve crimes," Cordero continued. "What a blade wiped clean tells me is a foreigner handled this knife, not a local. My guess is it was a clumsy attempt to throw us off the track of the real killer by implicating Justino."

"Well it wasn't the widow," Amparo said. "You were talking with her. That only leaves the Australian."

"Not quite," said Cordero.

"The African?" Amparo said.

Cordero didn't answer.

"The boy who raised the alarm—is he still at the kiosk?"

"He ran off with his soccer ball," said Sisko.

"What did he look like?" Cordero asked.

Amparo shrugged. "Like anyone of a dozen kids around this part of the village."

Cordero threw the question in a glare at Sisko.

"Small, thin. A kid, you know?" Sisko said raising his palms.

"What was he wearing?"

Sisko looked at Amparo and neither indicated he'd taken any notice.

"I want to talk to Justino," said Cordero.

Amparo took the key from the wall and handed it to him. "Be my guest," he said.

Cordero walked out, unlocked the door to the room in which Justino was locked, and entered. Justino was crouched in the corner as before and when he looked up tears streaked his face.

"Hello Justino. Remember me?" soothed Cordero. "I'm the one who took you home from here the other day. I'm going to do that again now. But first I have to ask you some questions."

"I haven't done anything!" Justino wailed. "Why do they keep saying I have?"

"Well they found a knife among your coconuts," Cordero explained. "I think someone put it there."

"That officer?" he asked.

"You mean the police cadet? Why would he do something like that?"

"He doesn't like me. He pulled me and pushed me."

"He shouldn't have done that," Cordero said. "I'll speak to him."

"You said that last time," Justino complained.

"I'll be more forceful with him this time." Cordero squatted near Justino but not so close as to scare him. Justino sniffled and pinched his nose.

"The boy who said you took his soccer ball—"

"I didn't take a soccer ball!" cried Justino. "I don't know where that ball came from. I didn't put it there. I promise!"

"I believe you, Justino. I'm not interested in the ball, just the boy who said you took it. What did he look like?"

Justino sniffed and tugged at his nose a second time.

"Look like?"

"Yeah," said Cordero. "Can you describe him?"

Justino clamped his eyes shut as though it was hard for him to think.

"He was small," he said, opening his eyes to Cordero. "Short, you know?"

"That's great, Justino. Did you notice what he was wearing?"

Once more the eyes clamped shut.

"Short pants and a T-shirt, I think."

"Great. Okay."

"And he didn't wear anything on his feet," Justino added. "They were real dirty. I saw that."

"You're doing well, Justino. It helps a lot. Did you notice anything printed on his T-shirt? You know, a design or something?"

Justino nodded.

"What was it?"

"It was something I don't know. I can't read."

"Could you write it for me?"

"I can't write," Justino said.

"Do you think you could draw the word for me?"

"No."

Cordero let out a faint, disappointed breath.

"Okay, Justino. You've been very helpful. Get up and I'll take you home."

"What about my coconuts?"

"We'll put your cart in the vehicle as well."

Cordero raised himself and helped Justino to his feet.

"There was a picture," Justino said.

Cordero stopped.

"What? Where?" he asked.

"On the boy's T-shirt."

"A picture of what?" Cordero asked.

Justino appeared to shiver.

"The face of a demon," he said.

"A demon?"

"There were big black teeth like they were going to bite you. And places above where the eyes should be. And a funny black nose and the cheeks of the demon's face. And claws!"

Cordero tried to piece the jigsaw of descriptions together.

"A demon you say?"

Justino's head bobbed up and down in agreement.

"Everything black?"

"And yellow," Justino said. "The demon's face was yellow, too."

Cordero rubbed a hand through his hair. *Black, yellow, teeth and claws*, he thought to himself.

Slowly an idea started to emerge.

"Could it have been a bat?" Cordero asked. "You know with its wings outstretched?"

Justino covered his face with a hand, re-visualizing the image in this head.

"Maybe," he said. "But I think it was a demon. That's why I was put in here."

• • •

Cordero took Sergeant Amparo's utility and drove Justino and his barrow of coconuts home. He explained to his mother that Justino had done nothing wrong: there had been another misunderstanding at the police station and Justino was very helpful in sorting it out. He was about to return to the police station when Estefana called. She'd found Antonio Gomes and detained him at the other end of the village to where Cordero had just taken Justino home.

When he pulled up outside the house where Eskolastika Suarez lived, Cordero noticed Estefana standing over a boy sitting on the ground under one of the avocado trees. He climbed down from the vehicle and approached, noticing Estefana's shirt was ripped and there were streaks of dirt on her trouser leg. A few articles of clothing that had been drying on a rope had fallen or been pulled to the ground.

"That's him over there," Estefana said. "A girlfriend of his lives here and she told me she was expecting him back from Maquili but he was running late. His mother told me he rode a red motorcycle so I waited. After about forty minutes he showed up. When he went into the house, I took the keys from the bike and knocked on the door. I guess he saw the uniform and took off. But he got tangled in the washing hanging over there."

"You look like you've been in a struggle," Cordero said. "You okay?"

"Yes, *maun*, I'm fine. He put up a bit of a fight but I subdued him. I cuffed him too."

"Great, Estefana. Well done."

Cordero walked over to the boy and squatted down in front of him. He looked to be about twenty years of age and embarrassed to be bettered by a woman not bigger than himself. His jeans and shirt were covered in specks of mud from the ride from Maquili and he only wore flip-flops on his feet. His hair had been tied in a pony tail but the struggle had loosened it so that it hung over his face. His hands were clasped behind him.

"Antonio Gomes?" he asked.

The boy didn't look up. "Who's asking?" he grumbled.

"My name's Cordero. I'm a police investigator."

Antonio raised his head and glared at Estefana through the loose strands of his hair. "What she attack me for, *maun*? I didn't do nothing."

"So why did you run?"

"Didn't know who she was, did I?"

"She's wearing a police uniform," said Cordero.

"Never seen her before," Antonio said and he spat onto the ground. "She don't look like no police officer to me. Police officers all men or else they're fat and ugly."

"What were you doing in Maquili?" Cordero asked.

"Visiting friends. What do you think?"

"I'll ask the questions, not you."

Antonio made a point of spitting a second time.

"You know an Australian by the name of Robert Evans?" Cordero asked him.

"Who's he, *maun*?"

"Man rents a room from the priest."

"I don't know any Australian-man-who-rents-a-room-from-the-priest," he said in a sing-song fashion. "Why you asking stupid things?"

"That's funny because you've been seen talking to this foreigner," Cordero said.

"Who told you that, *maun*? Whoever it was is lying."

"Okay. You and I are going to the police station," said Cordero. "Get up."

"What you say? I ain't done nothing wrong. What is this shit, *maun*?"

"I'm arresting you for assaulting a police officer, lying to a police investigator, and asking too many questions when I told you not to."

Cordero looked across at Estefana.

"Can you follow me on his motorcycle?" he said.

She nodded.

"Now get in my vehicle," he said back to Antonio. "And behave or you'll make me angry."

19

"I loved Hank, as I've told you, but I realised he could never give me what I needed," Mrs Frankston was swivelling in her chair in the front room.

"What's that?" asked Carter.

"You'll laugh," Mrs Frankston said.

"Try me."

"Normality," she said in answer to Carter's question.

Carter had taken the key to the study from her pocket and was heading toward the door.

"Who the hell is normal?" she said.

"I said you'd laugh."

"I wasn't laughing. I was making a point," Carter said, turning back to Mrs Frankston. "Look at us. I'm a cop, you're not. I've always been single, but you've been married and now you're a widow. Who's the normal one? No two people are alike."

Mrs Frankston looked up at her. "Well, we're both American women of about the same age, both now single, and both stuck here on this damn island," she said, allowing a thin smile to spread across her face.

Carter smiled too and nodded.

"That's all true," she said. "I can't argue with that."

As she placed the key in the lock of the study door, Carter noticed a feint humming sound coming from inside. She turned again to Mrs Frankston who was standing behind her now.

"Is that a generator I can hear?" Carter asked.

Mrs Frankston nodded.

"Hank had to preserve his specimens and to do that he had to control the temperature and humidity in there," Mrs Frankston said. "Things go off quickly in this climate and power comes and goes as you've noticed. He set up the generator to run air conditioning and a dehumidifier when the power was out."

"Has the power been out today?" Carter asked.

"No," Mrs Frankston said. "Hank probably put that on before he went out the night he was killed. I was under strict instructions not to touch his stuff. So, I didn't. You're about to enter his world, not mine."

"But a generator would need to have been refuelled to still be operating," said Carter, but Mrs Frankston just shrugged as though it was no concern of hers.

Carter unlocked the door to the room and was confronted by cool, dry air. She entered, realising immediately that she was looking at a field laboratory, rather than a simple study. Her FBI training had included instruction in taking biological specimens and processing these using microscopes and centrifuges, so the scene was not entirely foreign to her. She guessed correctly that the four plastic structures along one wall represented some kind of experimental aquaria with individual heating, chilling, lighting, and water circulation devices probably used to test which corals were showing more resilience to rising temperatures. At the end of the aquaria was a large plastic bucket with what looked like clumps of seaweed heaped in mirky brine. She noticed a centrifuge in one corner: it would have enabled the extraction of microscopic tissue from the coral polyps. A heavy compound microscope sat on a table, its eyepiece removed, and a Canon digital reflex camera attached with a mounting mechanism and camera adapter. Below the table was another water-proof Nikon digital camera, sitting atop a colour printer attached by a cord to a laptop which rested alongside the microscope. A second thick, black underwater camera casing lay on the floor next to the printer.

Around the room were scattered silica bags as a further humidity control and laboratory supplies: pipettes, glass microscope slides, petri dishes and dissecting tools as well as dozens of samples and pile after pile of notes. Among the samples were different kinds of corals, some of which had been cracked open, and seaweed arranged to dry on slips of cardboard. A shelf was lined with small glass vials containing a clear liquid Carter guessed would be alcohol or formalin. Each vile contained a sticker with a notation that made no sense to her. Rough sketches on sheets that had been ripped from different sized pads were strewn across the room and stacks of handwritten reports were lined up in rows on the floor. Mrs Frankston ignored the chaos and eased herself down into the chair at the table and clasped her hands between her knees.

A framed photograph on the table caught Carter's attention. It showed a beaming younger Susanna in a gilded frame bearing a sock and buskin either side of the base.

Carter picked it up and examined it.

"Nice photo," she commented.

"What? Oh, yes. It was taken at UC. I had it made up for Hank after we'd started…you know."

Carter replaced the photograph. She lowered herself onto one knee and flipped through some handwritten reports sitting on one of the piles on the floor. The top page read:

Visual inspection:
Snorkel depth 1-4y. Sample 60.

The second page:

Hand pliers. Preserved in DMSO buffer (25% DMSO, 200 mM EDTA, NaCl saturated, pH 7.0). Stored at 14F until DNA extraction.

The pages underneath contained similar notes Carter had no way of deciphering but some of which seemed to reflect notations on the viles. The bottom page showed:

Result: 38 scleractinian genera in addition to 8 non-scleractinian genera.

Below that was a line that read:

High ambient temperature and basic storage facilities may explain low amplification success.

The other piles contained pages with identical notes but with variations in the numbers.

"My parents became over-protective when my brother, Josh, died," Mrs Frankston was saying. "They didn't want me going anywhere, doing anything. I guess they figured they'd lost one child and didn't want to risk losing the only other one they had."

She inclined forward.

"Most of that was my mother, of course. When my father ran for the Senate, things became even worse because now he had a reason to protect the family's privacy. So, it became: 'You can't do this, Susanna', 'We don't want you doing that, Susanna'. I felt like I was living inside a prison, you know, and I was only allowed out when my father's campaigning for votes demanded the usual family-friendly photos. We'd all have to smile as though everything was okay."

Mrs Frankston pinched the root of her nose.

"But it wasn't okay. It wasn't okay at all."

Carter was listening as she examined a wall where dozens of photographs of corals and seaweed had been printed off and pinned up in some kind of order that was lost on her. At the end were two long columns of photographs that appeared to have been taken under the microscope and were headed by a note at the top that read '*Symbiont algae*'.

"Your husband take all these photos?" Carter asked.

"What?" said Mrs Frankston. "Oh, those. Yeah. Hank took a lot of photos. He kept complaining that Timor hadn't signed some international agreement regulating the trade in endangered plants and animals, so he wasn't able to take any samples back to the States with him. That's one of the reasons he wanted to stay—to try to negotiate around that. It's also why he took so many photographs. None of them interest me. They're all connected to his research and none to our time here together."

"No happy snaps?" Carter asked.

Mrs Frankston merely shook her head.

"I'll need to take these cameras and look through them," Carter said.

"Sure, fine. Go ahead," Mrs Frankston said, waving a hand. "I've no use for them."

She eased a strand of hair behind her ear.

"That's why I left for university in California," she continued. "I was suffocating at home. I just had to get away."

Carter moved alongside her and flicked through a journal that rested in the center of the desk. It seemed to contain more recent notations similar to those in the reports on the floor. One page began:

Samples vortexed for 5s and 90 uL supernatant removed...

"I had no idea what I wanted to study. I just wanted a *life*. I drifted into the first degree program that came along and got engrossed in life on campus. So vibrant after what I'd known at home! That's how I met Hank. He was an early career professor at the same place. He seemed so...so...adventurous, passionate... so full of life compared to what I'd become used to. And when he talked about his plans to do research in far-off places, it sounded so exciting."

"That doesn't sound to me like the normal life you say you want," said Carter, flicking through the journal.

"No," agreed Mrs Frankston. "It wasn't. That desire came later. After the sharks, the sand flies, and the rats in the toilet. The excitement wore off and I realised I was living *his* life not mine."

Carter licked a finger and turned another page:

Solution (5 M guanidine isothiocyanate....

"You know what any of this means?" she asked.

"What?" Mrs Frankston replied, engrossed in her memories.

"These journal entries," Carter said and showed the page to Mrs Frankston. "You know what this stuff means?"

Mrs Frankston took a cursory look.

"No," she said. "Not at all. Like I said, that was Hank's world not mine."

She took a deep breath and straightened in the chair.

"You ever felt like you were living someone else's life?" she asked.

Carter flicked through the journal to the most recent entry. It was headed:

Site 315/115 yDS.

The page contained similar notations to the others but with the addition of references to the word '*algae*' twice underlined. The notations ended in an exclamation mark.

"What about this?" Carter asked and she spun the journal around so Mrs Frankston could view the page. The woman gave it a glance and shrugged her shoulders.

"Does '*Site 315*' mean anything to you?"

"No."

Carter opened the last pages of the journal which seemed to hold separate entries. They listed all site numbers in order with shorthand directions from a shoreline feature such as a particular hut or a distinctive tree. None of it made sense to her.

She closed the journal and pushed away from the table. She gazed out the small, barred window, and thrust her hands in her pockets.

"My mother ran out on my father when I was just a kid," she said. "My father remarried but I never took to my stepmother. A few years later my father was shot dead trying to stop a couple of guys abducting my half-sister in a parking lot. Things got worse after that with my stepmother and so I left home. I've been living my own life since I was sixteen years old."

Mrs Frankston cast a sympathetic eye.

"That's awful," she said. "I'm guessing the life you're living is not the life you would've chosen to live."

"Everyone I've ever loved either left or was taken from me," Carter said. "Doesn't give you a lot of faith in relationships."

She unscrewed the camera from the microscope, picked up the Nikon from underneath the table, and made to leave the room.

"But I make do," she added.

• • •

Sergeant Amparo examined the red motorcycle that Estefana rode into the yard of the police station after she handed him the keys. He connected the bike to reports of an unfamiliar red motorcycle seen near a sacred house that had been broken into north of Beloi, and suspected Antonio Gomes was the mystery burglar. Cordero took the youth to the lockup, removed the handcuffs, and secured the door. He and Amparo agreed to give Antonio time to get used to the idea he was in serious trouble before talking to him. They figured the prospect of a stint in prison might loosen his tongue.

In the meantime, Cordero and Estefana drove to the lodge in the sergeant's utility. He would go and put further questions to the African but he had something to do first. She wanted to change out of the uniform ripped and soiled in the scuffle with Antonio.

After Estefana entered her hut, Cordero searched the grounds of the lodge for the boy who hung out there with his soccer ball. He had no luck so he crossed over to the kitchen and excused himself to a woman preparing food.

"Have you seen the boy?" he asked.

"Benni?" the woman said, closing the lid on a pot she was boiling on the gas-fired stove.

"If that's his name," Cordero said. "The boy who plays by himself in the yard."

"He's my son," said the woman. "What's he done now?"

"Nothing, *mana*," Cordero reassured her. "I just want to talk with him that's all."

The woman looked Cordero over and wiped her hands on the front of her dress.

"Benni!" she shouted. "Benni!"

There was a slapping of feet and the boy came scuttling from outside the rear of the kitchen. As Cordero suspected, he was wearing a 'Batman' T-shirt over his too-large shorts.

"This man wants to have a word with you," the woman said.

"Thank you, *mana*," Cordero said. "This won't take long." He looked down at the boy. "Let's go sit at a table where we can talk man-to-man."

The boy gaped up at his mother, his mouth slightly ajar.

"Go on," she said and the boy dragged himself off after Cordero, arms limp by his sides and a pained expression on his face.

They sat opposite each other, the boy climbing onto a seat too high for his feet to touch the ground.

"So I hear someone stole your soccer ball, Benni," Cordero said. "Tell me how that happened?"

The boy blinked but said nothing. He began to swing his legs.

"I know it was you because the police officers told me it was you," Cordero added. "You're the only boy in the village with that great 'Batman' T-shirt."

The boy wiped his T-shirt down and picked at his nose. But he remained silent.

"You know what I think, Benni?" said Cordero. "I don't think anyone stole your ball at all."

The boy's legs stopped swinging. The confidence in his face dissolved.

"I think you put it in that man's cart with the coconuts." Cordero placed the knife wrapped in the rag on the table between them. "Along with this."

Benni stared at the bundle on the table and his face began to buckle as though he was about to cry.

"You're not in any trouble, Benni," Cordero said. "I just want you to tell me why you did that?"

Benni snuffled a blob of mucous and rubbed his nose furiously with a hand.

"Did someone tell you to put this in the cart?" Cordero said, pointing at the bundle. "And claim the man had stolen your ball?"

Benni blinked a few times.

"You're not in trouble, remember," Cordero reassured him. "Did someone tell you to do that?"

The boy nodded.

"Who told you to do that, Benni?"

The boy looked across with pleading eyes.

"He said not to tell," he whimpered.

"I know but it's okay to tell me," Cordero said. "I'm a police officer."

"You don't look like a police officer," Benni said.

"Well, actually I'm a police *investigator*. That's an even more important type of police officer. A police investigator keeps more secrets than a police officer. So you can tell me. Whose idea was it for you to put this in the man's cart?"

Benni looked around to make sure no one could see him even though he and Cordero were the only two in the dining area. He pointed at a hut. It was Miller's.

"So the *malae* who's staying in that hut, *Senyor* Miller, told you to put this bundle in the cart and say the man stole your ball? Is that what you're telling me?"

Bennie nodded.

"Did he tell you to yell out and make a fuss until someone came?"

Benni nodded.

"Outside the kiosk near the police station?"

A third nod.

"Did the *malae* tell you why he wanted you to do that?"

The boy shook his head.

"Is *Senyor* Miller there now?"

"He went out," the boy said. "I saw him go."

"Do you know where he went?"

Benni shrugged.

"Okay. Thank you, Benni," Cordero said. "You've been very helpful."

The boy resumed swinging his legs.

"Do I have to give it back?" he asked.

"Give what back, Benni?"

"He gave me a dollar to put the things in that cart," Benni said. "Do I have to give the dollar back to him?"

"No Benni. You keep your dollar," said Cordero. "You've earned it."

20

"You told me you were a good Christian, *maun*," Cordero was saying.

He'd gone to the house of Welcome Jesus and pulled up alongside the yard where a goat was munching on leafy weeds and chickens were busy with their pecking. The African was in the house, stirring a stew of fish pieces and sweet potato in a pot balanced over a small bottled-gas burner. He had his back to the door as Cordero walked into the kitchen.

"I try to be, my brother," Welcome replied. "That's all the Lord asks of us. We all children of Adam and carry the mark of his Fall. No one perfect."

"Maybe so but that doesn't explain why you lied to me," said Cordero.

The man stopped his stirring but kept his eyes on the stew.

"Lied to you? The Bible tells us God hates a lyin' tongue. Proverbs 6:17, brother."

"I'm more interested in the Timor-Leste Penal Code which says giving false information to the police is a crime," countered Cordero.

"What you talkin' about, brother?" asked Welcome, turning side-on to Cordero.

"You said you were at the church the night Professor Frankston was killed but you weren't, were you?"

"Who told you that?"

"Never mind who told me," said Cordero. "It's true, isn't it?"

The man continued with his stirring and didn't reply at first. Cordero figured he was taking his time to think up an excuse.

"Yes brother, it's true but there's a reason I didn't tell you."

"What's that?"

Welcome swivelled around to Cordero holding a large wooden spoon in his hand. His face seemed to fall ever so slightly.

"Well brother, I worked hard to be accepted into this community," he said and touched his chest with his free hand. "Wasn't easy for a man from Africa brought here as a prisoner to be taken in by these folks. No one trusted me at first. But I found my way with the Assembly people and now everyone there respects me."

He lowered his eyes.

"Church folk don't take too kindly to sins committed below the belt. You know what I'm sayin'? But a man has needs. A woman too."

"Are you telling me you lied about where you were to protect your reputation and that of a woman?" Cordero asked.

"Not just any woman, brother. A good, God-fearin' Christian woman. That's the honest truth," he said.

He put the spoon into the stew and lifted out a sample to taste.

"You want some stew?" he asked. "Almost ready."

"I'd rather the *whole* truth," said Cordero.

"What you mean the whole truth?"

"I mean you also had an exchange with Professor Frankston that night, didn't you?"

Welcome put the spoon down on a bench beside his stove and wiped his hands. He locked eyes with Cordero and raised his chin.

"Yes brother, I did," he answered. "That no sin and no crime in the Holy Book or in your penal book."

"No, but lying about it is," said Cordero.

"I didn't lie about it," Welcome said. "I just didn't tell you."

"And why didn't you tell me?" Cordero asked.

"Same reason. I tell you that, you start askin' what I was doin' out there that time of night. They say the blanket unravels one thread at a time. Before I know it, I'm before my church as a man involved with a woman outside of marriage. I'm guilty of the grave sin of fornication. That woman is, too. Like I said, the congregation of the Lord don't take too kindly to that type of 'ting."

Cordero took a chair from near the wall, reversed it, and placed it in front of Welcome. He sat with his hands resting on the back of the chair.

"I'm listening," he said.

"I know what it's like to be an outcast. Didn't want that no more and didn't want it for the woman."

"Who are we talking about?" Cordero asked just to check.

"Her name's Lazara," Welcome said. "And she's a prayerful woman. Can't help her husband dead and needs help to raise her two boys."

"Help you're only too happy to give her in return for certain benefits," Cordero said.

"I ain't ashamed of that," Welcome said. "Like I said, we all have needs."

Cordero ran a hand across his face.

"What did you and Frankston argue about?" he asked.

"Who say we argue?"

"You returned angry. You must have argued about something."

The man shut the gas off under his pot. He leaned his rear on the bench and leered out toward the yard.

"Well, it was that damn boat, brother. I told him he gots to pay me money to get the propeller fixed and help me get by until it was. He say no. Say he had more important 'tings to do. He just walk off."

"And so you went after him, took his knife and stabbed him. You didn't slash him, you just aimed at his kidney knowing he'd bleed out or die of shock quickly. I'm guessing you learned those skills in prison."

"No brother. We have no knives in prison."

"What about a prison shank?" Cordero said. "And if you didn't have access to one, I'm sure your cellmates would have play-acted stabbing someone. You all would have hated the guards and wouldn't have had much else to do with your time but pretend to have your revenge on them."

"No brother, no shanks and no play-actin'."

Welcome rushed into another room and re-appeared with a

book with the words *Biblia Sagrada* embossed on the cover. It was a Portuguese copy of the Bible.

"I swear on this Holy Bible, my brother," said Welcome holding the book out to Cordero. "I did not kill that man!"

"Did you struggle with him?"

Welcome withdrew the Bible and lifted his head defensively. "I walk after him and grab his shoulder. That's it. I keep tellin' him I can't work without my boat. He get real angry, push my hand away and walk on. I don't go after him. Figure it no use. So, I go back to my woman."

"I'm going to check out your story," Cordero said, rising to his feet. "If you've been lying to me any more and I find out, you won't just be fronting your congregation as a fornicator. You'll be fronting a judge in Dili on a murder charge."

He placed the chair to one side.

"Enjoy your stew."

• • •

Estefana had changed into a clean uniform and lay on her bed. Carter was at the Frankston house, Cordero had gone to question the African, and Miller was nowhere to be seen. She was left alone and had time to think without interruptions.

Despite what Carter had said about the dogs simply being wild and possibly diseased, Estefana knew she was right to see them as a warning. She wasn't talking herself into something that wasn't true. Even if Carter was right about the dogs, none of what she'd said explained why they nearly tore her to pieces. It didn't explain why they were in a pack, why they were on the track to the house of *Mana* Lazara at precisely the time she came by, or why they had chosen to stop attacking one of their own and focus on her instead.

The incident only made sense if there were spirits involved, the spirits of the people who had been brought to Atauro by the Indonesians, left to starve or die of untreated illnesses, and suffered miserable deaths as exiles--the spirits of the people her father had buried in mass graves, people forever separated from their origin villages and so cut off from the kin meant to perform the regular rites for the dead.

Estefana rolled onto her left side, found no comfort there and tried her right. She couldn't relax. Her mind raced. She thought of her husband, Josinto, and how devastated he would be if anything happened to their children. He might even leave her for another woman who could give him healthy children to continue his family line. Where would she be if he left her? How would she cope? She knew that things like that happened. She gripped the sheet with both hands and pushed herself into a sitting position. She opened the mosquito net and reached for a bottle of water on a small side table, took a mouthful, replaced the cap, and lay down with the bottle clutched tight between both hands.

She recalled the man who had chased the dogs away. He hadn't swung a stick at the dogs or thrown rocks at them. He hadn't even been visible in the dark before the dogs ran off. He had commanded them only with his voice. '*Lakon tiha*', he'd said. 'Be gone'—and the dogs went. He'd said he was a *matan-dook*. She'd seen him demonstrate his power. If he could command the spirits that controlled the dogs, and they were the spirits of the people seeking revenge for what her father did, maybe he could lift the curse she felt was falling upon her and her children.

She sat up a second time, straighter now, and took another drink of water. If Cordero was going to insist that she stay on the island, she knew what she ought to do.

It was certainly worth a try.

21

Returning to the lodge Carter noticed the police utility parked outside and Cordero sitting at a table in the dining area drinking from a bottle of mineral water. She joined him. She placed the two cameras on the table, and he moved the knife in its wrapping to the side. She took the bottle from him and swigged a little water.

"What's that you have?" he asked.

"Frankston's two underwater cameras. Probably nothing but hundreds of shots of coral and algae but I thought I'd check," she said.

She handed over the bottle.

"Anything in his study strike you?"

"Not really," she said, looking around for someone to ask for her own bottle of mineral water. "Just a lot of technical stuff. The last entry in his journal ended in an exclamation mark which is interesting. But I couldn't make any sense of the scientific notations. Neither could Mrs Frankston."

"I'll take a look a little later," he said. "You have the key?"

She took it from her pocket and gave it to him.

"I can't see how research into coral would threaten anyone enough to cost Frankston his life," Carter said. She chewed her lip. "The motive must be personal somehow."

Benni's mother appeared at the door to the kitchen. Carter made a sign that she'd like some of the same some water that Cordero was drinking, and the woman nodded and went to fetch it.

"You speak to the African again?" she asked.

"Yeah," he said. "I did."

"And?"

He picked up the bottle and finished what was left of his mineral water.

"He admitted he was at the widow's house and that he'd had an argument with Frankston about compensation for his broken propeller," he said. "Said he'd kept it quiet so no one would find out he was having an affair with *Mana* Lazara. Swore on a Bible he didn't kill Frankston."

"You believe him?" she asked.

He lifted his shoulders.

"I called Sergeant Amparo and told him to have his young cadet take a look along the track to the house of *Mana* Lazara and around her yard," he said. "If the African did stab Frankston he wouldn't have taken the knife with him to her house. He'd have tossed it away somewhere along the way. And from what the woman told Estefana he wasn't gone long enough to have taken the knife any further along the road."

Carter nodded. The woman brought a bottle of mineral water and a glass to the table. Carter thanked her and drank straight from the bottle.

"I think I'm starting to believe her," Carter said.

"Who? Mrs Frankston?"

"Yeah," agreed Carter. "I'd say she did love her husband but couldn't abide three in the marriage."

"Three?"

"The other was the coral."

"I thought you said she was a flirt who was wrapping Miller around her finger," Cordero said.

Carter placed her now half-empty bottle on the table and leaned forward.

"I can't be right all the time or there'd be nothing left for you to do," she said. "And Miller doesn't need much encouragement to behave like a teenage boy in heat."

"Well, you're right there at least," Cordero said, motioning toward the knife.

"What's that?" she asked.

"It's a kitchen knife he had the boy who hangs around here plant in Justino's cart in a rather amateurish attempt to re-implicate him in the murder of Frankston."

"You are joking," Carter said, moving her bottle of mineral water and repositioning the knife in front of her for a closer look.

"He chose the wrong kind of knife and wiped it free of prints, which is something only a *malae* would do. So I knew someone had planted it. The kid who hangs around here owned up to the whole thing and said Miller had paid him to do it."

She stiffened.

"Where the fuck is he?"

"Out somewhere but he'll be back and when he is I'll explain the meaning of 'obstruction', 'fabrication of evidence', and 'falsely incriminating' someone to him," Cordero said.

"Wait," she said arching forward. "Do I have to explain the term 'diplomatic immunity' to you? He works for the Embassy. Taylor will see to it he slides free otherwise it would reflect badly on him. Leave it to me. I can put the wind well and truly up Miller better than you."

• • •

Carter had seated herself on a plastic chair outside her hut waiting for Miller when the wind strengthened and started to whirl leaves and grit around the yard. Estefana had left saying she had to see someone about something in connection with her father's time on the island and she was gone before Carter could ask who and what. She moved inside the hut out of the wind but kept the door slightly ajar to catch sight of Miller coming back from wherever it was he'd gone. She tried to make her anger ebb but found it revive again when she thought through the idiocy of Miller's behaviour.

Twenty minutes later he came in through the front gate of the lodge heading for his own accommodation.

"Gerard!" Carter said, walking outside to confront him. He either didn't hear her due to the gusts playing through the trees and bushes or else he was ignoring her.

"Gerard!" she repeated, and he spun toward her voice. "We need to talk. Come over to the dining area."

She led the way with Miller following. She pulled up a chair and sat: he drew out his own chair and sat across from her on the opposite side of the table. He looked stiff and ill-at-ease at first but soon bent over and began rubbing his hands together between his legs under the table.

"I've done something silly, ma'am," he said, eyes downcast. "I mean Agent Carter."

"Oh, I know that, Gerard," Carter said. "I want to know why."

"It's because you and the Timorese investigator were going to arrest Mrs Frankston for the murder of her husband," Miller said.

"We weren't going to arrest her," Carter corrected him. "We were going to ask her questions about arrangements she'd kept secret from us. She explained herself and we've left it at that."

His eyes shot up and met hers.

"But I thought—"

"You thought wrong, Gerard."

Miller was ashen-faced. A peel of thunder sounded overhead, and he jerked as though shocked by the sound.

"Have you been sleeping with Mrs Frankston?" Carter asked.

"What!" Miller exclaimed. "No ma'am. I would never do something like that. Her husband has just been killed."

He rubbed a hand over the bridge of his nose as though trying to erase an uninvited thought. He caught Carter's stare and frowned.

"She just, you know, looks so sad and vulnerable. I just wanted to help."

"So you'd draw the line at having sex with a widow but not at framing an innocent man for murder?" Carter put to him.

"It wasn't like that, ma'am," he said.

"All right explain to me what it was like, Gerard?"

Heavy raindrops started to fall and quickly turned into a torrent blanketing the lodge. Lightning lit up the yard and more thunder followed. Miller looked out from the dining area at the grounds which were taking on the appearance of a shallow lake. Water dripped from loose thatching on the far side of the dining area.

When he faced her again, Carter's eyes were boring into his.

"Well?" she said.

"When you and Mister Cordero left to go to Mrs. Frankston's house, I panicked," he said. "I noticed someone walk past the lodge with a cart of coconuts. You know the ones they cut the tops off so you can drink the water inside?"

"Go on, Gerard," Carter said.

"I don't know what came over me but I rushed into the kitchen. There was no one there. I saw a kitchen knife and picked it up. Someone had been chopping up a chicken. For dinner I guess. Blood had congealed on the carcass and I smeared some of it on the knife. To look like it had been used to…you know?"

"What then?"

"There was a dish towel lying on the floor. I wiped the handle of the knife and wrapped it in the dish towel."

"How did you get it into the cart?"

"Benni."

The downpour intensified.

"What did you say?" Carter asked, raising her voice to compensate for the torrent of rain hitting the roof.

"I said Benni. The kid who you see around the lodge. That's his name. Benni. I told him to take the dish towel and his soccer ball and put them both in the cart."

"Louder, Gerard, I can't hear you over the rain and I want to know the details."

"I told him not to open the dish towel or let the contents fall out," Miller said, his voice rising now. "I said when he'd managed to put both in the cart, to start yelling near the police station that the man pushing the cart had stolen his ball. I told him to not stop yelling until someone came out of the police station to investigate."

"And he did this why?"

"Benni and I are friends," Miller said as if it were obvious. "And I gave him a dollar to do what I said and to tell no one."

"Sounds like an ingenious plan, Gerard, except that the kitchen knife you chose was a single-bladed knife. Frankston was killed with a double-bladed knife. And wiping the prints told Cordero a foreigner must have been behind the plant because your average Timorese knows nothing about prints. So your whole plan wasn't ingenious at all. It was decidedly whacky from the start."

"I know, ma'am. I'm sorry ma'am. I was stupid."

"You were worse than stupid, Gerard. You were guilty of assembling false evidence to implicate an innocent man in a murder."

"I wouldn't do that ma'am. I figured that when they tested the blood they'd realize it was chicken's blood and so the man would be set free."

Carter leaned in across the table.

"What if they didn't test the blood, Gerard? This isn't exactly Quantico. There's no forensic lab on this island and there isn't much of one in Dili." She sat back. "If you weren't having it off with Mrs. Frankston, what motivated you to do it?"

Miller fidgeted and grew even more embarrassed.

"Ambassador Taylor has been on to me every day to arrange for Mrs. Frankston's repatriation. I called him when I thought she was going to be arrested." He looked at her, his face now flushed. "He was really angry. He said 'Gerard, put a stop to this nonsense immediately!' I didn't know what else to do."

"In case you haven't worked it out yet, Ambassador Taylor is an idiot, Gerard," Carter said. "But you can't pin this fuck-up on him. He didn't tell you to frame anyone. He wasn't here. You were."

"I know, ma'am. I'm sorry. I'm really sorry."

"You keep saying that."

"What else can I say?"

She watched him struggle with a sense of shame for a full minute. Her silence was a better punishment than further reprimand. When the time had elapsed, she stood to leave and pushed her chair under the table.

"I know Taylor can be a pain in the ass," she said. "But you work for the State Department, not him. You either need to grow up fast and get smart, Gerard, or you need to look around for another career before you do something really stupid like start a war."

He looked up at her like a young boy who'd just been reprimanded by his mother.

"What will you tell the ambassador, ma'am?" he asked.

"Nothing," she said. "The less Taylor knows the less likely he is to cause trouble."

22

Cordero entered the police station where Sergeant Amparo was sitting in his usual chair but with the window closed, rain bucketing against the pane.

"You're wet," he said, as Cordero shook off the raindrops he'd acquired running from the utility. "I think we're in for trouble. This is a big storm and every channel through the village is already full."

Cordero ignored the comment. "You ready?"

Amparo hoisted himself out of the chair, hopped across to the wall behind his desk where the key to the lockup hung, and led Cordero out.

"I'll go first," Cordero said. "The murder is the priority, and it may have something to do with what this boy was up to with the Australian."

Amparo worked the key in the door, opened it and stepped aside. Antonio Gomes was sitting on the edge of the bed, but he jumped up as they entered.

"What's this all about, *maun*?" he complained to Cordero. "You got nothing on me. I ain't done nothing."

Antonio glared at Amparo who backed against the wall furthest from the bed, allowing Cordero to take the lead in the questioning.

"Why did you run from a police officer and assault her when she caught up with you?" Cordero asked, standing in front of Antonio, arms folded.

"We've been through this, *maun*. I told you, she didn't look like no police officer to me."

He slumped onto the bed.

"She was wearing a police uniform," Cordero pointed out.

"So what? She could have stolen it," said Antonio. He looked around Cordero to Amparo. "When can I get out of this shit hole?"

Amparo said nothing.

"You said the person who told me he had seen you with the Australian was a liar," he said, ignoring Antonio's grumbling. "It was a priest. Father Robeiro."

"So what?" snapped Antonio.

"If you went to church more often, you'd know priests don't lie," said Cordero.

Antonio remained tight-lipped.

"Did the Australian pay you to do something for him?" Cordero asked. "And did he pay you to deny you knew him?"

Antonio let his head drop toward the floor. He started tapping his foot.

"It'll help your case if you cooperate, Antonio," Cordero said.

Antonio was suddenly up on his feet again.

"What case, *maun*?" he spat. "You got nothing on me! You say I did something; you show me the proof. You got nothing!"

Amparo pushed himself off the wall and joined Cordero.

"That your motorcycle outside?" the sergeant asked Antonio.

"Yeah. This is shit, *maun*! That a crime now to own a motorcycle?"

"No. But to break into sacred houses is," Amparo replied.

Antonio's mouth moved as though he was about to say something but instead, he sat down. Amparo waited.

"Don't know what you're talking about," Antonio mumbled finally.

"Four *uma lulik* have been broken into the past two weeks," Amparo said. "One in Akrema, one in Uaro-Ana, one in Biqueli, and one last night in Maquili. Each time a red motorcycle was seen in the area just before or just after the break-in."

"Not me, *maun*. Must be some other red motorcycle on the island."

"Where were you last night?" Amparo asked.

"Maquili. So what?"

"What were you doing there?"

"I told him," Antonio said, indicating Cordero.

Amparo edged Cordero out of the way and stepped in closer, his great bulk hovering over the boy.

"Well, you can tell me too," he growled.

Antonio flinched.

"Visiting friends."

"Who? What friends?"

"Friends, *maun*. Different friends, you know?"

"And where have you been the last two weeks?"

"Where?"

"You deaf? Yeah, where?"

"All over the place, *maun*. I don't keep track."

"What do you do for work, Antonio?" Cordero chimed in.

"This and that."

"Can you be more specific?"

"I do different jobs. Whatever people ask me to do. Tourists and shit."

"*Whatever* people ask you to do?" said Amparo.

"You know what I mean, *maun*," said Antonio.

"There are no tourists here on this island now, Antonio," said Cordero. "They all left when the wet season started. So, were you doing jobs for the Australian?"

Antonio merely shrugged while he stared at the floor.

Amparo signalled to Cordero to join him just outside the door to the lockup. There they huddled while the sergeant whispered out of earshot of Antonio. Cordero glanced through the door at the boy. "That's pretty dramatic," he said in a voice so Antonio could hear. Amparo whispered some more. Cordero nodded and they moved back into the room and over to the bed where the boy was sitting, his hands clutching the thin blanket.

"Okay, get up," ordered Amparo.

The boy looked up, uncertain now.

"What?"

"I said get up," Amparo repeated. "You're going to Uaro-Ana."

"What? Why?" Antonio asked.

"Because the elders there are the most pissed off their sacred house was broken into. And they're the most traditional. If they believe it was you who broke in, they'll feed you to the sharks. That's the traditional punishment for violation of an *uma lulik*. Even if there's no proof you did it, you'll do. They're going to have to appease the ancestor spirits somehow and you can be their somehow."

He grabbed Antonio by the arm and lifted him to his feet.

"What? Wait? You can't do that!" Antonio protested, dragging the blanket along with him.

"I can do whatever I like," the sergeant said. "You assaulted a police officer, remember? Who's going to hold me responsible if the elders feed you to the sharks?"

"Wait! No!" the boy cried as Amparo shoved him toward the door and out. Antonio let go of the blanket and his eyes sought out Cordero. "He can't take me anywhere! Tell him to stop!"

Cordero shrugged.

"I'm here investigating the murder of a foreigner. Sergeant Amparo is in charge of break-and-enters. I have no authority over him."

"This is bullshit, *maun!*" Antonio shouted.

The boy tried to wrestle free of the sergeant but without success.

"What if he cooperates, sergeant?" Cordero asked suddenly.

Amparo paused. Antonio had broken out in a cold sweat.

"Depends on what he tells us," Amparo said.

"What if he tells us what he knows about the Australian?" Cordero said. "He's the prime suspect in the murder case."

Amparo glared at Antonio whose expression said he might be prepared to do that.

"If what he says is useful," Amparo said. "But if he's bullshitting, I've had enough of him and he's off to satisfy the anger of the elders up the coast and get them off my back!"

• • •

Estefana hesitated outside the hut where the *matan-dook* had said he lived and fingered the crucifix on the necklace her husband, Josinto, had given her. She stared straight ahead without taking in anything of the hut, the yard, or the setting as she considered the arguments for and against what it was she was about to do.

A *matan-dook*, she knew, represented a link between the world of the living and the world of the dead, between people just like her and spirits like those of the dead her father had buried. A *matan-dook* could communicate between the two worlds, mediate the impacts each was having on the other, and maybe even dissuade the spirits from pursuing a course of action designed to inflict harm or punishment on someone they decided was the appropriate object of their wrath.

But how a *matan-dook* operated and when was shrouded in secrecy. If she insisted on an intervention on her behalf, Estefana could be accused of trying to contact the spirits without any authority to do so. At the very least, that could see her branded a sorcerer or witch and cause residents of Vila to become hostile to her as well.

What if she pleaded with the *matan-dook* for help rather than demand it? He might refuse but he seemed friendly enough. And he had rescued her from the pack of dogs threatening to attack her. There was a chance he would look on her circumstances with sympathy and agree to help.

Or would he?

She wasn't from Atauro and so he had no responsibility toward her. In fact, he might feel that to use his powers for the benefit of an outsider would jeopardise his status on the island and turn the spirits against himself.

The spirits!

Was all her talk about the spirits nothing more than hysterical nonsense she was feeling? Was it silly to believe any retribution would befall her for the deeds of her father, as Carter would have said? What was her education and training telling her and how did that weight up against her traditional instincts?

Maybe it was better to just return to the lodge, leave things be, and just wait and see what transpired.

There were good arguments to do that and good arguments not to do it. So, what *should* she do?

The more she thought about it, the more clouded and confused her thinking became.

She took a deep breath and walked into the yard and down to the door of the hut.

• • •

After Miller had sulked off to his hut and shut the door, Carter popped her head into the kitchen and asked for another bottle of mineral water. She said she'd be back in just a minute. She went to her hut, retrieved Professor Frankston's two underwater cameras, and came back to the dining area. She sat herself at a table, picked up the smaller of the cameras, and began flicking through the digital files.

They held photos of coral. Light brown corals and dark brown corals, purple corals and others that were dark green and light green. Occasionally there was a photo of dark red corals. Most were shaped like the branches of a tree, but others were tabular, mushroom-like or encrusting the seabed like a carpet. There were so many images of coral that they all began to look alike. But she was determined to check everything on the cameras and so kept flicking through another, and another, and another.

The mineral water arrived. Outside the rain pounded down—so much so she hadn't heard the woman from the kitchen approach. Carter finished with the first camera, and took a break. She poured the water into a glass and drank. She stared out on the soaking yard for a minute to refocus her eyes. She picked up the second camera.

More corals. There were purple corals and pink, blue, and orange. Some were shaped in bunches and others looked like small, underwater shrubs—some coloured, some bleached—pointing toward the surface of the water. Other files contained images obviously taken through the microscope: countless images of cell-like structures Carter presumed were microalgae—so many images she was becoming transfixed by them.

That was until suddenly, something altogether different appeared.

Toward the end of one file were four images of an outboard motor. One was an overall shot of the motor. Another showed a close up of the skeg sheared off completely. A third showed the blades of the propeller mangled and the last showed the mid section of the exhaust housing bent out of shape. There were no images of the boat to which the motor was attached but how many boats with damaged propellers would Frankston have taken an interest in?

She stared up at the rain dripping through the thatch roofing, wondering why the only images on either camera not of corals were of a damaged outboard motor. No one had thought to ask Mrs Frankston if she knew anything about a damaged motor. She rose, asked the woman in the kitchen for the loan of a coat against the rain, and took off to do just that.

23

"You're soaked through, *alin*," the *matan-dook* said, referring to her affectionately as a younger person as he pulled open the door of his hut to Estefana. "Come in and sit down. I'll get you a towel."

The old man shuffled off to a corner of the room, rummaged through a pile of mixed clothing and linen, then handed her a frayed blue towel.

Estefana thanked him and dried her face.

He offered her a chair and she sat.

"More dogs?" he asked.

"No *senyor*," said Estefana running the towel lightly over her wet clothes. "I'm afraid it's much worse than that."

The doubts and nervousness about visiting the *matan-dook* suddenly proved too much to contain any longer. She put the towel to her eyes and began to cry.

The man moved his own chair closer to Estefana and placed a hand lightly on her knee. "Tell me what bothers you child," he said. "Perhaps I can help. Take your time."

Estefana bunched the towel in her hands on her lap. She fiddled with it as she explained who she was, her father's name, and how he had been brought to Atauro by the Indonesians in the 1980s because of his opposition to their brutal rule. She recounted how her father was forced to bury other people from the mainland exiled to the island to avoid the possibility that they might help the pro-independence guerillas. She said she feared the spirits of those buried far from their homes would seek revenge on her or, worse, her children for what her father did.

"I never wanted to come to the island," she said. "I had to because of my job and now I'm being made to stay until the investigation into the murder of the American is solved."

She wiped her eyes with the towel.

"I heard a *matan-dook* was caring for someone arrested for the murder," she continued. "You said you are a *matan-dook* when you chased away the pack of dogs about to attack me."

She met his eyes.

"That's why I've come to ask if you'll help prevent a curse being placed on me, if only for the sake of the children I hope to bear one day."

The old man listened patiently, taking the details of her story in and not interrupting. When she stopped talking and started wiping her hair, he relaxed into his chair and waited in case Estefana had anything to add. She didn't.

"Would you like some tea, child?" he asked. "It will help dry you out."

Estefana nodded and the old man rose, lit a gas burner, and placed a pot of water over the flame. While it boiled he seemed to study her from a distance but said nothing. As the minutes passed she was convincing herself that this had been a very bad idea on her part.

The water started to boil. The man grabbed a mixture from a small bamboo basket next to the burner and threw it into the pot. He stirred the pot vigorously and poured a large mug of tea. He handed it to Estefana, sat down, and bent forward, resting on his thighs. She tasted the tea, cupped the mug in both hands, and avoided eye contact in case he had taken offence at what she was asking him to do.

"Drink more and I'll tell you what I know," he said to her. "It's just a herbal mixture. It will help you relax."

She took another sip of tea.

"Yes, I am a *matan-dook*," he said. "The boy you mentioned—the one who was arrested for that killing—it is true he is under my care. The reason for this is that he is *pontu*," he said, using the same term he had used with Cordero to distinguish someone with a mental disorder from someone who was *bulak* or crazy.

"You see his father traded in maize that had been exposed to poison," he continued. "He knew the maize was bad but he traded it, nonetheless. Several children in the village died after they'd eaten the maize. The spirits of the dead cursed this man by making his own son *pontu*. In that way the father would suffer as the parents of the poisoned children were suffering only for a longer time, every time he saw his son. This was a long time ago and the father will soon die himself. When he is dead, the curse will be lifted from the son. My role is to keep the boy safe until it is."

Estefana drank more tea, wondering where this was going.

"From what you have told me," the man continued, "your father was forced to bury the dead who were brought here. He didn't choose to do it. It was not his fault. That is the difference. That is why there should be no curse on you or your children."

He paused to let his words sink in. Estefana considered what he had said but her expression showed she remained unconvinced.

"You said 'should be' no curse," she pointed out. "You didn't say 'would be' no curse. How can you be sure the spirits don't blame my father? When he came home from Atauro he was not the same man that I remembered. And before long he died of a heart attack. I was quite young and he was not old!"

"I am old enough to remember the time when the Indonesians ruled this island," he said. "They were savage and cruel toward people. I'm not surprised it affected your father's health."

"But—"

He held up a hand to silence her and leaned in.

"What we think we know, we don't know. Not really. The real world, child, is the world of the spirits. Everything we see is only a shadow of that. It's like a tree: there is more underneath the earth than what is above it. When we look at shadows we can draw the wrong conclusions."

She placed her mug of tea on the floor and raised the hand that held the towel. "But those dogs!" she said. "Why did they attack me? Why now? Why there? They were the spirits of the dead coming after me!"

The man waited until she settled down and stopped objecting. She clutched the towel in her lap with one hand and fingered the crucifix around her neck with the other. He studied her, noticing how she began to sway ever so slightly as if to comfort herself.

"The spirits are agitated," he said, looking up toward the roof of his hut. "You can see it in this storm. It's their way of expressing anger."

"So I'm right!" Estefana declared.

"It's not you they're agitated about. It's the violence that has come to Vila," the man said. "There has not been a killing on this island for many years. But the foreigner was killed. He may not be the last."

He watched her reaction. Every movement she made indicated she was pained, confused, and very scared.

He sat upright, his hands still resting on his thighs but his eyes closed as though he was deep in thought. For a full minute he said nothing.

"If you want to make sure the spirits don't harm you," he said finally, "I can tell you what to do. But you will have to be very brave to do it."

She wiped damp strands of hair from her face and looked squarely at him as if to say she was ready for whatever it was he might propose.

"It could involve an encounter with the spirits," he said.

She took a deep breath. She nodded.

"From your necklace I can see you are Catholic and that cross is important to you," he said.

Estefana gripped the crucifix without thinking. "Yes. Yes it is. My husband gave it to me," she said. "We've only recently been married."

"Even better," he said. "You must go to the cemetery. Beside the south wall where the road runs along the side you will see a large white grave. It's above ground and beside it is a small replica of a church tower on which is a plaque that reads 'Padre José Guterres'.

You can't miss it. Padre Guterres was a kind priest who cared for those the Indonesians brought here in the first years after they invaded. He was born in Macau, so he too has been buried far from his origin village and no one has cared for his grave in years."

He leaned in.

"Around the outside of the grave was laid a white concrete skirting to separate it from the other graves nearby. But it is badly cracked now for want of care. You are to go there and walk around on that skirting four times. Watch your step carefully because of the broken concrete. Don't look up or take your eyes off the ground. Whatever you hear you are to ignore. If you feel the presence of the spirits you are to ignore that feeling as well. You must show that you are strong and determined.

"As you walk around the grave you are to say: 'I am Estefana, daughter of Aniceto dos Carvalho. My father was forced by evil men to do what he did on this island. He always regretted having to do it. I regret it as well and I wish peace to all here.'"

He eased back.

"On the last circuit you are to bury that necklace beside the tomb."

She gripped the crucifix more tightly in her hand.

"To offer something you love," he said, "is the price that will repay any debt the spirits may feel you owe."

• • •

"Okay I do know the Australian," Antonio confessed when Amparo let go of him and he'd sat down on the bed. "When he first came to Vila he asked some of the boys if they knew someone who could be trusted, had a motorcycle, wanted to make some money, and could speak English."

He rubbed his hands together between his knees.

"I spent a year in Dili working with tourists," he said and shot them a knowing glance which Cordero assumed probably meant he dealt in dope or hashish. "That's how I learned to speak English and that's how I came to meet *Senyor* Bob."

They waited but Antonio had stopped talking.

"And what did *Senyor* Bob pay you to do?" asked Cordero.

Antonio stalled.

"Well ah...."

He was weighing his options. Amparo edged closer, towering over him in a menacing fashion once more.

"Come on! Don't waste our time," said Cordero.

Antonio looked up at Cordero.

"He paid me to take a look inside the *uma lulik* in Akrema and the others down to Maquili," he said. "He told me to leave the one in Vila alone. He said that he was looking for something but if he tried to look himself he'd stand out because he was a foreigner."

"He must have told you what he was looking for," said Cordero.

Antonio dropped his head.

"He showed me some photos," he said.

"What of?"

"Flags, coins, cloth made from the fur of a sheep. All of it old, you know?"

"What sort of flags and coins?" Cordero pressed him.

Antonio showed his irritation.

"Like I said, *maun*. Old stuff. Old Portuguese stuff. He said it was stuff that might have come off a Portuguese ship hundreds of years ago."

"Did you find anything?"

"No. All I saw was old spears and *tais* covered in dust. And some drums and wooden carvings too. But nothing like the photos he'd shown me."

"If you had found something what did *Senyor* Bob tell you to do?"

"He said not to take anything. If I found something like he was after I was to take photos of it on my cell and show him. That's all." He looked at Amparo. "I didn't *steal* anything!"

"And he told you to keep your mouth shut about it?" Cordero asked.

"Yeah. Sure. He said it was just a deal between him and me and he'd pay me more if anyone asked questions and I denied he'd ever hired me to do anything."

• • •

They left Antonio securely locked away. In the front office, Cordero congratulated Amparo on the ruse he'd come up with concerning feeding Antonio to the sharks.

"Yeah, there's enough tradition in these kids to make them shit themselves when you put threats like that to them. Even my cadet—he's spent time in Dili, too, in basic training in Dili. But it doesn't change things. It's like it's bred into them."

Amparo took to his chair with a thud.

"But what does any of that tell you?" he asked.

"It tells me Evans was after something valuable enough to him that he'd hire a boy to commit several crimes. Maybe it was valuable enough for him to kill for as well."

He tossed the keys to the police utility up in his hands.

"What it was *Senyor* Bob was after I don't know," Cordero said. "But you can be sure I'm about to find out."

• • •

Carter dropped the sodden coat under the thatched eave from which water was cascading and dripping. She banged loudly on the front door of Mrs. Frankston's hut. Seconds later the widow opened the door, stepped aside, and invited her in.

Carter wasted no time producing the camera with the images of the damaged outboard motor on it.

"I think this motor belongs to the African's boat—the man your husband hired to take him out over the reefs," she said.

Mrs. Frankston looked at each of the images carefully and nodded. She looked at Carter uncertain of the point of the images she'd been shown.

"Do you have any idea why your husband would take these photographs?" Carter asked. "All the other images on the two cameras are of corals."

Mrs. Frankston smiled weakly. "What did you expect?" she said.

"Even so—"

"He told me there'd been an accident with the boat," Mrs. Frankston said, cutting her off. "But I didn't know about the photos. He just said he'd try and get replacement parts sent over from Dili and would compensate the African for his lost income."

"So he was going to pay for repairs and compensate Welcome Jesus?"

"Of course. He'd already given him money for the damage. Hank was very obliging in that respect. Why do you ask? What's this about?"

"I can't go into that now, Mrs. Frankston," Carter said. "Thanks for your help. I'll get these cameras back to you when I can."

With that she made for the door. Outside Carter was about to slip the coat over her head when Mrs. Frankston called out to her.

"Before you go," she began, standing at the doorway, one hand on the jam.

Carter lowered the coat.

"Yes?"

"The journal's gone," she said. Carter looked at her. "Hank's journal. In his study. The one you were flicking through the last time you were here? Well it's gone."

"How could it have gone? You don't have the key," Carter said.

"I think there was a spare. In case he lost the one you have. Hank was always very cautious when it came to his research."

Carter stepped clear of the trickles coming down from the eave.

"Could someone have come in and taken a duplicate key? Have you been out?"

"I went for a walk along the beach just before it started raining," Mrs. Frankston said. "I wasn't gone long. Maybe twenty minutes."

"Who else would have known about a duplicate key?" Carter asked.

Mrs. Frankston raised and lowered her hands.

"The only person I can think of would be Bob. Robert Evans. As I told you he and Hank would often go into the study to discuss Hank's research."

24

"Where are you now?" Carter asked as she reached Cordero on his cell.

Cordero could just hear her over the rain peltering down.

"Just leaving the police station," he yelled into his cell. "I'm driving down to have another talk with Evans. He was behind the sacred house break-ins, and I want to know why. Where are you?"

"At—"

Thunder cracked over the village.

"What? Repeat that."

"I said I'm at Mrs Frankston's. Can you pick me up? There's something you need to know too."

"On my way."

Cordero was soon splashing through pools of rainwater as he made his way to Mrs Frankston's. Carter was waiting out front, under the eave but looking like she was soaked through. She ran to the utility as he pulled up, jumped in, and threw the coat she'd borrowed over the seat and onto the floor in the rear.

"Shit!" she said, wiping her face with her hand.

"Welcome to the wet season," he said.

"You don't think I've seen rain before?"

"Not like this," he said. "It'll be this way for months."

"Great," she said. "Another reason I should be back in dry, sunny Arizona."

She dipped her head to peer out through the windshield.

"What do you need to tell me?" he asked.

She sat back and palmed her hair.

"The African told you Frankston refused to pay for the damage to his boat, right?" she said.

Cordero nodded as he drove off. He switched the windscreen wipers to 'high' and they flapped left to right frantically, but he still had trouble seeing through the sheets of rain.

"He lied," she said.

"What?"

"I said he lied," said Carter more loudly.

"What do you mean he lied?" Cordero asked.

"Frankston had taken photos of the damaged motor. Four of them. He was arranging to have replacement parts sent over from Dili and had already paid compensation for loss of income."

Cordero raised his eyebrows.

"That's not all," said Carter, holding on to the dashboard as Cordero plunged the utility into a deep pothole and wrestled it out the other side. "Someone's stolen Frankston's journal. The widow says there was a duplicate key she didn't think to tell us about. Says Evans would've been most likely to have known about it."

"Is that so?" Cordero said, smiling. "Well now, let's hear what Evans has to say for himself."

He drove to a halt outside the presbytery and cut the engine. The priest's jeep was nowhere to be seen.

"He may have run," Carter suggested.

"Maybe. Or Father Robeiro might have it," said Cordero engaging the park brake. "Come on!"

They chanced their luck in the downpour to the door of the room Evans was renting. Cordero knocked. No answer. Carter skipped around the puddles, made for the window along from the door, and cupped her hands to the pane to peer through.

"There's someone lying on the floor!" she yelled.

Cordero banged harder.

"Police! Open up!"

Silence from inside.

He tried the lock on the door. It gave without the slightest pressure.

Robert Evans lay beside his bed, blood splattered under his head. Cordero knelt and felt for a pulse.

"He's alive!"

Carter joined him. "Let me check," she said.

Cordero called the health clinic to tell them they were on their way and why. While he did, Carter worked her hands carefully around Evans' head and neck. She checked his body and rolled him over.

"He's been coshed, hence all the blood." She surveyed the room quickly. "There!" she said and pointed to the walking stick Evans used which had been tossed part-way under the bed. "Grab it as well."

"Help me get him in the vehicle," Cordero said.

He lifted Evans by the shoulders, Carter by the legs. The man started to moan as they carried him out. They slid him onto the rear seat of the utility. Cordero went back for the walking stick. Five minutes later they laid Evans on a stretcher in the health clinic and a nurse came to attend to him.

• • •

Cordero paced the front room of the clinic while they waited for news on Evans' condition. Outside the rain had stopped and sunlight was breaking through the clouds and creating a drift of light mist through the village. Goats and chickens had re-appeared to forage and children were frolicking among the puddles.

"So he lied about Frankston not paying him for the motor," mused Carter.

"He lied about a lot of things," said Cordero. "And kept on lying."

After twenty minutes the nurse ushered them into a small room heavy with the pungent smell of detergent where Evans was propped up on a bed, a thick roll of bandages tied fast around his head.

"Concussion, three stitches, and a big bruise but he'll live," the nurse said and left them to the patient.

Evans looked up awkwardly as they approached.

"Bloody hell," he said. "Bit of a mess, eh?"

"Who did this?" asked Cordero.

Evans made to inspect the stitches in his head but thought better of it and withdrew his hand. He offered no answer to Cordero's question and stared down the bed at nothing in particular.

"We know you hired Antonio Gomes to break into four sacred houses," Cordero said.

Evans tried to smirk but even that inflamed the pain in his head.

"Never trust youth," he said. "You may have heard it said that while there's no honour in being a thief, there is honour among thieves. Don't believe that of the young. Young folks regard freedom as much more important than honour and they'll steal, bash and *snitch* to keep it. I'm guessing that boy fessed up. Bastard!"

"Sergeant Amparo threatened to hand him over to elders of one of the sacred houses he burgled to feed to the sharks," Cordero said, matter-of-factly.

Evans nodded slightly.

"I guess that'd do it too," he said.

"Breaking into a sacred house is a serious offence in East Timor," Cordero continued, ignoring the remarks. "We've reason to believe you also stole Professor Frankston's journal. That's another offence. And at the moment, you're our prime suspect in the murder of Frankston."

Evans eyes widened and he grimaced as a result.

"You threatening to feed me to the sharks as well?"

"No but I'd talk if I were you," suggested Cordero.

"Shit a brick," Evans protested. "I didn't bloody-well kill anyone. What do you take me for, mate?"

Again, he went to examine his forehead with a hand and again pulled it away.

"But I've cocked it up a treat, haven't I?"

He glanced at Carter who was standing on the opposite side of the bed from Cordero.

"Sorry, love. 'Cock up' is just an Australian expression for messing something up through incompetence."

Carter ignored the explanation.

"My colleague asked who struck you," she said.

He exhaled long and loud.

"That bloody African," he said. "He came bounding into my room saying the cops were on to him about something or other. Said we had to get what we came for and go."

He lifted a hand off the bed.

"*We*," he said and emphasized the pronoun. "I liked that. I didn't know what he was on about—you know, the bit about the cops on to him? For what? He saw that I was reading Frankston's journal. Demanded I give it to him. I told him to get stuffed. He tried to grab it. The rest is a bloody blur as you might imagine."

"I think it's time you told us what exactly you came to Atauro for," said Cordero.

Evans twisted too quickly to face Cordero and winced in pain. He reached for some tablets on a side table, popped two in his mouth and took a swig of water. He made a face and swallowed hard.

"Ever heard of the *Flor de la Mar*, mate?" he said.

Cordero didn't react.

"Didn't think so. Pull up a chair. It's a long story."

• • •

The rain was easing when Estefana arrived at the cemetery. She looked around—there was no one else in sight; she was alone. She wasn't sure if that was a comfort or a cause for concern. Alone, there was no one to bother her: alone, there was no one to call on if she needed help.

She made the Catholic sign of the cross across her chest, took a deep breath, and strode in through the rusting iron gates before there was time for her fear to build.

The *matan-dook* had told her to look for a white mock church tower beside an above ground tomb on the south side of the cemetery. She saw it immediately, rising above lesser gravestones, urns and monuments. She walked down the muddy, uneven path to the resting place of Padre Jose Guterres. Some of the tombs she noticed were adorned with statues of angles, pictures of Jesus or the Virgin Mary, or simple Christian crosses. Reminders of death, symbols of grief, were all around her and unnerving.

She stumbled and nearly tripped over a crumbling footstone. She clutched at a small columbarium on an adjoining grave to steady herself and knocked a vase out of its slot. A large black rat sheltering there scurried away over the crumbling borders of nearby graves.

A cold shiver went up her spine and she could feel the fine hairs standing up on her neck. She wiped a hand over her face, collected herself, and continued on.

Movement in the trees startled her. She tried to calm a racing heart by telling herself it was only night birds coming out now the storm had passed.

But her hands were shaking and she felt suddenly cold all over. She wiped her hands on the sides of her uniform. She thought of Josinto and the children he and she longed to bring into the world. He'd said he wanted a big family but not too big—not the twelve or more common in Timor but maybe four or even six. She thought of her father and the gruesome job he'd been forced to undertake by the Indonesians. She thought of the dead he had to bury on an island where none of them would find rest.

She held the crucifix around her neck so tightly it left an imprint on her fingers as she stepped gingerly toward the grave where the *matan-dook* had instructed her to conduct the strange ritual to appease the spirits.

25

"The *Flor de la Mar* or Flower of the Sea," Evans was explaining, "was an early sixteenth century Portuguese *nau*—" he looked across to Carter "—that means a carrack or ocean-going sailing ship, love. It had a history of leaks and breakages but it was sent to help the Portuguese in their capture of the Malay Sultanate of Malacca. In 1511 it was sailing to Sumatra when it was caught in a storm and sunk. No one has yet found the wreck even though a few of the sailors made it to safety."

He lifted his head gingerly to the ceiling.

"But they say it was carrying the equivalent of over two billion dollars in bullion in today's terms. Can you believe that? Two billion!"

Cordero folded his legs, impatient if Evans was embarking on a long, rambling lecture. Carter had chosen to remain standing.

"That's a nice story but Sumatra's a long way from here. What's any of this to do with why you're here on Atauro?" Cordero asked.

"Well the *Flor de la Mar* was not the only *nau* to ply these waters," Evans said, attempting a grin. "I wrote a book about Portuguese colonial adventures in these parts, remember? And they landed here…in Timor I mean…in 1515. After that there were regular ship movements to drop off missionaries and supplies on their way further north or to pick up sandalwood and head back home to Portugal."

He tipped a finger to the side of his nose indicating he was about to reveal a secret.

"Most of those ships carried bullion in the form of gold or silver coins to trade for silks, spices and ivory."

"I'm at a loss to see how this connects with you here on Atauro," Cordero said.

Evans pressed his hands to his sides and lifted himself in the bed, wincing in pain as he did so. He took a few seconds to settle before continuing.

"You'd know of Bidau, in Dili," he said. "The old folks tell a story there handed down for generations about a Portuguese *nau* that was shipwrecked out in the Wetar Strait in 1512. Only a priest and three sailors managed to make it to the mainland. The priest, of course, insisted they save an image of the Virgin Mary—nothing else—and it's said that's all they washed ashore with. The priest went on to build a church and the sailors married local women and started a community there on the coast."

His eyes narrowed.

"But what if other sailors, let's say less bloody pious types, took some valuables and in all the confusion as the ship went down took off to the north instead of south? That would have brought them to Atauro. Am I right?"

"So you're saying—"

"Hold on, mate. I haven't finished." He reached for more water and sipped a little before replacing the glass.

"If there were only two or three of them, the whole island wouldn't have noticed. Their impact would have been local. Right? Well among the Humangili down here in the southern part of Atauro is a kinship subgroup called *Soluan*. Not many of them left these days and spread out up and down the east coast. Now according to a creation story told by some of the very, very old *Soluan* elders, their patriarch arrived from the mainland after spending several days adrift at sea."

He touched the bandages around his head lightly as if to check they were still in place. He grinned.

"But get this, mate. The patriarch is said to have spoken Portuguese."

"How would anyone have identified Portuguese that long ago?" asked Cordero.

Evans brushed the comment away.

"You strike me as an intelligent man, mate. I bet you've heard that myths are not historical records. They're stories made up to justify social arrangements and behavior within a community. Are you going to tell me that Eve was created out of a rib from Adam when both men and women have to same number of ribs? Whoever came up with that one should have paid more attention in anatomy class."

He wiped a hand delicately across his face.

"As stories, myths evolve over time to suit changing circumstances. So maybe when the Portuguese arrived—swords shining and trumpets blowing—the *Soluan* adapted the story to give their patriarch a Portuguese tongue and so give themselves one up on their neighbors. Or maybe—" he paused for effect "—they finally realized that words unintelligible to them but passed down through the years as sacred due to their association with the patriarch were in fact Portuguese words."

"So you're saying you came here in search of bullion?" asked Carter.

"Yes, love, bullion. Or something of similar value like ingots of gold or silver. Who knows? But how else would a couple of shipwrecked sailors get accepted by the locals as patriarchs unless they brought something highly unusual with them?"

"If they did in fact arrive here," said Carter.

"Yeah," he said and glared at her. "A bloody big 'if', right? And that could explain why nobody's ever bothered to find out."

"Why look on the reef?" Cordero asked.

Evans fixed him with a glare.

"If they'd made land by boat, the boat—or what's left of it—would be known about. Honored, in fact, as a sacred relic. But there's no record of that ever having been done. So my working assumption is their boat was wrecked on the reef and they swam ashore. Coming out of the sea like that would have added to their mystique. But they couldn't have swum holding a box full of precious anything. They'd have brought a few samples—coins or whatever—to impress the locals and stashed the rest somewhere out in the coral. And out in the coral there'd be no fear of the stuff drifting away with currents or in the tide. That's what I had a hunch, no, more than a hunch, a gut-feeling, an *informed* gut-feeling, was out there."

• • •

Estefana began to walk around the grave as the *matan-dook* had instructed. She prayed the Lord's Prayer as she went, loud enough that anyone—anything—close to her could hear until she remembered what the *matan-dook* had told her to recite: 'I am Estefana, daughter of Aniceto dos Carvalho. My father was forced by evil men to do what he did on this island. He always regretted having to do it. I regret it as well and I wish peace to all here.' She repeated those words on her second circuit, keeping her gaze down as the *matan-dook* had also instructed.

She ignored the night birds rustling in the trees along the roadside outside the cemetery and she tried to control her fear by concentrating on the words she was meant to say. She took a deep breath, exhaled, and started on her third circuit.

Before she'd gone two steps she was alarmed by a sound.

Bark!

She imagined it was one of the dogs that had attacked her prowling the cemetery grounds and calling the other dogs in the pack. She cowered to present a smaller target. She scanned this way and that through the headstones but could see no dog.

Bark!

This time the sound seemed to have come not from the cemetery but from above. A spirit? A demon? She froze.

She studied the trees along the road outside the cemetery.

Bark!

The sound drew her attention to one tree in particular.

Bark!

There it was—not a spirit and not a demon unless one or the other had taken the form of a Scops owl. That was possible but the bird took flight and flew silently away. A spirit or a demon would have stayed and stalked her.

At least that's what she told herself.

She renewed her circuit of the grave. And that's when she saw it.

Rainwater had formed a channel which flowed from the slightly higher ground on the neighboring row of graves. The channel had coursed under the cracked concrete surround of the grave of the priest and pushed the handle of a knife out into the open. Without touching the knife Estefana flicked it out entirely with a chip of concrete broken off from the rest. It was a small, double-sided hunting knife. She could see blood smeared along the blade.

She knew it could be nothing other than the blood of Professor Hank Frankston.

• • •

"If what you say is true," Cordero put to Evans, "why would you believe anything remains out there?"

Evans tried to laugh but it was too painful and so he stopped.

"If the surviving sailors had gone after it too quickly they would have raised suspicions and risked losing it all," he said. "And besides, if the locals believed them to be demigods of some sort, the sailors would have been feted. You know what I mean, mate. They'd be invited to enjoy the charms of the local women—that sort of thing—and just imagine how distracting that've been for poor bloody sailors miles from home and years at sea. What good was the cargo to them then? They could've died before hauling it up. Or maybe their demigod status worked against them and they were made human sacrifices either by the *Soluans* or some rival group."

He turned to Carter. "They used to do that here, love."

Carter's showed no reaction.

"And that means knowledge of the location of what they'd hidden would have gone with them," he concluded.

There was a pause.

"Why not use acoustic detection to try and locate whatever you thought might be out there or underwater imaging technology?" asked Carter. "Why engage in such an amateurish hunt yourself?"

"Amateurish," he repeated and scoffed. "Simple fishermen, and plenty of them, are coming across valuable cargos in these waters all the time, love. You don't need to be bloody Jacques Cousteau. Besides, money doesn't grow on trees and I'd been sacked, remember. And quite apart from all that, I had no desire to draw attention to what I was doing."

"If you were so sure there was something out there, surely you could have raised funds for a proper search," said Cordero.

Evans sniffed.

"If I was right in my assumptions about something being hidden on the reef...*on the reef—*" he said a second time for emphasis "—we're talking Timorese territorial waters. I'd have received kudos aplenty but no bloody salvage rights. I can't live on kudos, mate."

"So you would have stolen whatever you'd found?" Carter said.

"I would have seen to it that I came into my just deserts, love. And I don't mean in honor and prestige. I'll leave that sort of shit to the Frankstons of this world. I'm too old to be impressed by a pat on the back. I wanted cash in the hand."

"Why did you pay Antonio Gomes to break into the sacred houses?" Cordero asked.

"I wanted to see if they contained any Portuguese relics," said Evans. "That would have strengthened my theory and narrowed the location of my search. But I met Frankston. When I got to talking to him I realized he'd already surveyed most of the reef north of here so that meant I concentrated on the area from Vila to Maquili. The boy kept searching sacred houses because that's what I'd paid him to do originally."

"Was Frankston in on it?"

"Frankston! Bloody nut-case he was. All he was interested in was bloody coral and seaweed and shit. I raised the issue of shipwrecks and bullion with him—in general terms, of course—to see if he was interested. He wasn't. All he ever talked about was coral this and coral that. Pain the ass in many ways."

"Why did you take the journal?" Carter interjected.

Evans heaved himself up uneasily in the bed a second time.

"The days before he was killed he was diving off Maquili. When I saw him the night he was killed he had a smile on his face a mile wide. I asked him why and he said: 'I found it! I damn well found it!' I asked him what he'd found and he told me I'd have to wait until he'd published his results to find out. I couldn't imagine anyone—not even him—getting that excited about bloody coral so I figured he might have found bullion along the lines I mentioned to him when we first met."

"Is that the real reason you were in Maquili the other day when you said you'd gone birdwatching?" Cordero asked. "You were in Maquili because Frankston had been working off the coast there?"

"Yeah," conceded Evans. "I wanted to check it out. Check the availability of boats there to take me out over the reef." He looked up. "But at that stage I didn't have the journal to tell me where to look. And besides, I am a twitcher like I told you," he said, using the colloquial term for birdwatcher. "Comes in handy if I want to go somewhere out of the ordinary without anyone asking too many questions."

"Go on," said Cordero.

"When I saw Antonio go by in that police vehicle, he looked like something the cat dragged in," Evans said. "That female copper followed on the boy's motorcycle. So I knew he'd been taken in and I knew it wouldn't be long before he talked. So I went to see Mrs. Frankston. Thought I'd give her some bloody bullshit story about needing to go into her husband's study to collect something of mine. But just as I arrived, I noticed a young man leaving her house."

Cordero meet Carter's eyes and she mouthed 'Miller' silently and shook her head in annoyance.

"When he was gone, she came out and took off down the beach for a walk or something. I knew where Frankston kept his keys. I found one and grabbed the journal before she came back."

"And you were reading the journal when the African came by?" asked Cordero.

"Only the last page. The rest was scientific claptrap."

"But you could interpret it?"

"Most of it," Evans agreed. "Frankston insisted on explaining it to me in considerable detail. It was his pride and bloody joy. And, of course, I was keen to learn."

"You said the African grabbed the journal off you before he struck you with your walking stick—"

"Is that what he hit me with?" Evans interrupted. "Bloody bugger!"

"He took the journal?" asked Cordero.

"I guess so," said Evans. "If you didn't find it in my room."

"He can interpret the scientific notations?" Cordero asked.

"He had to be taught to read the site locations because he was in charge of the boat. If Frankston wanted to go to, I don't know say, 'Site 85/80yDN', the African had to know where that was. There were directions to each site position at the back of the journal because there were so bloody many it was easy to forget or confuse them. '80yDN' would mean 'eighty yards due north' of that position."

"Where was the last site reference?" Cordero asked.

"The last?" Evans stared at the foot of the bed and mechanically recited: "'Site 152/60yDS.'"

"Which means?" Cordero pressed him.

Evans was lost in thought and took a moment to answer.

"What? Oh! Maquili. It means sixty yards due south of a site off Maquili that would be listed at the back of the journal."

"What was the last substantive entry in the journal about—the one that ended in an exclamation mark?" asked Carter.

Evans grinned.

"That, love," he began, "was Frankston's big find. His big, bloody find! The bugger had discovered a type of coral, in conjunction with another bloody type of microscopic algae, he thought would send the world of marine biologists into a flipping frenzy!"

He broke into a raucous laugh until the pain from his injury forced him to stop.

"All for bloody nothing," he said to himself.

"Would the African know that?" asked Cordero. "About the coral, I mean? Would he have been able to interpret those notes?"

"Not on your life," Evans said. "Frankston only taught him to read the location codes. That's all he needed to know. The rest of the journal would have been indecipherable to him. He'd have no idea!"

"Did you have the keys to Father Robeiro's jeep today?" Cordero asked.

"Yeah, why?"

"The jeep's gone. The African must have taken it."

"That'd be right. There was some diving and snorkeling gear in there as well. He's gone to Maquili, silly bugger."

"Does he know how to use the diving gear?"

Evans shrugged.

"He's seen Frankston do it often enough. Me too. I guess at a pinch—"

He raised a hand as if to say 'maybe'.

Cordero looked across to Carter who shook her head indicating she had no further questions. Cordero stood and they made to leave.

"All for bloody nothing," Evans repeated. "Just a bloody pipe dream."

Cordero paused at the door.

"Why didn't you tell Antonio to break into the *uma lulik* here in Vila?" he asked.

Evans raised his eyes to meet Cordero's.

"Too close to home, mate," he said. "Would've given the game away if he'd been caught."

Cordero nodded.

"Pity," he said and turned to leave.

"Why?" asked Evans.

"I went to look inside it," Cordero said. "I found part of an old flag."

Evans' eyes widened.

"You were asking me about flags before. What kind of flag did you find?" he asked.

"Old. Very old. It was a section of an heraldic cross," said Cordero. "Enough to show it was the cross of the Order of Christ. The flag of Prince Henry the Navigator."

"Well I'll be damned!" said Evans. He stared up at the ceiling and whistled. "So I was bloody right!"

He sat there, open-mouthed, before thinking to ask more questions but by then Carter and Cordero had gone.

26

"She found it in the cemetery," Sergeant Amparo was saying to Cordero on his cell. "Don't ask me what she was doing out there—she wouldn't say. She just brought it in and gave it to me. Said it had been wedged under some broken concrete around a grave but the heavy rain must have dislodged it. And before you ask, she picked it up with a kerchief and no one here has touched it. If it'd been wiped, there'd be no blood stains on the handle, which there are. So there'll be prints intact as well."

Cordero circled the front room of the clinic as Amparo was speaking.

"Where's Estefana now? With you?"

"She just left. She didn't say where she was going. I think the lodge. She was drenched and seemed a little unnerved by it all."

"I'm with Evans at the health clinic," Cordero said. "He was bashed on the head by the African. They'd colluded in a hunt for bullion Evans imagined was wedged somewhere out on the reef. The African took Frankston's journal, which Evans had stolen from his study, along with the priest's jeep. I'd say he's had an hour's start or more. He's set out for Maquili."

"Maquili?" Amparo grunted. "Well he won't get too far. The road's all mud and slush now and a bridge's been washed out about four miles this side of Maquili cutting the road. Damn Indonesians," he cursed. "Cut down so many trees there's landslides all over this island all the time now."

"Road not passable at all?" asked Cordero.

"Not to my vehicle or any other. Accidents have caused a few casualties too, apparently," said Amparo. "Had to send Sisko to sort it out somehow. He'd be able to get at least as far as the wash-away on the motorcycle."

"Where can I get another motorcycle?" Cordero asked.

"You won't," Amparo answered. "Everyone will be busy moving old folk, kids, animals around due to the storm damage. Anyhow, as I said, Sisko can only make the wash-out on a motorcycle. He won't get over the ravine with the bridge gone."

Cordero re-considered the plan forming in his head.

"Can you get into contact with him?"

"For the moment there's coverage. Sure."

"Tell him to keep an eye out for Welcome Jesus and to arrest him if he finds him. But tell him to be careful. It's probable the African has killed once already."

"Okay. I'll let him know and call you if he finds anything."

"Oh, one more thing," Cordero said before Amparo ended the call. "The African told me his real name is Eduardo Selewesi. He told Evans he'd been sent here originally because he was a rebel in the Mozambique Liberation Front. Are there any records you know of that would show if that's true and, if it's not, why the Portuguese brought him here in the first place?"

"The Portuguese destroyed a lot of records when they fled in 1975," Amparo answered him. "The Indonesians destroyed the rest. But there was another African here when I first arrived. From Angola. He's dead now. He'd been a prisoner with Welcome and knew him well enough. We were talking one day when Welcome walked past carrying a Bible under his arm like he was on a mission to save souls. The Angolan scoffed at him. He said Welcome liked to pretend he was something he wasn't. Said Welcome claimed to be a former rebel when he was nothing but a thief. Robbed a Portuguese trader, put the guy in hospital, and was picked up drunk in a whorehouse in Maputo two days later."

Cordero could hear Amparo laughing.

"Put him in hospital how?" he asked.

"Who knows?" replied the sergeant. "Didn't say. Not even sure the story is true."

• • •

"Seems a lot of people have something to hide around here," Carter said.

They'd gone to the lodge to await news from Sisko that he'd managed to apprehend the African. They were sitting in the dining area over coffee.

"Nothing unusual about that," replied Cordero. "Everybody has a secret or two."

"Even you?"

"Even me," he said.

He lifted his coffee cup.

"And I bet you do too," he added.

She leaned in across the table between them.

"Tell you what," she said. "You tell me yours and I'll tell you mine."

He put his cup down, rubbed a hand across his face, and looked out on the sodden courtyard. She could hear his foot tapping on the floor. He looked up, considering things before responding.

"Come on," she urged him.

He held her gaze.

"I robbed a grocery store once," he said.

"You what?" she asked, not expecting that for an answer.

He fidgeted with his coffee cup on the table.

"I was only eleven, maybe twelve. It was not long after my father moved the family to Australia."

She relaxed and folded her arms.

"Go on," she said.

"In those days' supermarkets were not common. Corner stores—kind of family run things—operated in most suburbs in Australia. There was one near where we lived. Run by Mister Peters, although I think his real name was Petrov or Petrovsky. You know, he'd anglicized it to fit in."

He picked up his cup and put it down again.

"He worked hard, real hard. He'd be open early, close late. Twelve, fourteen hours a day. Seven days a week. And he was not young."

He stopped and straightened, his hands pushing up on the chair either side of him.

"And?" she encouraged.

"And one day I was walking by and I saw him through the big pane window at the front of the store. He seemed to be arguing with a woman about something. I noticed his big brass cash register—remember those?—anyhow it was open and he was pointing at something she'd put on the counter and then into the register. I couldn't hear what they were saying. I just kept watching. Eventually Mister Peter's waved a hand out toward the rear of the store and the woman picked up whatever it was she'd brought in and followed him through a doorway behind the counter. There was a curtain that blocked off the back room from the front where all the merchandise was on show so you couldn't see from one to the other without moving the curtain aside."

He averted her eyes.

"The cash register was open and there was nobody else in the store. I went in and took some money—not all of it so he wouldn't notice at first, just some notes from the bottom of each pile in the tray. Than I ran out into the street before Mister Peters and the woman re-emerged."

She was watching him intently.

"How much did you take?"

"Thirty-seven dollars," Cordero said.

"You remember the exact amount? He nodded.

"That was probably his profit for the week in those days," he said.

He shook his head and drank the last of his coffee.

"Why did you do it?" she asked.

He put his cup down and rubbed his mouth.

"I'm not sure. My family didn't have a lot of money but we didn't need what I took. I think I was just angry to have been taken from Timor to a strange place where I didn't know anyone and didn't have any friends."

He cast his eyes down as though the guilt weighed on him still.

"What did you do with the money?" she asked.

He laughed.

"When I made it home I hid it at first. In the pages of some books I had. I took it out and counted it a couple of times and thought about what I could spend it on. Maybe a new pair of sneakers, you know, like the other kids at school wore. Or a football I could entice other kids to play with me with. But I ended up putting it in the poor box in the church. I couldn't return it or Mister Peters would know I stole it and I'd get into trouble. But I didn't want to keep it. I knew it wasn't right."

He met her eyes and laughed once more.

"Maybe that's why I became a police officer. I wanted to protect the hard-working Mister Peters of this world from people like me who'd rob them of their livelihoods."

She unfolded her arms.

"You could have put it in an envelop and just left it in the store," she said.

"Didn't have an envelop and didn't want to go back in that store in case Mister Peters saw me and smiled at me," he said. "He was always nice like that."

He picked up his cup but saw it was empty.

"I've never told that to anyone before," he said, and replaced the cup in its saucer.

"But you're telling me. Why?"

"I don't know," he said. "I feel like I can, that's all."

He shrugged.

"You're quite something," she said.

"Why? Because I robbed a grocery store when I was a kid?"

"No," she said. "Because what you did still bothers you all these years later."

He drummed his fingers on the table not knowing how to respond to that.

"Your turn," he said, to change the subject.

She put a hand to the side of her neck and balked at first. Her hair fell loose and she swept it into place. She placed both hands on the table.

"A few months after I started work in the Flagstaff office—"

She stopped abruptly as Estefana appeared and ran up to their table. Without being asked Estefana repeated how she came to find the knife but not what she was doing in the cemetery in the first place. Her account was rushed and sketchy.

"You've done well," Cordero said. "Sergeant Amparo told me."

Estefana blushed but Carter sensed it wasn't from embarrassment at the praise. She guessed that her friend might have more to say but was coy with Cordero there.

"Why don't you go and play with that kid over there," Carter told him. "He seems to like you."

"What?" He spun around to look where she was pointing. "Why?"

She glared at him.

"Just do it. Okay?"

He read her expression as insistent, though he didn't know why, wiped his hands on his trousers and lifted himself off the chair.

"I'll leave my cell here, okay? Yell out if Amparo calls with news from Sisko," he said and walked off to kick the deflated ball around the muddy yard with Benni.

"So what were you doing in the cemetery?" Carter asked.

Estefana turned away, a sheepish expression on her face.

"Come on," urged Carter. "We're friends. You can tell me and I won't say anything to him," she added, lifting her chin in Cordero's direction.

"I went to see the *matan-dook, mana*," Estefana said. "I told him about my fear for my children." She rubbed across her eyes. "I asked him if he would help me."

Carter waited.

"And?" she prompted.

"He said I should perform a ritual to appease the spirits. He said I should walk around a particular grave in the cemetery four times keeping my eyes on the ground no matter what I might hear or feel around me."

She eyed Carter directly.

"That could have been the spirits taunting me, *mana*." She

looked away. "After the fourth circuit, he told me to take my necklace and bury it beside the grave."

Unconsciously she fingered the crucifix.

"He said to offer up something of great value would honor the spirits and they would be pleased with me."

"Interesting guy this sorcerer," Carter said to see if her choice of words would elicit a response she could use to persuade Estefana this was all nonsense. Estefana didn't take the bait.

"He's not a sorcerer, *mana*. Not like you mean," Estefana corrected her. "He's a healer because of his power to communicate between the world of the living and the world of the dead."

Carter nodded the comment away, picked up her coffee cup, and drank the last of it, even though it had gone cold.

"I see you're still wearing your necklace though," she said.

Estefana let go of the crucifix and put her hands on the table. Carter sensed fear and disappointment.

"So what's eating you now?" she asked.

"Eating me, *mana*?"

"You know what I mean. What's got you upset?"

"I didn't complete the ritual, *mana*," she said.

"Why not?"

"Because I saw the knife. I knew it was the one you said killed Professor Frankston—double-edged, remember? Plus I saw the blood. So I took it to the police station straight away rather than complete the ritual."

Carter leaned forward over the table.

"And why did you do that, Estefana? Why did you take the knife rather than complete the ritual?"

Estefana stared at her.

"Because you are a police officer, that's why," said Carter. She put a hand over Estefana's. "First and foremost, you're a *police officer*. Your character and your training are stronger than any fears you may have about spirits."

The expression on Estefana's face said she was struggling to be persuaded by that interpretation.

"You may be right, *mana*. But it's not me I'm most worried

about." She pulled her hands away from the table and hunched over in her chair. "It's my children."

Carter made no comment.

"And now," said Estefana, "the spirits will be even angrier with me because I deceived them into thinking I was performing a ritual for them but instead I ran off to the police station."

She looked up, eyes welling with tears.

"It's worse now!"

Carter rubbed her face in frustration.

"Okay," she said. "I'll tell you what. We need to get hold of the African. He's the one most likely to have killed Frankston so he's our first priority. When we get him, I'll go to the cemetery with you and you can complete the ritual. If any spirits want to harm you, they'll have to deal with me first!"

• • •

"When I spoke to the *matan-dook* about Justino," Cordero was saying, "he told me he was a little crazy but not *bulak*, real crazy, like the one, he said, who talked a lot but knew nothing. I should have picked up on the clue."

They were at the table in the dining area. Estefana had gone to freshen up in her hut.

"What clue?" asked Carter.

"Talked a lot but knew nothing," Cordero repeated. "He must have been talking about the African and his constant references to Jesus and the Bible."

Carter chewed over the association. "I'd like to talk to this *matan-dook* myself," she said but Cordero ignored the comment.

"He lied to Evans," he said, referring to Welcome Jesus. "And no doubt others, about being brought here as a rebel freedom fighter when in fact he was a thug. He fooled the Assembly of God people into believing he'd had a profound religious conversion when what he wanted was acceptance and, even more, a cover to visit widows where he could comfort them in return for sex. He lied about Frankston refusing to pay for the damage to his boat. He lied about where he was the night of Frankston's death. He lied about encountering Frankston. And he bashes Evans on the head, takes Frankston's journal and steals the jeep."

He stretched his legs and folded his arms.

"I'd say that's a strong case for his guilt in the murder, wouldn't you?"

"It makes him an inveterate liar, that's for sure," said Carter. "But there's one or two things I'm not sure about."

"Like what?"

"He's been living here for forty years. He's settled. Why upset all of that now? And at his age?" she said.

Cordero leaned in across the table.

"Because he saw a chance to make money. A lot of money," he replied. "After a lifetime of poverty that would have been quite a temptation. Agreed?"

"Agreed. But also quite a risk," she said. She pursed her lips. "And why not kill Evans? That blow to the head was enough to knock him out but that's about all. If our African was a ruthless killer—and there's nothing in his background to say he was—why not finish Evans off? That'd leave no one to associate him with the journal, the jeep, or the dash to Maquili. He could have been home free."

Cordero's cell buzzed. It was Sergeant Amparo.

"Sisko found the jeep," Amparo told him. "Crashed into the ravine where the bridge washed away. According to other villagers stranded out there it happened only recently. Sisko said there was no one in the jeep but the windows were smashed and he noticed blood in the cabin and on the bottom of the driver's door which took the brunt of the collision into the ravine. He said there were drops of blood heading off in the direction of Maquili. Could be our fugitive only injured himself and has decided to walk the rest of the way."

"Can you send Sisko after him?"

"Sorry, no. He's the only officer I have out there. Other people were injured when the bridge collapsed and they came off their motorcycles. You know what it's like: two or three or more can be crowded onto the one bike. Some of the injuries are serious. Some are only kids. Sisko's trying to sort it all out and get the injured to the clinic somehow."

"How far would it be from where the jeep was found to Maquili and how long would it take to walk there?" Cordero asked.

"From the washout to Maquili would be about four miles. Slipping and sliding through the mud would slow him down on top of any injuries he might have sustained. So I'd say it'd take him two, maybe three hours. More if he's trying to carry anything heavy or bulky."

"And I can't drive your vehicle along that road?"

"You wouldn't get any further than Sisko is now."

"Can I get a boat?"

Amparo sighed.

"It's high tide," he said. "All the boats will be out fishing. It'll be hours before anyone comes in."

They fell silent, considering where that left things.

"You could walk," Amparo offered.

"Walk?"

"Yeah. Villagers do it regularly. Along the coast. It's a lot shorter than the road over the ridge. About three, four miles all up. Takes about an hour from here. I've done it myself several times but not with an injured ankle. There's a track that runs from the southern end of the beach at Vila. Well, sort of a track. Most of it's scrambling over rocks. But there's only one problem."

"What's that?" asked Cordero.

"Like I said: it's high tide. People only do the walk when the tide is low. Too dangerous when it's high like now."

27

"In that case we walk!" Carter said when Cordero had told her what Amparo had said. She sprung to her feet. "Let's move."

"He said it was too dangerous at high tide," Cordero responded and burrowed more firmly into his chair.

She stooped to his eye level, but he shifted to avoid direct contact.

"And so you're just going to sit there and let a suspect get away? You're a police officer, Tino. Danger is an occupational hazard," she admonished him.

"It's not danger that bothers me," he said. "It's getting stranded along the way which'd create even more delays in getting to the African."

"Right. So, we'd better not get stranded," Carter said and straightened.

"What's this 'we' business?" he said, meeting her gaze now.

"You'll need someone to keep an eye on you," she said. "It's dangerous at high tide, remember?"

"Too dangerous for you," he said. "You'll have to stay here."

"Look, you're not my boss, remember?" she said. "I work for INTERPOL."

"This has nothing to do with INTERPOL," he insisted.

"A murder suspect is likely to seize a boat and head for Indonesia with possible stolen cultural heritage items. Sounds like a perfect case for INTERPOL to me."

He shifted uncomfortably, knowing he was losing the argument.

"I could make better time without you," he grumbled.

"That's rich," she said, "given that you weren't going to get out of that chair at all."

Cordero rose, pocketed his phone, and picked up the keys to the police utility. She read his body language.

"Either I go with you, or I follow on behind," she said. "But one way or another I'm going."

"Okay, okay," he said, knowing it was pointless to resist any longer. "Go tell Estefana to keep an eye on Evans and let her know what we're up to. We'll drive down to the beach. I'll wait in the vehicle."

"Uh-uh," she said, holding out her hand. "I know you Cordero. Either you come with me while I talk to Estefana, or you give me the keys. I wouldn't want you to take off thinking I was right beside you when I wasn't."

He shook his head, smiled at that, and tossed her the keys.

• • •

The southern arm of the beach at Vila was a stretch of copper-coloured sand, covered in weed brought in by the tide together with assorted rubbish, odd sandals, and fishing tackle either washed overboard from cargo boats plying the Wetar Strait or brought ashore from among the debris swept into the sea from culverts running through the village. Waves came in high and violent and pounded the shoreline, leaving little room to navigate between the water and the onshore cliffs.

By the time they'd made it to the end of the beach Cordero stopped. He was already puffing. Carter pulled up beside him, showing fewer signs of fatigue.

"What is it?" she asked. She had to raise her voice above the crashing of the surf.

"I'm looking for the start of a track of some sort," Cordero shouted. "Amparo said you scramble over rocks and the outline of a track appears up ahead."

"So, let's scramble," she said and tore off ahead.

The rocks were a jumble of hard, sharp edges at irregular angles. To make progress meant timing the gap between a wave striking and the wave receding before it heaved and hit again. Too fast across risked slipping and being torn to pieces on the rocks: too slow meant getting drenched if lucky or swept out into deep water if not.

Carter faltered at the bottom of a crag. She'd rushed and slipped sideways but quickly corrected herself by grabbing an overhanging rock shelf and rebalancing.

"Careful!" Cordero yelled.

After that she took more care but was quick and nimble still. Cordero had the worst of it, his heavier upper body a liability when trying to keep his balance, and he began to lag behind.

After five minutes of clambering over rocks, Carter saw a track along a short expanse of marshy foreshore. She looked for Cordero who was making his way gingerly in her wake.

"There's a track up ahead," she yelled, and he raised a hand to signal he'd heard. She leapt from one rock to another in between waves before jumping onto muddy slush partially sheltered from the sea. She bent double, caught her breath, and waited for Cordero.

"How much more of this?" she asked when he finally joined her.

He sucked in air greedily, arms propped on his knees.

"We haven't come a mile yet," he said. He checked his watch. "It's only been fifteen minutes."

She nodded and started off. One hundred yards further on the track fell away and they were negotiating lethal rocks and deadly breakers again.

• • •

Miller hadn't left his hut for a few hours. He'd been lying on his bed taking Carter's advice to consider his future. He'd always wanted to work in the foreign service; since a young age he'd had dreams about doing great deeds abroad and coming home a hero. These were boyish dreams—the stuff of headline news, adventure comics, and action movies.

He'd read up on great moments in world affairs: Reagan's speech in West Berlin in 1987 challenging the Soviets to tear down the Berlin Wall; JFK guiding the country through the Cuban missile crisis; the great Allied leaders of the Second World War planning to destroy Nazism and remake the world. He daydreamed about doing something similar although what it might be always eluded him.

It was the call of exotic locations that moved him more than anything. He'd grown up in North Dakota—flat, featureless country where all the men wore dungarees and sat around complaining about the price for sugar beets and cereal crops. As a teenager, Miller's prized possession was an atlas his out-of-state uncle sent him for his fifteenth birthday. His favourite pastime was flicking through the pages and letting his imagination convey him to places he was only just discovering.

Was it all a childish fantasy that he'd carried, unchecked, into adulthood? Did he really have the makings of a diplomat—not the lust for foreign lands but the discipline, common sense, and maturity that the job required? Maybe Agent Carter was right: he wasn't cut out for it. He'd confused his loyalties and allowed Ambassador Hudson Taylor to control his every move even when he—Miller—felt Taylor's calls were questionable. He'd implicated an innocent man in a murder investigation, and that was a scheme he'd conceived stupidly and carried out poorly.

He wanted to talk about it with someone. But who? Taylor completely dominated the Embassy and would soon be dominating him in any heart-to-heart discussion they might have. The other Embassy staff Miller worked with either sucked up to Taylor for their own career advancement or distanced themselves as far as they could from anything to do with him. Besides, he was here—on Atauro— and they were there—in Dili. Carter had a poor opinion of him so he couldn't talk further with her. And he'd had little to do with the two English-speaking Timorese police officers who'd come with Carter and anyway theirs was the world of policing not diplomacy.

His mind shifted to Mrs. Frankston.

Susanna seemed open and honest with him. She was about the same age and was easy to talk with. She was smart and had traveled to, and lived in, strange and challenging places. He liked Susanna and she seemed to like him. They were friends.

He sat up on his bed and looked out the window of his hut. The rain had stopped. He hadn't noticed. There was nobody else around, nobody to tell him what to do or keep an eye on him. He'd go and have another chat with Mrs. Frankston.

On his way out of the grounds of the lodge he ran into Estefana who'd gone to the kitchen for some bottled water.

"Hello *maun*," she said.

"Hi," he replied.

"Going somewhere?"

"Just out for a walk. What about you?"

She told him where Carter and Cordero had gone and why.

"I'm just about to visit *Senyor* Evans at the clinic and wait for them to return," she said.

"Okay," Miller replied. "See you later."

• • •

Another, longer series of sharp, slippery rocks lay ahead. Here the waves crashed with such force that the crossing was even more dangerous than before. Carter led, staying crouched, thinking that to do so would keep her center of gravity low. If she was struck by a wave, she figured, she'd be able to withstand the impact until she grabbed a handhold on the rocks.

It didn't work.

A huge wave exploded over her just as she hesitated on a jump. She was knocked sideways into a jutting boulder and tipped into the water with the swirl.

Cordero scrambled to reach her. He positioned his feet firmly on the rocks and grabbed a section of ledge with one hand for support. Carter was floundering as the water swelled and withdrew in a great sucking motion that pushed her back onto the rocks and then further out to sea. She gasped for air and flayed about attempting to steady herself. She was failing. Cordero leaned across as far as he could.

"Grab my hand!" he yelled.

Another wave struck over them both and he almost lost his footing.

"Grab!" he repeated, as she was struggling for breath.

She reached out but missed. She tried again, snatched his hand but it slipped straight through her own. She coughed water and almost choked as she tried to fill her lungs with air.

He somehow managed to extend his hand a little further. It hovered just above her head.

"Grab!" he shouted.

She suddenly felt a solid shape beneath the waterline on which to place her foot and hoisted herself out of the water with all the energy she could manage. She caught his hand. The grip held.

He pulled her up to where he was straddling the rocks. Another wave hit and he drew her in tight to his own body with the free arm and held her fast until the water receded. When it had, he guided her quickly away from the waves and off the rocks. They collapsed together, both soaked and exhausted.

"Thanks," was all she was able to say.

"Let's take a rest over there," said Cordero, indicating a clump of pandanus palms in a small clearing away from the roiling sea. They crawled over. His shirt and trousers clung to his body as hers did to her body. Their shoes squelched with water. Under the aerial roots of the palms, they slumped again to the ground. Cordero sucked in air while Carter managed a laugh.

"I shouldn't have let you talk me into this," she said.

He laughed at that too, as he sat up, tore off his shoes, and emptied the water from them.

"Well, we're here now," was all he said.

Carter nodded and took off her own boots. They agreed to a five-minute break. Both fell silent.

Out of nowhere an old woman appeared. She looked to be in her seventies, perhaps even older. She wore a grubby head scarf and a long, drab sarong, the bottom of which was not even damp. On her feet were mismatched flip-flops. What could be seen of her hair was grey and her skin looked like petrified wood.

She stooped down under the fronds of the palm. She held a coconut she carried for refreshment, a straw made from some kind of grass sticking out of a cutting in the top.

"What you doing, *labarik*?" she asked, referring to them as children.

"We're heading for Maquli, *senyora*," Cordero said.

"Seems to me you sitting on your ass," she said and laughed. Her teeth and gums showed red from a lifetime of chewing betel nut.

"You need this?" she said offering the coconut.

"I'm fine, thanks," Cordero replied. She offered it to Carter who smiled and shook her head.

"Come with me," the old woman said. "I'm going that way too. Try to keep up. There's a lot of things I need to do today."

The old woman lit a hand-rolled cigarette she pulled from the folds of her head scarf and took off without a further word. They followed her across more rocky formations along the water's edge. The old woman puffed smoke occasionally while she worked her arms and legs like a spider. Carter had trouble keeping up with her while Cordero tried to use the woman's footholds as best as he could remember them from his vantage point far behind.

After thirty minutes the old woman left the rocks and headed across a stony patch of ground toward a ridgeline. She stopped and waited for Carter and Cordero to catch up. She was standing on the beginnings of a track.

"This track takes you to Maquili village," she said, pointing. "Up over that hill there. My hut is this way." She pointed along a narrow ravine to the west. "You follow this track and you come to Maquili. Even you can't miss it," she said eyeing Cordero with a grin.

The old woman started off as Cordero translated the instruction for Carter's benefit.

"*Orbigadu senyora!*" Cordero called his thanks after her but she merely lifted her coconut by way of acknowledgement.

"How are you holding up, Tino?" asked Carter.

"How am I holding up? What about you? Did you cut yourself on those rocks?"

"No. Luckily. But I'm damp through and my legs are bruised." She glanced at the old woman who was working her way through the trees. "Did she really say 'hill'?"

"Yeah. *Foho-oan* in Tetun," he said. "It means baby mountain. You know, hill."

"Well this *foho-oan* seems a little high to be a hill to me. But I'm from Missouri." She slipped her boots off one by one and again drained the water from them. "Let's hope she's right and Maquili's on the other side."

She slid her boots back on.

"Come on," she said. "Bad guys have a habit of not waiting for the cops."

28

From the top of what the old woman had called the hill, Carter and Cordero looked down on Maquili about two hundred feet below. It was a village of around a hundred concrete block houses among which were scattered several older plank and thatch huts that resembled hazelnuts from a distance. On the southern fringe of the village was a low massif and between it and the hill on which they were standing the settlement spilled down to the sea which glistened bright blue under a clear sky.

Maquili was the site of one of the earliest settlements on Atauro and there were few signs that it had changed much in a long time. The Indonesian-era dirt road from the high inland ridge wound down the western edge of the settlement and ended at a white stucco church and two large concrete buildings of a drab, official kind. This, it seemed, was the center of Maquili. There were no roads beyond the church, only a serious of walkways through small corrals and fenced-off garden plots with rough-hewn styles to enable a thoroughfare. Cooking fires drifted thin plumes of smoke here and there, but few people could be seen. An eerie silence hung over the village broken only by the rhythmic pummelling of the waves which echoed up the ravine.

Cordero and Carter followed the track down to the edge of the village and thread their way through the corrals and gardens. A man emerged from one house and went quickly to work on his small crop of sweet potato as though he had been called away briefly from a task he'd already begun. Cordero approached him.

"*Lisensa, senyor,*" Cordero said excusing the interruption. "I am a police investigator."

The man straightened, a bunch of weeds in his hand, and looked Cordero over—the damp clothes from scrambling over the rocks, sand encrusted on his trousers.

"You don't look like a police investigator," the man said. "Where's your uniform? Where's your vehicle?"

"Investigators don't wear uniforms, *senyor*, and a bridge came down on the road in the storm." He pointed vaguely toward the sea. "I walked from Vila along the coast."

The man glanced at Carter, a question in his eyes.

"This is my colleague. She's American," Cordero said to keep it simple.

"She looks even less like a police officer than you," the man said. "Go away. I don't believe you."

"We just need to know if you've seen an African, about sixty years old, pass this way," Cordero said.

"This is Atauro, not Africa," the man said and bent down to resume his weeding.

Cordero raised his hands in exasperation. Carter urged him on further into the village.

Chickens scattered before them. They made their way through one tiny corral where a boy was tossing bundles of bamboo leaves over a rickety fence to a few skinny goats. The boy looked to be no more than ten years old and wore a faded checkered shirt and grubby jeans.

"*Bondia, alin*," Cordero said.

The boy paused, holding a branch of bamboo.

"*Botarde*," he said, emphasizing the word which corrected Cordero's greeting of 'good day'. It was well past noon and so 'good afternoon' was in order.

"Sorry, you're right," Cordero conceded. "Have you seen an African man come this way? He's old."

The boy stared at Cordero, non-committal.

"I'm a police investigator," Cordero said to reassure him.

"You don't look like a policeman," the boy said.

Cordero ran a hand through his hair.

"I know but I am, okay? Have you seen an African? He may

have been carrying some goggles or something to go into the water."

The boy looked at Carter.

"Don't worry about her," said Cordero. "Have you seen someone like the man I described?"

"Old like you?"

"Older," said Cordero. "Much older."

The boy thought for a moment. He pointed toward the beach.

"Down there?" Cordero asked.

The boy nodded.

"How long ago?"

The boy jerked his shoulders.

"He hasn't come back?"

"He sat down with San Pedro," the boy said. "I think he's there."

• • •

"Hello Mrs Frankston. I mean Susanna," said Miller in a soft, almost pleading tone.

She was sitting at the table when he appeared in the open doorway. She looked up quickly from a brochure she'd been studying and affected an expression of delight.

"Why hello Gerard," she said. "How nice to see you. What brings you here?"

She was wearing shorts and a T-shirt, nothing more. Miller was guarded about where he looked.

"I was wondering if I could have a word with you," Miller said. "The others are away and I kind of find it easier to talk to you anyway."

"Away? Away where?"

"I'm not too sure of the details," Miller said as he took her offer of a chair. "The other officer—the Timorese woman—told me they think the African killed your husband. He assaulted Mister Evans and took your husband's journal. He also took a jeep and started out for Maquili. But the rain's destroyed the road and the other police officer, the local one, went there to sort it out. He phoned to say he'd found the jeep abandoned but the road was impassable. "

"What local police officer?"

"The young one," said Miller. "The one who rides the motorcycle. I don't know his name."

Mrs Frankston moved the brochure in front of her off to the side.

"Agent Carter and Mister Cordero have had to walk to Maquili along the coast," Miller added.

"Walk? How long would that take?"

"I don't know exactly but I don't think they'll be back for quite a while," Miller said.

"So that sergeant who stays in the station is the only officer left in the village?"

"That policewoman who came with us is here, but she's been told to keep an eye on Mister Evans at the health clinic."

"No one else?"

Miller shrugged. Mrs Frankston grabbed the brochure.

"Do you see what this means, Gerard? I can go!" she said.

Miller made a doubtful face.

"I thought you had to stay until the investigation was completed," he said.

"But if the police are after the African for the murder of my husband, the investigation has been completed. Don't you see? Besides, you told me the Ambassador wants me in Dili."

She tapped the brochure.

"All the fishing boats are out because it's high tide," she said. "But the resort hotel in Beloi has a water taxi. I can be in Dili in less than an hour."

"But Mrs Frankston—"

"No buts about it, Gerard. When I get to Dili I'll go straight to the Embassy and tell your Ambassador what a wonderful assistance you've been to me."

She pushed herself up and scurried into the bedroom.

"I'll just take a small bag. The rest can be shipped over later."

"But Mister Cordero has your passport," Miller pointed out.

"I'm only going to Dili, Gerard," she said. "And I'm sure the Ambassador could fix me up with something temporary beyond there."

"Wait—"

"No time for that now, Gerard. I need to change into something more appropriate, book that water taxi, and arrange a *tuk-tuk* to take me to Beloi. I'll call you when I get to Dili."

• • •

The foreshore at Maquili was devoid of the fishing boats normally beached at low tide and the nets hung out to dry along the sand. A large, white statue of Saint Peter the Fisherman, his right arm raised to the sea, his left holding a key—symbolizing the Keys to the Kingdom given him by Jesus—stared off into the distance across the Wetar Straight. At the left foot of Saint Peter was a large concrete rooster. Nothing and no one else was on the beach except Welcome Jesus who sat on the far side of the statue, hunched over his knees.

Ten yards from the statue, Cordero signaled Carter to circle round to the other side of the man while he approached him directly.

"I hear you comin', brother," Welcome said in a guttural voice. "You got nothin' to fear from me."

As Cordero drew nearer, he noticed a string bag at the feet of the African holding goggles, flippers and the journal taken from Professor Frankston's study. Beside the bag lay a three-pronged spear and a stain in the sand from a wound seeping blood from the man's leg.

"I 'tought I'd be able to get me a boat," Welcome said. "They not jealous of me down here. But my timin' all wrong. They all out fishin'. And now you here."

He shifted the injured leg.

"My leg hurts. I can't run, brother. Can't even walk far anymore."

Carter joined them, raking the spear out of reach with her foot. The African smiled up at her but it was a pained, defeated kind of smile.

Cordero sense the fight had gone out of the man and sat down next to him on the other side of the statue, clasped his hands, and let out a sigh of relief.

"Why did you do it, Welcome?"

The man's shoulders heaved, and he scraped a hand across his face.

"I gone crazy. Like I drunk a bottle of *Tipo*," he said and looked at Carter. "That's real strong rum they make in Mozambique. Ruin many a man."

He gazed out at the sea.

"But I don't drink *Tipo*. Can't buy it here. It was Satan temptin' me and I gave in to him."

"Tempted you with what? The treasure?" asked Cordero.

"Like Satan temptin' Jesus in the desert after the fast of forty days and nights, brother. But Jesus tell him to go. Get out!" He met Cordero's gaze. "I let him in."

He turned his gaze back to the sea.

"Ain't nothin' good happen to me all my life," he said. "I was poor in Mozambique and I been poor here. That's a hard weight to carry, and I had to carry it on my own after my sweet wife, Natalia, died. She was my anchor, and now I'm cut adrift on Satan's sea of sin."

He flicked flies away from the seeping wound on his leg.

"Yes, I was thinkin' of treasure," he admitted. "I figure I have me some nice 'tings in this life before I join Natalia, you know?"

"You can't read the notations in that journal, can you?" Cordero said.

The man squinted down at the bag to his side.

"Can read the site codes," he answered. "That's all I need."

"Evans can read the rest," said Cordero. "But you didn't ask him about them, did you? Do you know what kind of treasure Professor Frankston found?"

Welcome glanced sideways at Cordero, his face drained of expression.

"Coral," Cordero said. "It was a unique type of coral he'd found. Or rather the algae within it. That to him was treasure. It had nothing to do with shipwrecks and bullion."

The African tightened his jaw and turned away.

"I'm not lying to you, Welcome," Cordero said. "Not like you've lied most of your life. You lied to Evans about why the

Portuguese imprisoned you here. You lied to join the Assembly of God church in order to gain the confidence of women. You lied about your movements on the night of Frankston's death. Lying has become a way of life for you."

The man nodded and lowered his head.

"See this rooster here," he said and extended a hand toward the concrete form at the feet of the statue. "That's because San Pedro betray Jesus three times. It should be me there. I betray him more than three times."

He tried to straighten his injured leg.

"Is Mister Evans okay?" he asked. "I don't mean him no harm. Satan just took me over for a second and I reach out and hit him. Hit him out cold, brother. I check him and he seem alright. So I left him there, took the keys to his jeep, the journal, and here I am. Is he okay?"

"He'll live," said Cordero. "Why did you kill Professor Frankston? Was that to get the journal and go after what you thought was the treasure?"

The African stared at Cordero, the whites of his eyes large with indignation.

"We all brothers," he said. "No mark of Cain on me. I never kill nobody!"

"Like I said, you lied about where you were the night he was killed. Why do you expect me to believe you now?" Cordero demanded.

"Because I ain't lyin' now! Sweet God Almighty!"

"You lied about him not paying for your damaged boat," said Cordero. "I'm not sure you've told me one true thing the whole time we've talked."

"I lie about the boat engine 'cause I need to keep the treasure secret," said Welcome. "If you knew what we arguin' about, the treasure was a secret no more."

"And what *did* you argue about?"

"That night I heard him comin' up the road. He was whistlin', you know? He always whistlin' when he was happy with what he found out on the reef. So I went to ask him why he was so happy.

He said, 'I found it, Welcome!' like that, you know? I ask him what he found. He said I have to wait until he wrote about it. I thought he must be talkin' about the treasure that Mister Evans had told me about."

He brushed a hand across his head.

"So I say, 'If you write about it, everyone will know'! He just laugh. I said I get a boat from someone and we go and bring it up from the reef next day. He laugh again and say 'I'm goin' leave it right where 'tis, Welcome. Right where 'tis'!"

"And so you took the knife from his belt and stabbed him," Cordero suggested.

"No!" Welcome objected. "I go to my woman and he go whistlin' along. Do I look like a killer to you? I done a lot of bad 'tings, brother, but even San Pedro here guilty of that. I never kill no one!"

"We've found the knife, Welcome. It won't be hard to trace it to you."

Welcome settled down. He showed no signs that news of the discovery of the knife surprised or concerned him.

"Ain't no tracin' to me, brother, 'cos I ain't never touch no knife. As God in heaven is my judge I'm tellin' you the truth."

Cordero checked with Carter. She raised her eyebrows but said nothing.

"What were you planning to do if you had found sunken treasure out there?" he asked Welcome.

The man raised his shoulders.

"Go the other side of the island and hide a while maybe. There's parts there no one goes. Not Portuguese, not Indonesians, not Timorese police. Wild folk there, you know?"

He glanced off to the side.

"Or maybe I go to Indonesia dependin' on what I was able to bring up from the coral and how much fuel the boat have. Maybe make Alor," he said, referring to a nearby Indonesian island. "But I not thinkin' bout that too much. Like I say, Satan guidin' me and Satan don't always tell you his whole plan."

Cordero watched the turbid water swirling close to the beach.

"Tide's going out," he said. "The fishing boats will return soon and we can take one to Vila after they've unloaded the catch. You're coming with us, Welcome. But first let's check that injury to your leg."

29

They took Welcome Jesus to the health clinic in Vila for a quick check on his injured leg and, following that, to the police station. They returned to the lodge to change out of the damp, spoilt clothes. Carter ran into Miller as they came through the entrance. He was flushed and edgy.

"I need to tell you something, ma'am," he said.

"Not now, Gerard. I'm soaked through," she said and strode past him.

"But ma'am, I mean Agent Carter," Miller spluttered. "It's about Mrs Frankston."

Carter swung on her heel.

"You're going to tell me you've been to see her," she reproached him. "Straight after we'd had that talk earlier. I can't believe you, Gerard!"

"No, ma'am," he said. "I went to my hut after our talk and stayed there for hours. Thinking over what you'd said. I went to see her but only just now. I've just come back."

"I can't fathom you, Gerard. I told you—"

"She's gone!"

"What?"

"She's gone to Dili, ma'am."

"She's what!"

"I told her that you and Mister Cordero had walked to Maquili to pick up the African for the murder of her husband," Miller began. "You should have seen her face light up when I told her that. She seemed to think it meant she could go now. To Dili, I mean. She's booked a water taxi from the resort hotel in Beloi. I couldn't stop her. I'm not a police officer. I've no authority. She left ten minutes ago in a *tuk-tuk*."

"Shit! One of these days you'll learn to keep your mouth shut, Gerard," Carter said. "Cordero!" she yelled.

She'd relayed a shorter version of Miller's information. Cordero called the hotel resort and the maritime police in Beloi and put a stop to the water taxi leaving the wharf. He told Carter he'd go after Mrs Frankston himself as soon as he'd changed into dry clothes.

Carter wasn't paying him her full attention, chewing a fingernail while he spoke.

"What? Oh, okay," she said.

Cordero hurried off to his hut to change.

"I'm going to do some more checking up on her while you're gone," Carter called after him. She turned to Miller. "Something's been bothering me, Gerard," she said. "How would you like to do something right for a change?"

"Yes, ma'am, I would."

"Get in touch with the Embassy. I *do not* mean Taylor! Get onto one of your smart colleagues. Maybe Davidson, the cultural attaché. I want all he can dig up on Susanna Sheridan's time at the University of California, Berkeley. Okay? Every little thing. And I want it within the next hour and a half. After I change, I'm going to the health clinic. I'll be thirty minutes."

She took off as Miller reached for his cell.

"Oh, and one other thing, Gerard," she said over her shoulder.

"Yes, ma'am?"

"For Pete's Sake stop calling me ma'am!"

• • •

"She didn't answer my questions on the way back," said Cordero. "In fact, she didn't say a thing. She just sat there with her arms folded and sulked."

He'd called Carter and told her to meet him at the police station. He'd gone out front to walk her in while Sergeant Amparo kept Mrs Frankston company.

"Well maybe she'll talk now," Carter said, opening the door.

Amparo was behind his desk, flipping a pencil over to amuse himself. Mrs Frankston sat in the middle of the room, a scowl on her face. Cordero pulled up a chair in front of her. Carter sidled to the wall behind Amparo's desk and leaned a shoulder against it.

"I'll ask you once more, Mrs Frankston," Cordero said. "Why did you run?"

"I didn't run, you silly man. I told that Embassy official what I was doing. That's hardly running. You weren't here to tell. You'd gone after the African for killing my husband. So as far as I was concerned, the case was closed and I was free to go."

She tightened her arms across her chest, crossed her legs, and began to jiggle a foot.

"That's not your call to make, Mrs. Frankston," Cordero said.

She shrugged.

"You've been cooperative up to this point," Cordero said. "But you must realize that leaving for Dili without permission does raise suspicions."

"As I said, Mister Cordero, you weren't here to ask permission from," she countered.

Carter pushed herself off the wall, put a hand to Cordero's shoulder, and came around to stand face on to Mrs. Frankston.

"How well do you know the cadet police officer, Sisko?" she asked.

Cordero glanced at Carter.

"Who? Oh, you mean that young policeman." Mrs. Frankston waved a hand. "Hank asked the sergeant here for someone to keep an eye on the place while he was out on the reef. I told you that before. He didn't want anyone disturbing his specimens or his diving gear or the data he'd collected. That young man came around from time to time, but I didn't have much to do with him."

"If you didn't have much to do with him, why was he seen leaving your house the morning your husband's journal was stolen?"

Mrs Frankston shook her head and jiggled the foot more vigorously.

"Remember Evans saying a young man had left the house just as he was arriving to retrieve the journal?" Carter said, inclining her head toward Cordero. "We assumed that was Miller. I went and checked. I asked Evans if he could describe the man he saw. He laughed and said that wasn't hard since he was dressed in a police uniform."

She glared at Mrs Frankston.

"Well? Why was he in your house?"

"He'd come to see if I was okay. That's all. What's wrong with that?"

"What's wrong with that is you didn't bother to tell us when you reported the journal missing."

"I said I'd gone out for a walk. And I had."

"Yes, but that's all you told us. Why didn't you mention Sisko's visit?" Carter pressed her.

Mrs Frankston adjusted herself in her chair to show her annoyance at the questioning.

"Am I on trial here?" she demanded to know.

"We're merely asking questions as part of our investigations," Cordero said to reassure her.

"Doesn't sound like that to me!" she snapped.

"I've been doing a little more checking up on you, Mrs Frankston," Carter continued.

"Well good for you, Agent Carter."

"I believe that during your time at UCLA you got involved with a dramatic society. So involved, in fact, that you spent most waking hours with actors and directors."

She took a sheet of paper from her pocket.

"Let's see now. You played a minor role in *Death of a Salesman* in your second year and the character Stella Kowalski in *A Streetcar Named Desire* in your third year. That's quite a leap. Kowalski was a key role. You must have been good. You certainly received favourable reviews. Very favourable, in fact. One reviewer called you a…how did he put it?…'rare instinctive' actress."

Carter lowered the sheet.

"How's that relevant?" asked Mrs Frankston. "What are you implying?"

"That maybe you've been acting the whole time. Maybe you've been playing the grieving widow for Investigator Cordero's benefit, the lonely, bored but dutiful wife for mine, a vulnerable innocent when it came to Gerard Miller, and the vamp, perhaps, when it came to Sisko."

Mrs Frankston jumped to her feet.

"Really! That's absurd and offensive! You can rest assured Agent Carter that I will lodge a complaint against you with the Embassy when I get to Dili."

"Are you now acting the injured party?" Carter said ignoring the outburst.

Cordero rose and prodded Carter to move aside.

"Let me apologise for my colleague, Mrs Frankston," he said. "Rest assured the Timorese police are not questioning your character or your behaviour. We only ask that you remain here, in Vila, until we have completed our investigation as we have requested all along. If you'll allow me, I'll drive you to your house."

"Don't bother!" said Mrs Frankston, picking up her overnight bag and making for the door. "I'll walk!"

Carter moved to the door of the police station and watched Mrs Frankston storm out to the front of the compound and off down the road. Cordero asked Amparo to take the fingerprints of Welcome Jesus and get them and the knife to Dili for checking as soon as possible. Sisko had not yet returned from the mayhem on the road to Maquili and so the sergeant would have to take the items to the maritime police in Beloi himself. Cordero left the keys to the utility with him and joined Carter to walk to the lodge.

"That was dramatic," he said.

"She's the drama queen, not me," Carter replied.

"I thought you told me you believed her," he said.

"I told you I was *starting* to believe her. I never said I made it all the way."

"What started you digging into her past at university?"

"The day I looked through her husband's study? There was a photograph of her on his desk. On the bottom of the frame was a sock and buskin."

"A what?"

"Sock and buskin. You know—the laughing mask and the crying mask that symbolize theatre. Well, they weren't there to represent him. He was a marine biologist. So they had to be there to represent her. Liberal arts student remember? That's what you study when you're not really studying anything. So maybe the sock and buskin represented a sideline she got involved with. It nagged me."

"But what prompted you to act on the nagging?"

"It was an accumulation of things Miller had said. Remember when he brought her to the health clinic to see off her husband's body? He mentioned how devastated she looked. When I took him to task over the knife he'd planted, he said he was trying to help because she appeared so exposed and defenceless. And when he told her about us going off to Maquili, he said I should have seen her face light up."

"Okay. So?"

"'Light up'. Those were Miller's very words," she said. "Like on a stage, you know?"

He frowned as though not entirely convinced by her reasoning.

"You and I are trained to look through appearances to motives and facts, Cordero," she said. "People like Miller aren't. What if they were all performances on Mrs Frankston's part? What if she was acting the whole time?"

He lifted his eyes off the road and looked ahead.

"So you think she put Sisko up to it?" he asked.

"I don't know," Carter said. "She might have done it herself but played him to get rid of the knife or lay a trail of evidence to Evans or the African. Who's to say? I just know there's more to her than she's let on."

"If Sisko is involved, it's going to be hard to prove," Cordero said.

"I know," Carter agreed. "But there's one place we can start."

"Where's that?"

"Let me call Estefana and I'll tell you."

• • •

The widow Lazara was hanging out washing as they approached her hut. Estefana had told Carter where she lived, and they had made a detour to visit her. Cordero introduced himself and Carter and said he just had a few questions to ask and none of them concerned the African.

"Well, what do you want to know this time?" the woman asked, continuing to wring wet clothes from a bucket.

What Cordero wanted to know was more correctly a question Carter wanted answered.

"Earlier today," Cordero began after Carter's prompting, "I asked Sergeant Amparo to send his cadet over this way to look along the track from the road to your house for a knife."

Mana Lazara stopped her wringing and puffed herself up.

"You chasing me now?" she said and looked ready to hit Cordero with a wet scrunched up T-shirt.

"No, not at all," said Cordero, trying to sound reasonable. "I just want to know if you happened to notice the cadet. He's name's Sisko. He rides a police motorcycle."

The woman lowered the wet bundle and scrutinized Cordero and after him Carter. She lifted the T-shirt and twisted it as hard as she could.

"I know him and I seen him," she said finally. "Why you asking me about him?"

"Was he searching the area?" Cordero asked.

She brushed aside the suggestion with a wave of the T-shirt.

"Him?" she huffed. "He didn't search nothing, nowhere. He parked his motorcycle down by that palm tree, leaned on it some in the shade, and rode away."

"How long would you say he was there?"

"I keep telling you police officers I don't have no watch." She threw the T-shirt over a bush to dry and picked up another article of clothing to wring. "He was there about as long as it takes to boil water!"

Cordero thanked the woman and they set off for the lodge.

"And that tells you what exactly?" Cordero asked. "Beside the fact that he's a lazy cadet which I could've told you."

"It *suggests* to me," Carter corrected him, "that he didn't look for the knife because he knew where it was all along."

30

Carter sat hunched over a mineral water while Cordero paced the yard by the dining area on a call to Amparo.

"Okay, thanks," he said. "Don't tell him where you've gone or why. Just tell him you need him to keep an eye on Antonio Gomes and the African until you're back." He ended the call. "We're in luck," he said resuming his seat. "Amparo hasn't left yet. He found something Sisko always handles and he'll take that off to be tested for prints as well." He poured some of the water into his own glass.

"Wouldn't his prints have been taken when he joined the police?" she asked.

"This is Timor," he said. "If they were—and that's a big 'if'—retrieving them could take days, weeks even."

He drank a little.

"Sisko went off to look into the collapsed bridge *before* Estefana brought the knife in to the police station," he said. "He hasn't been told about her finding it. So as far as he's concerned the murder weapon hasn't been located."

He finished the water in his glass.

"It could still be the African, you know," Carter said. "Or Evans."

"I know. But the African's in custody and Evans is in no condition to leave the health clinic just yet," Cordero replied. "If Sisko is involved, he's out and about and he could take off anywhere."

"If he killed Frankston, he could have wiped his prints from the knife," Carter pointed out. "He is a trainee cop, after all."

"I know that too. But he's only *in training*. And the type of training he's done so far in community policing doesn't place much emphasis on that sort of thing."

He studied her expression.

"Something tells me you're working on a plan," he said. "I know you always come up with a plan."

Her smile said she took a good deal of satisfaction from that remark.

"If Mrs Frankston put him up to it, she's not going to admit it," she said. "So we can't rely on her cooperation and she's probably too smart to implicate herself. He likes Estefana. I noticed how he was looking at her when we were hanging out the washing the other day. So, if Estefana agrees, I'll coach her into what to say and we'll send her over to have a friendly chat to him. That's step number one."

"Step two?"

"Let's not get ahead of ourselves," she said. "Let's see what step number one throws up first."

Cordero frowned.

"If Sisko is our man, whatever you've got in mind could be dangerous for Estefana," he said.

"I've talked to you about police officers and danger," Carter said. "Estefana is a police officer. And a capable one. She'll be fine."

He stood to leave.

"Okay," he said. "I'll relieve her at the health clinic. I hope you know what you're doing."

With that he was gone.

"So do I," said Carter to herself.

• • •

"*Mana!*" Sisko said. "What are you doing here?"

Estefana was sitting in the chair usually occupied by Sergeant Amparo when Sisko returned from the bridge collapse. She was flicking through one of the sergeant's magazines, trying her best to appear interested in the contents.

"The sergeant had to go out somewhere but he didn't say where," she lied. "Said it could take a while. My colleagues are resting after they walked to Maquili so I was told to come here and keep an eye on the two prisoners until you showed up."

"They brought the African back?" Sisko asked, placing his helmet on the sergeant's desk.

"Yeah," she said.

"Well it's great to see you," Sisko said and pulled up a chair alongside her. "I was out on a big job on the road to Maquili. There'd been so much rain it washed away a bridge. The jeep the African took had crashed into a ravine and motorcyclists had slid off the side of the road too. Lots injured." He puffed up. "But I sorted it out."

Estefana creased her brow. She lowered her eyes and took a deep breath.

"Is there something wrong, *mana*?" Sisko asked. "Maybe I can help."

"I haven't helped in the murder investigation at all," she said. "That investigator, Cordero, isn't impressed." She swept an imaginary hair behind her ear and stared straight at him. "All he has me doing is watching suspects and running errands. I'm worried when he gets to Dili his report will damage my career."

She shrugged and leaned forward.

"That's why I've been unhappy since I arrived here," she added.

"But I thought you worked for the American," he said.

"She doesn't think much of what I do either. I'm supposed to translate for her but Cordero speaks English and ever since we came to Atauro she's just ignored me."

"I never did like her," Sisko said and jumped up to rummage through a drawer under the desk. "I'll make some coffee."

"I heard them talking earlier," Estefana said. "They said once they find the knife used to kill the American they'll conclude the investigation and return to Dili."

"Conclude the investigation?" he repeated.

"Yeah," she said. "They've got enough on the African to charge him but need a murder weapon to satisfy the prosecutor in Dili."

Sisko stopped what he was doing and thought about what that could mean. If this young police woman found the knife rather than him, there'd be no suspicion attached to its recovery. He could wipe the knife of prints, the African would be taken for trial in Dili, and he could put this whole mess behind him and get on with his life.

"I wish I knew where that knife was," Estefana was saying. "If I found it they'd have to take me seriously. They'd have to say I was a good police officer."

Sisko spun around.

"Maybe I could help you look for the knife," he said.

"What do you mean?" asked Estefana.

"I searched that area where the American was killed," he said. "I know it." He leaned forward and whispered. "I know where I didn't look too, you know, when I got bored and gave up searching." He straightened. "We could go now."

"I don't know," she said doubtfully.

"What's there to know?" he asked.

She twisted her bottom lip and took one end between her teeth.

"You think we'd find it?"

"No harm in trying," he said.

"What about the two out back?" Estefana asked.

"What about them? They're not going anywhere. The key's here on the wall."

"Wait a minute," Estefana said. "If you help me, and if we do find something, what do you expect from me? I'm married you know!"

"*Mana!*" Sisko said and spread his arms. "I don't know what you're thinking but I'm not like that. I don't want anything. I'd be happy to know I helped you."

Estefana feigned a weakening resolve.

"You really think we'd find the knife?" she asked.

"Who knows?" Sisko said. "But if we don't, it hasn't cost us anything. Come on. We'll take my motorcycle."

"I don't know," said Estefana, stalling.

"Come on," encouraged Sisko. "You don't want that police investigator thinking you're useless. Come on. Let's go. I know you're a smart girl. Let's see if we can show him just how smart you are."

• • •

Sisko pulled the motorcycle up at the spot where Frankston's body had been found in a ditch on the side of the road.

"I searched up and down this road, *mana*," he said, lifting the helmet from his head.

"But you know what? I didn't search the cemetery down there. I figured no one would want to go where the dead are buried to get rid of a knife and I sure wasn't going in either." He slipped off the bike. "But someone might have thrown it in."

He helped her dismount.

"Let's go look."

Estefana was nervous about going into the cemetery. She imagined the spirits of the dead would be angry that she had begun, but not finished, the ritual the *matan-dook* had suggested she undertake and was now back deceiving again. But she'd come this far with Sisko and to pull out now could invite a more immediate danger.

She followed him up the road, arms hanging slack by her sides. He stopped at the gate.

"If someone tossed a knife in here from the road it'd be over by that south wall," he said, pointing with the helmet in his hand. "It couldn't have been thrown further. Follow me."

They threaded their way through the rows of headstones and graves.

"Here," Sisko said less than twenty yards from the wall. "Start looking around here."

Estefana reluctantly played the game. She noticed Sisko was spending more time looking at the general area around the cemetery or gazing at her figure than he did examining his own chosen area to search.

"Let's get closer to the wall," he said after a few minutes. "You look around that big grave there. The white one with that funny church steeple. I'll concentrate on these other graves."

Estefana retraced her steps from the earlier visit. Keeping her fear in check, she circled the grave, rummaging through the broken concrete on its border.

"Nothing here," she called.

"You sure?" Sisko asked.

"Yeah," she replied. "You find anything?"

"Nah. Let me have a look."

He came over and scanned the opposite side of the grave to the one where he had hidden the knife. He straightened and stretched.

"Hard work, huh?" he said and smiled.

He wandered around to the other side of the grave and began raking the broken concrete more carefully. He stopped where she'd found the knife and took to one knee. He felt around, prodding under a split layer of concrete.

"Anything?" she asked.

He didn't reply.

He prodded again, more frantically now.

"You find something?" Estefana asked again.

Suddenly he was on his feet.

"What's the matter?"

"This is stupid," he said, his tone suggesting he was irritated to the point of anger. "We're never going to find anything here. You were crazy to make me think we could."

"I didn't—"

"Let me think," he barked at her.

He rested on the wall of the cemetery for a minute.

"If we don't find anything they'll send me off to the health clinic to guard that stupid *malae*," Estefana said, careful to stay in role. "Let's keep looking. What's the matter with you?"

"Nothing," he grumbled. "This is bullshit. Come on. Let's go."

With that he stormed off and left her having to run to keep up.

31

Cordero closed his cell and returned to the table Carter occupied.

"Amparo said the maritime police boat just left. That means the prints should be checked this evening. If the knife wasn't wiped, we'll know soon enough if either the African or the cadet is our man."

Estefana had rejoined them and given an account of Sisko's behaviour at the cemetery and his reaction when he discovered that the knife wasn't where it should have been. That confirmed their suspicions, but it didn't clarify Sisko's part in Frankston's killing and wasn't enough hard evidence to prove anything if it had.

"You did a great job, Estefana," Cordero told her.

He'd told Amparo what Estefana had said and asked him to find a way of keeping Sisko busy until morning.

"Did Amparo confirm that Sisko's still in the dark about the knife being found?" Carter asked.

"Yeah," Cordero said. "So what's the second part of your plan?"

"Sisko may think someone's come by, seen the knife, and taken it home," Carter said. "Or maybe someone found it and is holding on to it until they get a chance to hand it in. Either way he'd be thinking of locals who live there, pass through, or visit the cemetery."

"Okay, so?"

"Call Amparo again," she said. "Tell him to have Sisko leave the keys to the motorcycle at the police station tomorrow morning. He can say he'll be out most of the day with the utility and you need the bike. Tell Amparo to make himself scarce tomorrow. Sisko's job is to stay and guard the African and Antonio Gomes."

Cordero frowned as though yet to see where this was going.

"That means Sisko's on foot," Carter said. "He won't get too far if he tries to run. But let's see what he does when the sergeant isn't there to keep an eye on him."

"That's it?" asked Cordero. "That's your plan?"

"It's part two," said Carter. "The plan is a work in progress."

Cordero tried to conceal his doubts about this whole approach. He wasn't having much success and it showed.

"You got a better idea?" Carter tilted her head and asked him.

"Well I want to be a little less passive than that," he said. "I'll go early tomorrow morning to the area around the cemetery. I want to know how the *matan-dook* knew to direct Estefana to find the knife. If I'm in the area I can also keep an eye out for Sisko if he leaves the police station to go door-to-door for anyone who happened to find a knife. We'll keep Estefana at the health clinic with Evans. If Sisko thinks she's double-crossed him, he's unlikely to try anything given the presence of staff there."

He adopted his best appealing face.

"I'd sure like to know what Mrs Frankston has to say about her relationship with Sisko," he said and raised an eyebrow.

Carter grinned.

"I'm ahead of you on that," she said.

• • •

The *matan-dook* was working something on the gas burner as Cordero approached the hut.

"Coffee?" the man said. "I heard you coming." Cordero looked around behind him. "No one approaches my hut this early," the old man explained. "They're either tending their gardens or walking away from here and into the village."

He pointed Cordero to a chair and poured two cups of black coffee. He handed one cup to Cordero, picked up the second, and sat himself.

"You have more questions?" he asked.

"Yeah. Do you have any sugar?" Cordero asked, trying to keep it casual.

"No," was the answer.

It was the following morning, just on sunrise.

Cordero tried the coffee. It was strong and far better than what they served in the lodge even without the addition of sugar.

"I hear you arrested the African," the man said.

"Yeah," Cordero replied. "The crazy one you said talks a lot and knows nothing."

The old man smothered a laugh.

"It's all that Jesus talk he does. Doesn't stop him doing what he wants." He scratched his head. "I don't understand that stuff. Those Assembly people say their god made them so they can do good or do bad. So why do they get upset when people do bad?"

"They say it comes down to free will," explained Cordero. "Good is good and bad is bad. The choice is yours. How you choose is how you're judged. It's up to you."

"Makes no sense to me," said the man. "Why punish people if they choose an option their god put before them?"

"You feel the same about Catholics?" Cordero asked.

"They say a Catholic can go to the priest and say, 'I did wrong' and he says 'Okay, don't do it again'. They say if you are a Catholic you can do that as many times as you want. So, choosing bad is just part of life. Makes more sense to me." He sipped his coffee. "But not a whole lot more."

Cordero wriggled in his seat.

"How did you know where the knife was planted?" he asked. "You're not going to tell me the spirits told you."

The *matan-dook* smiled.

"I told you. I move around at night. I'm quiet. It's a skill. No one hears or sees me."

"If you saw someone plant the knife, you must have seen who it was," said Cordero.

The old man shook his head.

"I didn't know it was a knife," he said. "It was dark. I saw a shape bent over trying to conceal something. I knew because of the way the head turned left and right as though checking no one was there. I couldn't make out who it was."

"But it struck you as odd?"

"I didn't think any more of it. I hadn't seen any fighting, and I didn't see any body. So, I didn't take much notice—just thought it strange that someone would be in the cemetery like that at that time of night."

He drank more of his coffee.

"When I heard the next day that the American had been killed out there," the man continued, "I figured whoever I saw must have been involved and that whatever they were trying to conceal had something to do with it."

"It was a man you saw?" Cordero asked.

The old man shrugged.

"Or a woman who wore pants," he said. "Many do these days, you know."

"Could it have been the African?"

"No. He's a big man. The figure I saw was smaller."

"Why didn't you come forward with this information earlier?" Cordero asked.

The man lifted his head, blinked, and pursed his lips.

"The American was not one of us. I wasn't responsible for him like I am for my own people."

Cordero decided not to argue the point.

"So why did you tell my young female officer to look there?" he asked.

"She is Timorese. And she was in distress," he said and drained the last of his coffee. "The American was dead. There was nothing I could do for him."

Cordero also finished his coffee, placed the cup on the nearby bench, and brushed his clothes.

"Was the idea of the ritual simply an excuse to direct her to the knife?" he asked.

"You have spent too long among foreigners, *senyor*," the man said. "They always look for one simple cause for all things. Why does water flow down? Gravity, they say. Why do trees grow up?

Sunlight. They never allow that these things might make their own choices. If you ask a foreigner why the water flows here, in this particular place and not there, or why a tree grows the way it does and not some other way they'll tell you it comes down to chance. That's not an explanation. It's an excuse."

He smiled, tossed out the dregs of his coffee, and collected the empty cups.

"Our ancestors knew that things are much more complex, that people, animals, and plants all have their inner selves, that the world we can see and the world that is closed to us are connected. You and I and that coffee you just drank are all connected. The living and the dead are two expressions of the one existence."

He stood to go back inside his hut.

"That girl's problems are in her own thinking. The only solution for her must conform to that thinking. Anything else, like the suggestions of foreigners or people like you who think like a foreigner, she will reject. She fears the danger is great so she'd expect anything that might counter it must also be great. That's why I told her to offer her necklace to the spirits: it seemed to be of great value to her. The ritual I told her to perform is important to put an end to what troubles her. It is part of who she is whether she knows it or not. But where the ritual took place is of no consequence and so its location, even its form, could serve other purposes."

• • •

Carter put her forearm on the frame of the open door to the house the Frankstons had rented and peered in. Mrs Frankston was sitting at the table, staring into a cup of coffee steaming in between her hands.

"We know your boyfriend killed your husband," Carter said. "Or covered up the killing for you. I'm here to find out which it is."

"He's not my boyfriend," Mrs Frankston said without looking up.

Carter strode into the room and leaned over the table in front of the woman.

"Well, the two of you were up to something and you're about to tell me what it was," she said, in a cold, flat tone. "I'm not on this island in any official police capacity so if you don't talk or, if you do and start lying and acting a part, I'll come over this table and cause you some serious harm. You understand me?"

"You don't have to threaten me," Mrs Frankston said calmly. "You saw through me. You made me realise how appalling I've been. To everyone. I've been thinking about that since I left the police station."

She lifted her eyes.

"I'm ashamed of myself."

Carter pulled a chair out from under the table and sat, leaning in on her forearms.

"So, tell me about you and Sisko," she said. "I don't have a lot of time."

Mrs Frankston took a gulp of coffee, held it in her mouth, and swallowed.

"He started coming around after Hank asked the police to check on the place, as I've said. He spoke English. Not well but well enough. Sounded like he'd picked it up from tourists."

Her hands left the cup, and she sat back.

"He was funny, and I didn't have much company, so we started impromptu language lessons. I'd spend ten minutes on his English. He'd spend ten minutes on my Tetun. It was all very innocent."

She smiled at the memory.

"But as Hank neglected me more and more in favour of his damn corals, I grew bored, lonely, frustrated, as I told you." She looked Carter in the eyes. "I wasn't lying or playing a part when I told you all about that. You must believe me."

A fly landed on the table between them and Mrs Frankston brushed it away.

"So, I started to think that if I could make Hank jealous, maybe he'd take more notice of me. I started to give the young officer a bit more…encouragement. It never went too far, you understand. I'd just touch his hand if he could pronounce a difficult word or grab him playfully by the shoulders and shake him if he made a mistake. I thought if he was relaxed and familiar in my company Hank would notice. You know?"

The fly returned. This time she ignored it.

"But he started getting the wrong idea. Started taking things too far—small things at first like patting me on the shoulder but soon he'd put his arms around me and pull me into him. I'd already started thinking about flying to Dili and leaving Hank here. The way Sisko was behaving only added to my sense of urgency to go."

Her eyes were teary now.

"But I had no idea he'd kill Hank. Honest. I started to think that he might have had something to do with it after he left here yesterday but, believe me, whatever he did had nothing to do with me."

"Why did he come here the other day and what did you talk about?" Carter asked.

"He came by for no reason," Mrs. Frankston said. "I was sorting through some paperwork. He wasn't making much sense. He kept telling me what a beautiful woman I was, how much he longed to be with me. He tried to grab hold of me several times and I pushed him away. I was scared. Trust me I was scared! He can get angry for no reason and, I don't know, sort of turn somehow. I told him my husband had just been killed and he was being totally inappropriate. He just looked at me and grinned. 'I told you I'd take care of everything', he said. I told him to go or I'd start screaming and he left. When he was gone I went for my walk to calm down."

Carter fixed her with a skeptical eye.

"You're asking me to believe you, to trust you're telling me the truth now. Why should I, especially after you tried to run away?" she said.

"I wasn't *running*," she insisted. "I was *going*. That's all. Like I said at the police station, if I was running why would I have told Gerard what I'd arranged to do? Why would I be here now? My door's not locked and there's no one standing guard outside."

She reached across to Carter.

"I did play up to Sisko and look what's happened. I played up to Gerard in the hope he could help me get out of here but that only made me a suspect in my own husband's murder. I'm through play acting and I'm through telling lies. You've reason to doubt me and I don't know what else I can do to make you believe me. But I didn't have anything to do with Hank's death and that's the honest-to-God truth."

"Why didn't you tell us any of this before now?" Carter asked.

A tear ran down Mrs. Frankston's face.

"Because of Hank," she said. "Like I said, I felt ashamed. I'd betrayed him. And that led to his death."

• • •

Cordero lurked around the houses and huts near the cemetery trying to appear inconspicuous as the sun rose higher in the eastern sky and the day warmed up. Other than a few people making their way into the village center the only other signs of life were chickens and a few stray goats. There was no sign of Sisko and after two hours of waiting and watching Cordero was ready to give up and go back.

Sisko had been told to sleep in the police station because of the need to keep watch over the African and the youth being held there. It had been a restless sleep. Amparo had found a reason to leave him alone again this morning, and the cadet was drinking strong coffee at the sergeant's desk. He was trying to figure out where the knife had gone and what its disappearance meant for him.

This all began with that woman, he said to himself. *That bitch*!

His thoughts were interrupted when a cell suddenly come to life. He shifted some papers on Amparo's desk and found the sergeant's cell underneath. Amparo must have left it there when he'd driven off in a hurry. Sisko checked the caller ID. He didn't recognize the name.

"*Bondia*," he said into the cell. "Cadet officer Sisko Ketakura here."

"Is Sergeant Amparo there?" the voice on the other end asked.

"No. Here's just left the police station on a job," Sisko said. "He left his cell here. Can I help?"

"I'm Officer Correia from police headquarters in Dili," the caller said.

"Yes?" Sisko replied.

"I have the results of the prints Sergeant Amparo asked for."

"Prints?" said Sisko. "What prints?"

"The ones on the items he sent over yesterday."

Sisko's head started spinning.

"Hello? Are you still there?" Correia asked.

"Yes, sorry. Go ahead," Sisko said.

"The prints on the knife match the prints on the mug," Correia said. "There's no match with the prints on the fingerprint card."

"You're talking about the knife used to kill the American over here?" Sisko asked, straightening in the chair.

"I don't know what it was used for I'm only telling you the results," Correia said. "But how many blood-stained knives has your sergeant sent over?"

Sisko ignored the question.

"You said the mug," he repeated. "What mug?"

"The one with the Real Madrid emblem," Correia said.

"Just a minute," Sisko said.

He hurried over to his own desk, scattered the piles of papers on it and shifted the radio to one side. There was no sign of his coffee mug.

"Are you there?" Correia was asking.

"Yeah," said Sisko absently. Through the window he could see Amparo pulling up in the police utility. "Yeah. Okay, I'll let him know. Thanks," he said and ended the call.

• • •

"Bastard locked me in the washroom when I came back to the station!" Amparo was shouting into his cell. "Just managed to break out. He let Antonio and the African out. Antonio's nowhere to be seen. The African must have taken some prodding because I heard Sisko yelling at him to get out and run. He's taken my vehicle and the keys to his motorcycle. I've no idea where he's gone!"

Before Cordero could answer he noticed another call coming in.

"Hold on a minute," he told Amparo.

The second caller was Carter.

"I was just entering the gates of the lodge when I was almost run over by that police utility. He's taken her!"

"What? Who?"

"Mrs Frankston! Sisko was driving! Like a madman! He must have pulled up at her house just after I left. She wouldn't have gone willingly. He's grabbed her, Cordero!"

"Which way was he going?" he asked.

"North, out of Vila," Carter said.

Cordero said to meet him at the police station and ended the call.

"I'm coming now!" he told Amparo and ended that call as well.

32

Cordero was running to the police station when he noticed Welcome Jesus sitting under a jackfruit tree, its bulbous egg-shaped fruit dangling precariously above his head. The man smiled as Cordero approached.

"What are you doing here, *maun*?" Cordero asked and stopped.

"That young officer kick me and the boy out of that place, brother," he said. "I 'tink he gone crazy. I hear someone shoutin' in the washroom. The sergeant maybe. That young officer's tryin' to cause problems around here, I 'tink."

"So why are you just sitting here?"

"I figure I'm in enough trouble as 'tings stand, my brother," said Welcome. "I don't want to be no fugitive. I know how well you track folks down."

Cordero caught his breath.

"Okay," he said. "Come with me to the station now. I'll tell Sergeant Amparo it was none of your fault."

"Yes, brother and thank you, brother," said Welcome rising to his feet. "Like that blessed apostle on the road to Damascus, I seen the Lord's blazin' light, you bet!"

• • •

As he entered the yard of the police station, Cordero caught sight of Carter yanking open the front door and disappearing inside. He stormed in a few seconds later. Amparo stood unsteadily at the front of his desk, taking the weight off his injured ankle. Carter was already pacing the room, her chin cupped in one hand.

"Any idea where Sisko's heading?" Cordero asked Amparo.

Amparo staggered over to the map on the wall. Every time the foot below his injured ankle touched the floor he grimaced. It was clear that he'd re-injured himself trying to break out of the washroom Sisko had locked him in.

"Aren't many roads on Atauro," Amparo said. "The one to Maquili is blocked by that bridge collapse. There's the main one up north to Biqueli but you need to go through Beloi to get there. I called the maritime police in Beloi and they're keeping an eye out for him. There's a road west that forks on the other side of the island. South is Anartuto and Atekru on the coast. I've called the officer in Anartuto and told him to keep watch at the crossroad. North is Arlo but the storms washed part of that road away and it's impassable. Sisko and I were talking about it only yesterday."

He adjusted his stance as Cordero and Carter crowded around him to view the map. The African, who had followed Cordero into the police station, raised himself on tiptoe behind them to look over their shoulders.

"You learn anything new from Mrs Frankston this morning?" Cordero asked turning to Carter.

"Only that she teased him to try and make her husband jealous and Sisko took it the wrong way. I think her abduction confirms she was telling the truth."

Cordero nodded.

"What about this road?" he asked Amparo and pointed.

"That goes to Mount Manucoco," said Amparo. "About halfway up, at least. Beyond that it's a track. I don't know why he'd go there although I think he does have some kin up that way. Mentioned something about it once or twice. I didn't take much notice."

"That a hard road to be travelin', brother," said the African from behind them. "I seen the mud washin' down from that road on visits to some church ladies out that way. Hard road to travel is what I say."

Without looking at Welcome, Amparo nodded his agreement.

"Okay. That'll slow him down quite a bit," said Cordero. "Any chance he's armed?" he asked Amparo.

"We don't arm cadets, and nothing's been taken from the gun locker."

"You said he'd taken the keys to the motorcycle," Cordero said. "You have a penknife or a screwdriver here somewhere?"

"Should be one here somewhere," said the sergeant. "Why?"

Cordero didn't answer.

"I can't take you with me," he told Carter. Before she could protest, he held up a hand. "I know all about your thoughts on danger and police officers. But this time there's too much danger and room for only one officer on the motorcycle."

• • •

Cordero took the screwdriver Amparo found for him and hurried out to Sisko's motorcycle. The sergeant leaned against the doorframe watching. Carter stood by his side with the African peering over their shoulders again.

Cordero tore the cover off the bike's ignition switch and joined the two exposed wires with the blade of the screwdriver. The bike kicked over but didn't start. He tried again and succeeded. He mounted the bike and tossed the screwdriver to Amparo, but it was Carter who caught it.

"Where did you learn that?" the sergeant asked.

"I grew up in Australia," Cordero said and revved the bike.

"Stealing motorcycles?"

"No," Cordero spun the bike around toward the gate kicking mud up with the rear wheel. "Losing keys!" he shouted and was gone.

• • •

As soon as he pulled off the compressed dirt of the main road north to Beloi, Cordero could see what the African had said about the road up the mountain. Sheets of slushy mud had oozed down the side road and he had to work the motorcycle hard to avoid slipping and dropping the bike or getting bogged. His shoes and the bottom of his pants' legs were soon encrusted in mug and he could feel flecks of muck on his face. His arms were sore and his backside ached from the bumping and jostling on the bike.

A little further up the incline the road surface appeared less like black soup and more like a brown sponge. He could make out ruts the utility had driven deep into the slush suggesting Sisko was having a hard time negotiating the climb as well. Where he could, Cordero kept to the side of the road to get more traction on the congealed surface. Often the rear wheel would slide and he'd swear out loud as he struggled to correct the bike.

Swearing was his only consolation on a difficult ascent to the top.

Manucoco towered over the southern part of the island. As Cordero climbed, coconut palms and banana trees gave way to a forest of strangler figs, eucalypt and fire trees. The roar and growl of the motorcycle sent flocks of birds scattering from the treetops and the odd goat scrambling for cover.

The sun was higher in the sky now and the day was scorching and humid. Cordero wanted to stop and clean his face of grime and sweat but he dared not. As he climbed higher the engine began to splutter. He suddenly feared that the motorcycle would run out of fuel but there was no time to check the tank. He'd go as far as he could and so he pushed the machine harder.

Around a sharp bend where the forest thinned he saw the utility, abandoned. The road had degenerated into a foot track. The driver's door of the vehicle and the passenger's door were open as though the occupants had fled in a hurry. Cordero cut the engine and lay the motorcycle on its side. He wiped his face with a kerchief and stretched his fingers and hands to get his circulation flowing freely again. He pocketed the kerchief and stole up on the rear of the vehicle.

33

The cabin of the utility was empty, and the key was in the ignition. Cordero took to the track through thinning brush, sago palms and spindly acacia trees. Soon he heard voices: a female's—distraught, pleading—and a male's—swearing and shouting orders. Cordero emerged at the edge of a clearing. Sisko and Mrs. Frankston were on the far side overlooking a sheer drop-away. The cadet was manhandling Mrs. Frankston by her upper arm, her hands cuffed behind her. Her legs and skirt were covered in mud from where she'd struggled and slipped.

She was terrified: Sisko looked almost deranged.

The clearing was soggy and so would offer no purchase if Cordero charged. There was no way he could sneak up on Sisko or reach him and take him before he had a chance to push Mrs. Frankston over the edge.

"Stop, *maun*!" he yelled and Sisko jerked around, his left hand firmly clenched around Mrs. Frankston's thin bicep. For the first time Cordero noticed a watch with a metal band on Sisko's wrist and he recalled the scrape Howard Brooks said he'd noticed on Hank Frankston's collar bone.

"Stay where you are!" Sisko shouted. "I mean it!"

"Come on, *maun*," said Cordero as he edged closer. "Let her go."

"I said stay where you are! Come any closer and I'll push her over!"

"Then what? It'll be you and me and you don't stand a chance," said Cordero, and realized by the way Sisko's nose flared that it was wrong to challenge him in that way. "Why do you want to harm her?" he said, hoping to set the cadet's mind on something else. "She hasn't done anything to you."

"She was tempting me, *maun*!" Sisko bawled at Cordero. "Taunting me! She said she'd have sex with me if I helped her. But she never meant it. It was a trap!"

He jerked back.

"You promised me, bitch!" he shouted in Mrs. Frankston's ear.

The woman shook her head.

"I didn't promise anything!" she screamed. "You took it the wrong way!"

"Fuck you!" Sisko shouted as he nudged her closer to the drop. She peered over. The cliff fell away to a jumble of jagged rocks a hundred feet below. She screamed and dug her heels into the ground, attempting to resist him.

"Officer Ketakura, please," said Cordero. "Let her go."

"Fuck you!" Sisko yelled again. "And fuck her! *Hawa's* possessed her!"

"What? Who?" asked Cordero.

"*Hawa, maun! Hawa*! Don't you know? That's why we're here where *Hawa* lives. He can have the bitch!"

Cordero had no idea what Sisko was talking about but it was what he might do that was the more urgent concern.

"Listen, Sisko!" he said in an attempt to buy time.

Cordero's mind flashed back to what the *matan-dook* had told him only a few hours earlier: that solutions to people's problems had to conform to their way of thinking.

"You're a police officer," Cordero said. "I'm ordering you to let her go!"

"I was *training* to be a police officer!" Sisko said, almost in tears now. "Not any more. Not after I killed that foreigner."

Cordero moved a little closer.

"Stop, *maun*! Stop I said!" Sisko screamed.

Cordero held out his hand to indicate he'd do what he was being told.

"Why did you do it?" he asked. "Why did you kill her husband?"

Sisko angled Mrs. Frankston away from the edge the better to face Cordero. The fingers of the hand which held her opened and closed around her arm. He wiped his face with his free hand.

"Her husband," he repeated. "He wasn't a husband to her. She told me!"

"What did she tell you?" Cordero asked.

The cadet shook his head in torment.

"She said he didn't care for her!" he shouted.

"How do you mean?" Cordero pressed him, inching forward.

"And she was no wife!" Sisko burst out, ignoring the question. "She tempted me too, *maun*! Touching me, tickling me. A wife shouldn't do that to another man. She never dressed like a wife should either. But I'll make her pay. You'll see!"

"So she led you on," said Cordero. "Is that what you're saying?"

Sisko nodded as the sunlight caught tears on his cheeks.

"Like she wanted to be with me, *maun*! With me!"

"Is that why you killed the American? So you could take his place?"

Sisko shook his head, furiously this time.

"You don't get it, *maun*!" he yelled.

"Well tell me," said Cordero. "What did you argue about?"

Sisko caught a deep breath, his chest lifting. He gazed up as though reliving the experience in his head.

"I saw him walking that night," he said. "I was walking home. Amparo told me to leave the motorcycle. Said I was getting lazy riding it around all the time." He scoffed at that. "The fat pig!"

He glared at Cordero.

"So I walked. I heard the foreigner whistling in the darkness. He was happy. But I wasn't! She'd told me she didn't want to see me anymore. That very day! After all the time we'd spent together!"

He took another lungful of air.

"I figured it was because of him. So I stopped him. Asked why he didn't care for his wife like a husband should. He said I didn't know what I was talking about and pushed past me. I ran in front of him. I said if he didn't care for his wife, I did. He should leave her and I'd marry her!"

His face contorted and he started to sob.

"And after that?" Cordero asked.

"He laughed at me, *maun*! In my face. Laughed like what I was saying was a joke, like I was a joke! Said I didn't know what I was talking about. Said he would soon be famous around the world. Why would any American woman ever want a Timorese *lakonnain* like me?" he said, meaning loser.

"So you took the knife and killed him?"

Sisko sniffled, relaxing his grip on Mrs. Frankston.

"He started to walk on," he said. "Laughing. I saw the knife in his belt. The next thing there was blood all over the knife and over my hand, over my shirt, and he was lying on the ground. I don't know how it happened. I didn't mean to kill him. It just happened!"

Mrs. Frankston tried to wriggle free. Sisko yanked her a little further from the edge as he tried for a better grip.

"You stabbed him twice," Cordero said.

"Once, twice!" Sisko yelled. "I told you I don't know. I lost my head!"

"If you didn't mean to do it why didn't you report it as an accident? As manslaughter?" he asked.

"Killing an American?" Sisko said in derision. "Like you said I was with the police. I'd have had no chance. They'd have made an example of me. To keep the Americans happy."

Cordero kept Sisko talking while he grappled with a way to free Mrs. Frankston and hopefully take the cadet alive.

"So you hid the knife," he said. "Why in that priest's grave?"

"I was covered in blood, *maun*. His blood! Where could I go and not be seen? First thing I thought was locals don't like cemeteries. Only go in to make offerings to their dead relatives. Priests don't have relatives. I thought no one would go near that grave."

"Makes sense, I guess," Cordero said to encourage Sisko to keep talking. "After you hid the knife, what did you do?"

"I was scared. I went home and got out of my uniform. I couldn't think straight. I only remembered the knife the next morning and thought maybe I should move it. When I went to get it, I saw that crazy guy near the cemetery. Justino. He looked like he'd been in a fight or something. All dirty and bloody, you know? He reminded me of my own shirt with the blood all over the front. So I figured I'd take him in and say he'd killed the American. Everyone knows Justino's crazy enough to do something like that."

He glared at Cordero.

"Everyone except you!"

Mrs. Frankston tried to break free by kicking at Sisko's legs. He shook her violently, refocusing his attention on why he'd brought her to this spot.

"That's enough talk," he said. "This bitch is going to pay!"

He heaved her toward the edge but she stumbled and slipped through his grasp. He bent down to pick her up. Out of the corner of his eye he detected the earth to his right begin to shift. First leaves that had drifted onto the topsoil stirred although there was no gust of wind and then the mud beneath the leaves slewed and split even though no water appeared to flow.

He looked closer. Suddenly a hand-like a claw protruded. From under a pile of weeds a disfigured head appeared, the hair mattered with mud, the face covered in dirt and grime.

"Fuck!" Sisko yelped.

He eased his grip on Mrs. Frankston and she scrambled violently to break free of the corpse-like thing emerging from the ground.

It rose, silent but for the sucking sound of the mud resettling in the cavity. Half way up it grabbed a rock, pushed the rest of its body free, and staggered toward Sisko.

"Fuck!" he cried a second time and raised a hand to protect his head. "No! Shit! No!"

Mrs. Frankston was clambering away. Cordero charged forward, one hand outstretched.

"Stop, Justino! Stop!" he cried, but the boy had already swung the rock across Sisko's head and sent him hurtling to the ground.

"It's okay, Justino," Cordero said. "It's okay. Calm down."

Cordero reached for the rock and Justino surrendered it without resisting.

"He called my name," Justino appealed to him, his whole body slick with mud. "He's the one who hit me. But I'm strong now. The earth makes me strong. I hit him back!"

"You did good, Justino," Cordero said. "Now stand aside."

He put a hand on Mrs. Frankston's shoulder. "You okay?" he asked and she twitched a nod.

He squatted beside Sisko. The cadet was unconscious and bleeding from where Justino had hit him with the rock--but he was breathing. Cordero checked the trouser pockets for the key to the handcuffs. He found them in the right-side pocket, shifted across and released Mrs. Frankston from the cuffs.

He noticed her face was pale, her hands trembling, and her eyes wild with fear.

"You sure you're okay?" he asked.

Again she jerked her head that she was.

"I'll just be a minute," Cordero said, and squeezed her shoulder gently.

He examined Sisko more carefully. His pulse was strong and the wound to his head seemed not too serious. Justino had scrabbled away after the rope he'd adorned with the rat and the snake skin.

"Justino," Cordero called. "Help me get him up and into my vehicle. It's down at the start of the track. Not far. I think he'll be okay."

He stood as Justino lumbered over and propped his arms under the cadet's shoulders.

"Mrs. Frankston. Could you go ahead of us and get some water from the police utility, please?" Cordero asked. "It's in a flask on the backseat."

There was no response.

Cordero peered over his shoulder.

Mrs. Frankston had collapsed and lay prostrate near the hole Justino had emerged from.

34

Cordero was stirring sugar into his coffee when Carter walked in off the road. Her hair was wet, and she had a towel draped over her shoulder. Under it was a T-shirt and under that, a ragged pair of shorts.

The sun was up, the day was warming, and the morning was calm and very pleasant.

"*Bondia*," Cordero said. "You're up early."

She leaned over the railing that fenced off the dining area and brushed the hair from her face.

"Went for a swim," she said, jiggling her shoulders. "It's a beautiful morning."

"A swim?"

"Have to work off the aches and pains from that walk to Maquili," she explained.

"I didn't know you brought a swimming custom with you," he said.

"I didn't," she replied, a cheeky smile playing on her face. "I swam naked."

He fumbled the spoon and knocked the coffee cup over.

"You've spilled your coffee," she said.

Cordero quickly mopped up the spill with a napkin and refilled his cup.

"How'd things turn out last night?" she asked. "With Sisko?"

Cordero had driven Mrs Frankston and Sisko Ketakura down from the mountain to the health clinic where Carter had met him. Mrs Frankston was treated for trauma, given sedatives, and kept in overnight for observation. Carter had decided to stay with her until she was sure she had settled. The blow to Sisko's head required stitches after which Cordero had taken him to the police station to be charged. He'd also driven Justino home and hadn't seen Carter after leaving the clinic.

"He didn't have much to say," Cordero said. "Kept babbling about *Hawa*."

"*Hawa*?"

"Yeah, *Hawa*. It's a name Sisko repeated when he had Mrs Frankston on the edge of that drop. I asked Amparo what it meant. It's from Hresuk—the language of the Humangili community around here. Sisko is Humangili."

He stirred sugar into his newly filled cup of coffee.

"*Hawa* is a spirit some Humangili associate with Satan," he continued. "They believe he dwells in the mountain. Sisko was thinking he'd send Mrs. Frankston back to *Hawa* because it was *Hawa's* idea she try to seduce him. Amparo figured it may have been an attempt to make peace with the spirit of Professor Frankston by eliminating the woman Sisko believed had caused him to take the man's life."

"Another vengeful dead to appease," Carter commented.

"I've just come from the health clinic," he said.

"Oh. How is she?"

"She seems as fine as could be expected this morning," Cordero said of Mrs Fankston. "I think they'll let her go around midday. She said she wanted to thank you for staying with her last night."

Carter shrugged.

"She asked me to get her a change of clothes from the house," Cordero said. "The place stank! I couldn't wait to get out of there."

"Her husband had set up a generator out back to run power to his study—which was really a laboratory—including an air conditioning unit. Back up for when the power went out," Carter said. "It was for his samples. He turned it on the night he was killed, probably as a precaution before he went out. My guess is that Miller saw it humming away and kept it refuelled on his visits. She didn't refuel it maybe because she was never shown how. All Frankston's seaweed samples will turn to slime now and there'll be no way to confirm his findings."

Cordero merely shook his head.

"I gave her back her passport and told her she was free to go. Miller was heading over there to help her get to Dili when I sat down here."

"Of course he was," she said. "What about Evans?"

"He's leaving today as well."

"Without charge?" she said, surprised.

"Oh, he faces a hefty fine for violating sacred houses when he gets to Dili. Some of that money will come to the elders here. He'll also be barred from re-entering East Timor for several years."

"What about stealing the journal?"

"Mrs Frankston doesn't want to press charges. The journal's been returned and it doesn't seem to mean much to her anyway. She said she'd send it to the university in Hawaii that funded her husband's research here."

"I guess you're going to tell me that Welcome Jesus walked free too," she said.

"Well, actually—"

"He could've killed Evans and he re-stole the journal and the jeep," she protested.

"True but neither Evans nor Father Robeiro want to press charges. Also, now that Sergeant Amparo has a police station to run on his own for a while, and with that newly damaged ankle, he offered Welcome a job cleaning and sorting. Welcome was happy to accept."

Cordero sampled his coffee and uttered a satisfied sigh.

"What about the boy who did the break-ins?" asked Carter.

"Antonio?" Cordero smirked. "Amparo will keep an eye on him now. He won't get up to too much trouble. My guess is the sergeant will have given him a clip around the ears and told the elders the boy's been severely punished and won't be breaking into any more sacred houses."

Carter lowered her head.

"What'll happen to Sisko?"

"Results of the prints on the knife and off his mug have sealed his fate. Oh, and the wristwatch may show it caused the scrape on Frankston's collarbone. We'll leave that to Brooks to determine. So what happens to him now is up to a prosecutor and a judge in Dili," he said. "He was right to think they'll make an example of him. He's probably looking at fifteen years at least in prison on the mainland."

He drained his cup and examined the jug of coffee for another. He'd emptied it already.

"Where's Estefana?" he asked.

"She was getting up to have a wash when I left." She looked off to their hut. "I'm going to the cemetery with her this morning. She wants to complete that ritual she was told to perform."

"I like that *matan-dook*," Cordero said. "I think he actually is a healer in many ways. He seems to have a good handle on what makes people tick."

Carter's hair had fallen over her eyes and she brushed it off. The sunlight caught a warm glow in her face.

Cordero admired the effect, admired her, and produced a nervous cough.

"We're a good match, you and me," he said.

"What?" she replied, her tone suggesting he may have crossed a line.

Cordero shifted in his seat.

"You know, as investigators I mean," he said to recover himself. "We're a good team."

"You didn't say 'team,'" she corrected him. "You said 'match.'"

"Well, I meant 'team,'" he said. He drew his legs in under his chair and lowered his head to hide his embarrassment.

She stared at him for a long moment.

"Save me some coffee," she said pushing herself off the railing. "I'll be back when I've cleaned up and changed."

"I'll order more," he said. "Breakfast?"

"Yeah. That too. I'm hungry. Can you order me fruit salad and some bread rolls, please? Yogurt too if they have any."

She started to walk off to her hut.

"There's more," said Cordero.

She stopped and glanced over her shoulder.

"Jada called this morning. My superior, you know? He said I can consider myself suspended after I hand in my report."

She retraced her steps, frowning as she did.

"For working with me?"

"That's not quite how he put it," said Cordero. "More disobeying his direct orders."

"Well shit. He can't do that!" she insisted.

"He can and he has."

She studied him for a few seconds.

"You don't seem too upset," she said.

He raised a hand as if to say 'Who cares'.

"He needs to be seen asserting his authority, I guess," said Cordero. "But it won't last long. He's short of trained investigators and the last thing he wants is to lose me. I'll be put out in the cold for a few months. But he's keeping me on half pay so I don't go anywhere."

He flicked a hand to attract the woman in the kitchen who was wiping her hands in the doorway.

"Or until the next big case comes along," he added. "Besides, I could use a break. Maybe do some swimming, myself."

He sat back, looking more at ease.

"I did kind of push and prod you to do certain things," she said. "You can be a bit obtuse, you know."

"Obtuse?"

"Yeah. It means—"

"I know what obtuse means."

She lowered her head and made circles in the dirt with a foot.

"You hold it against me?"

"Not for a moment!" he said.

She winked at him.

"I'm glad," she said. "Well, we've got something in common."

"What's that?"

"Ambassador Taylor seems to think I'm responsible for putting Mrs Frankston's life in danger." She sniggered. "I'll be in for a scolding when we get to Dili too."

"Mrs Frankston told me she'd put in a good word for you with the Ambassador," he said.

"Lot of good that'll do," scoffed Carter. "Taylor is not one to take the opinions of women to heart."

"You worried about what he might do?"

"I'm only worried I'll burst into laughter when he puts on his serious face," she said and made to leave.

"Wait!" he said.

Again, she stopped.

"You didn't tell me your secret, remember?" he said. "You started to say something about having just started work in Flagstaff."

She lowered her eyes and shook her head before raising it with a smile.

"I developed a craving for chocolate," she said. "But I'm over it now. You can't eat chocolate in Timor because it's too hot and the chocolate melts."

He considered that as she walked off.

"Hold on. Arizona's hot too!" he said but she was already halfway to her hut.

• • •

They were headed down the road that led to the cemetery. It was mid-morning and already muggy under a cloudless blue sky. Estefana had given herself the poor excuse for a shower that the lodge provided and dressed in a clean uniform. Under pressure from Carter, she had also picked at a breakfast and finished a cup of coffee.

They were walking quietly until Carter broke the silence.

"Are you up for this?" she asked.

Estefana barely nodded.

"I'll be close by the whole time," Carter said to reassure her. "You'll be fine."

"I didn't complete the ritual, *mana*," Estefana said, her voice quavering. "That will have angered the spirits more."

"Well you are going to complete it now, Estefana," Carter said. "And put these spirits to rest."

Estefana was doubtful.

"The spirits may not like you coming along, *mana*," she said.

"All my life I've been told someone or other wouldn't like what I planned to do," Carter said. "It never stopped me and it won't stop me now. Besides, I'll stay outside the cemetery. You'll do the ritual on your own."

They were almost at the cemetery gates.

"I'll wait here and make sure nothing distracts you," Carter said. "Or harms you, okay?" she added with emphasis as she rubbed Estefana lightly on her shoulder.

Estefana walked inside and off to the grave of Padre Jose Guterres with its replica church tower and cracked concrete surround. She stopped when she arrived at the grave and stood perfectly still, causing Carter to wonder if she was about to abandon the ritual and run back. But she didn't. After taking a deep breath she took the first tentative steps in the initial circuit, eyes fixed firmly on the ground as the *matan-dook* had instructed.

At the foot of the grave she paused. A breeze was picking up and she gazed quickly at the trees along the wall separating the cemetery from the road. Another deep breath and she circled a second time. She was mumbling something now but Carter was too distant to hear what it was she was saying.

She rounded a third time and finally a fourth.

After the last circuit, Carter watched as Estefana closed her eyes and pressed the necklace to her breast. Once more she was saying something. Was it a prayer? Was it the name of her father or Josinto? Carter had no way of knowing and felt she had no right to know in any case. This was Estefana's trial to endure not hers.

Estefana knelt, took off the necklace and kissed the crucifix. She buried it beside the grave.

She crossed herself and quickly ran to where Carter was waiting. They exchanged strained smiles before rejoining the road to the village.

"Well now you've done it," Carter said.

"I hope so, *mana*," Estefana replied.

Carter stopped abruptly.

"No. You've done what the *matan-dook* told you to do, so now it's finished. Okay? You've completed your task and the spirits of the dead won't be bothering you any more," she insisted. "You got that?"

Estefana allowed a little of her tension to ease and she put an arm inside Carter's.

"Or bother my children," she added.

"Or your children," echoed Carter.

"Thank you, *mana*," Estefana said.

They continued on their way.

Two women with bamboo baskets balanced on their heads walked past in the opposite direction and exchanged a greeting. Chickens ran in front of them and a piglet wobbled across the road chased by two small children giggling in pursuit.

The quiet, unremarkable life of Vila with its placid villagers, coconut palms, and slow rhythmic slapping of the waves onto the nearby beach, was returning to normal.

"*Mana*?"

"Yes, Estefana," said Carter.

"Do you think I am foolish to want children?"

"No! Not at all. What makes you think that?"

"Sometimes I feel a little confused, *mana*. Things are changing in Timor but I tell myself that to be a mother is what I was born to be and I accept that and I'm happy. To me it's like that tree."

She pointed to a large palm up ahead.

"Below the trunk are the roots. They are the spirits of our ancestors. The trunk itself is who we are—where we were born, the family we are born into. The leaves at the top appear when you accept who you are and because the tree is then complete, it bears fruit. That's how I see things anyhow."

She turned and faced Carter.

"When you talk about how important it is to be free, to me that's like seeds blowing around trying to find a home. I don't want to live like that, *mana*, without roots. Without embracing who I am and what my role is. Does that sound silly?"

Carter had stopped and was raking the pebbles on the road with her boot.

"No, Estefana," she said. "I'm sure a lot of women feel like that. Take Mrs. Frankston. All she wanted was to set down roots, but her husband wanted to keep moving around, doing his research, finding new things. I think it's good that you want to have a family and that you'll be happy as a mother."

Estefana smiled broadly.

"But that's not what you want, *mana*?" she asked.

Carter kept her gaze low so that it was difficult to see her face.

"No," she said and continued walking. "Not just yet."

About the Author

Chris McGillion is a regular visitor to East Timor where he has been involved in media development initiatives and conducted research into the communication of agricultural science in remote mountain communities. He is a former journalist whose work has been published in Australia, the US and the United Kingdom and has taught politics, philosophy and communication skills at four universities in Australia. He has authored or co-authored a number of non-fiction books on subjects as diverse as US-Cuban relations, clerical sexual abuse, and religious sociology. He lives in the Blue Mountains west of Sydney, Australia.

www.ingramcontent.com/pod-product-compliance
Lightning Source LLC
LaVergne TN
LVHW031537060526
838200LV00056B/4535